The Holy War in Modern English

John Bunyan's 1682 Classic
Paraphrased by Leslie Noelani Laurio

Copyright 2018 Leslie Noelani Laurio

All rights reserved.

ISBN: 9781731487995

CONTENTS

Preface - pg 6
Chapter 1 - pg 10
Chapter 2 - pg 21
Chapter 3 - pg 30
Chapter 4 - pg 45
Chapter 5 - pg 60
Chapter 6 - pg 71
Chapter 7 - pg 81
Chapter 8 - pg 88
Chapter 9 - pg 100
Chapter 10 - pg 109
Chapter 11 - pg 118
Chapter 12 - pg 126
Chapter 13 - pg 135
Chapter 14 - pg 143
Chapter 15 - pg 150
Chapter 16 - pg 155
Chapter 17 - pg 163
Chapter 18 - pg 169
Chapter 19 - pg 175

A very few footnotes from Samuel Adams' 1795 annotated Holy War have been added to this etext.

To the Reader

It seems strange to me that story tellers and people who love to write about history never write about Mansoul's wars. Man cannot possibly know who he is until he knows about these things.

I know there are all kinds of stories, both local and foreign, and they're told as fancifully as the writer wants. Some writers make up things out of their own imaginations with such cleverness and wit, that even though people know they're just making things up, they gain a following and even influence the way their followers think.

But, fair reader, I have something else in mind. The story I'm going to tell you is so well known by some people that they could tell you the story themselves with tears and joy. There are many people who are familiar with the town of Mansoul and her troubles.

So listen to the story I'm going to tell you about the town of Mansoul and what happened to her -- how she was lost, taken captive, enslaved, and how she turned against the very one who wanted to save her. She opposed her Lord with hostile means and allied herself with his enemy! This is a true story, and anyone who tries to deny it would have to falsify the best records. How do I know it's a true story? Because I was in that town myself, both when it was first set up, and when it was pulled down. I witnessed Diabolus in control of that town, and Mansoul under his oppression. I was there when Mansoul claimed loyalty to the traitor, and submitted willingly and wholeheartedly to him.

Yes, I was there when Mansoul trampled divine things underfoot and wallowed in filth like a swine. I saw her pick up weapons to fight her own Prince Emmanuel, who had been so wonderful to her. I was there and, I'm ashamed to say, I was even pleased at the time to see Diabolus and Mansoul cooperating so well together.

Don't accuse me of making up stories, or call me a writer of fanciful fiction. I can state with absolute certainty that what I'm about to tell you is absolutely true.

I saw the Prince's armed men come down with troops of thousands to besiege the town and take it back. I saw the Captains with my own eyes, and I heard the trumpets with my own ears. I watched as his soldiers covered the ground and set themselves in battle formation. I'll never forget that day as long as I live. I saw the King's colorful banners flying in the wind, and the enemies inside the city conspiring together to ruin Mansoul and destroy her very soul.

I saw siege mounds built up against the walls of the town, and cannon arranged to batter down the walls. I heard the grenades whizzing by my ears, heard them as they landed, and I saw the destruction they left behind. The ancient god of Death covered Mansoul's face, and I heard Mansoul cry out, 'Woe to me, for when I die, I shall be lost forever!'

I saw how the battering rams tried to beat open the Ear Gate so that the enemy could beat down the entire town. I saw the hand to hand combat, and heard the Captains shouting. I identified the wounded and noted who was killed -- and I knew which of the dead would come to life again. I heard the groans of the wounded, while others fought on recklessly with no fear. While the shout of, 'Kill! Kill!' was ringing in my ears, the gutters ran, not with blood -- but with tears. The Captains, when they weren't actively fighting, would molest us day and night. Their constant call, 'Get up! Come on, let's take the town!' kept us all on edge so that we couldn't rest or even sit down.

I was there when the gates were crashed open, and I saw Mansoul despair as her last hope was gone. I watched the Captains march into the town uncontested, to fight and cut down their enemies. I heard the Prince tell the Sons of Thunder to go up to the castle and capture the enemy, and I watched them bring him down and drag him through the town, chained and in shame.

And then I saw Prince Emmanuel take possession of his town of Mansoul. After she received his pardon and began to respect his laws, Mansoul became a greatly blessed and gallant little town.

When Diabolus and his companions were rounded up, made to stand trial, and finally executed, I was right there. I was even standing by when Mansoul executed those rebels with her own hands. I saw Mansoul, now dressed beautifully in white, as the Prince called her 'the delight of his heart' and put delicate gold chains around her neck, and lovely precious rings on her fingers. I heard the people of Mansoul weeping, and I watched the Prince dry their tears. I heard some people groaning, and others rejoicing. There's no way I can tell you everything I saw, but you can see that I know what I'm talking about, and Mansoul's unparalleled wars are no fable.

Mansoul had been coveted by both princes -- one wanted to bless her, and the other to destroy her. Where Diabolus would stake his claim and cry, 'This town is mine!' Prince Emmanuel would plead that he had a divine right to his Mansoul. Then they would go to war, and Mansoul would think, 'These wars will be my undoing!'

Poor Mansoul! Her wars seemed endless as she was passed from one contestant to the other, and then became the victor's prize, and then the loser would shout, 'If I can't have her, I'll tear her to pieces!' Mansoul's very home was the battleground and center of the fighting. She didn't just hear the noise of battle from afar, or fear the possibility of swords, or only witness small skirmishes -- she was right in the midst of it. She could see the blood on the sword blades, and hear the cries of those who had been wounded. Her fear was real -- she had to live it. She not only heard the trumpets, but saw her bravest soldiers gasping for life on the ground. She could never speak flippantly about it with people who can never be serious, or chat lightly about it among people who have neer seen real fighting, whose disagreements only end in heated but harmless words.

Poor Mansoul! The outcome of those wars would determine her eternal fate, whether health and happiness or ruin and disaster -- and it would be for forever.

So don't count me as one of those people who amazes you by telling you to gaze at the stars because each of them is home to some alien creatures. How can I know if there's a world in each star or planet?

But I've taken up too much of your time. Open my book and you'll see something of significance that's even more rare and wonderful than the stars. Keep my clues in mind, but apply them carefully if you want to know the hidden meaning of my story.

John Bunyan's Note

Some say that I didn't really write Pilgrim's Progress -- as if I would claim fame and reputation on the basis of someone else's work, and become rich by robbing another. They say that I'm so fond of recognition that I wouldn't hesitate to write more lies just to see my name in print. But that is not true. I haven't been that kind of low creature since God converted me. Pilgrim's Progress came from my own heart, to my head, then trickled into my fingers and pen onto the paper. The idea and the words were my own. I didn't tell anyone about it until I had finished it. Nobody added even five words to it; the whole thing is my work, and mine alone.

It's the same for this book that you're now reading. It came from my heart, head, fingers, pen -- the same as the other. I declare that no man in the world can say with truth that he wrote this book except myself. I don't say this to brag or to seek men's praise. I say this to keep people from being tempted to scandalize my name. Note that the letters of my name can be rearranged to form the phrase 'Nu hony in a B.'

A Tale of the Holy War

Chapter 1

One time as I was on my usual travels of various places, I happened to come to that famous country called Universe. It's a large, spacious country that lies between the two poles at the center of the four points of the heavens. It's a lush, green place with hills and valleys, well-situated, abundant with food, lively with people, and having plenty of fresh air.

[Note -- This describes the world in its present state.]

The people aren't all the same race, they don't all speak the same language, or have the same culture or religion. In fact, they're as different from one another as the planets are different from each other. Sometimes they're right and sometimes they're wrong, just like any place else.

[Note -- Before Adam and Eve's fall, all was harmony and beauty, but sin introduced discord.]

I spent such a long time there that I learned the language, customs and manners of the people I was with. I enjoyed it there so much that I would have been happy to spend the rest of my life there and die among them, but my Master called me away on business.

In this country of Universe, there's a lovely, charming town -- an organized coalition called Mansoul. It has some charming buildings, lots of space, and many advantages. There is no other place quite like it anywhere.

It lies just between the two worlds. Its original founder and builder was a King named Shaddai, and he built it for his own pleasure. He made this town the glory of all his other projects, he pulled out the stops and made it delightful beyond anything else in that entire country. Mansoul was such a great place when it was first built that the gods themselves, when they came down to see it, sang for joy. Not only was it a beautiful town, but it was destined to be the capital city and rule over all the country around it. All the villages and regions around it had to come to Mansoul to do homage. The town of Mansoul had orders and authority from her King to require services from the surrounding area, and to subdue anyone who refused to do service for her.

[Note -- most authentic records: Scripture; Shaddai: God; the gods who sang for joy: angels]

There was a famous and elegant palace in the middle of the town -- strong enough be more of a citadel, or castle, pleasant enough to be a paradise, and large enough to contain the entire world. King Shaddai intended this palace to be a home for himself and no one else, partly for his own satisfaction, and partly because he didn't want strangers in there terrorizing the townspeople. King Shaddai also used this place as an armed fortress, but allowed no one but the citizens of the town to work there and maintain it.

[Note -- palace: the heart]

The walls around the town were so strong and sturdy that, if it hadn't been for the townspeople themselves, nobody could ever have broken through. The King was wise enough to know how to build walls that could never be breached by even the most evil tyrant unless the people themselves gave their consent.

[Note -- walls: the body]

This famous town had five gates by which to enter or leave, and they were as impregnable as the wall. These were Ear Gate, Eye Gate, Mouth Gate, Nose Gate, and Touch Gate.

There was always plenty of everything in Mansoul, and it had the most just and fair laws in the whole world. There was not one thief, villain, or traitor in the whole town in those days. The citizens were all men of integrity and united in cooperation, which is unusual in any town. And as long as the people were loyal to King Shaddai, they had his approval, his protection, and his friendship.

Well, one day a mighty giant named Diabolus assaulted the town of Mansoul in order to seize control of it and make it his home. This giant was the king of darkness, and he was a volatile, demented tyrant.

[Note -- Diabolus: a fallen angel, an evil spirit; Satan]

This Diabolus is indeed a great and mighty prince, and yet needy and destitute at the same time. In his early years, he was one of King Shaddai's servants. In fact, the King had given him a high and powerful position in charge of his best territories and dominions. Diabolus was made 'son of the dawn' and had a prominent role. His authority brought him glory and fame that should have satisfied his Luciferian heart -- if it hadn't been as insatiable and inflated as hell itself.

When he had had a taste of greatness and honour, he began to rage in his heart for an even higher position, and he plotted how he might set himself up as lord over everything in the realm except for King Shaddai himself. But Shaddai had already put his Son in that place. So Diabolus thought what might be done to take over, and then shared his plan with his evil companions, and they agreed to join him. They decided to try to kill the King's Son so that his place and inheritance might be theirs. At the appointed time, these traitors assembled together, and began their assault. The King and his Son knew everything that went on in their kingdom and were well aware of these plans. The King loved his Son and was greatly angered and offended. Before the traitors had made their first attack, the King nipped it in the bud, convicted them all of treason, rebellion, and conspiracy, and cast all of them out of their places of trust, advantage, and honour. He banished them from court and turned them out into vile pits, bound up in chains to wait for the judgment he had appointed, when he would punish them forever.

Now that they had been cast out of their privileged place and knew that they had lost the King's favour forever, this only fueled their hatred and rage against King Shaddai and his Son, the Prince. So they roved about, wandering and raging from place to place, hoping they might find something of value to the King that they could spoil in order to get their revenge. They ended up in the spacious country of Universe and made their way towards Mansoul. Knowing that this town was one of the most treasured projects and delights of King Shaddai -- since they had been there when the King built it -- they took counsel and decided to make an assault on it. When they arrived at Mansoul, they gave a terrific shout of elation, and roared like a lion who has spotted his prey, and said, 'Ha! Now we have found his prize, how can we best be revenged on King Shaddai for what he did to us?' They sat down and had a council of war to consider the most effective plan to win the town of Mansoul for themselves. This is what they discussed:

1. Should all of them approach the people of Mansoul, or just a few?

2. Should they show themselves in their current ragged and destitute aspect?

3. Should they be upfront and tell Mansoul their intentions, or assault them with lies and deceit?

4. Might it be best to remove some of the principle townspeople who might offer resistance by shooting them and getting them out of the way in order to give their own plan a better chance of success?

Here's how they answered those issues.

1. It would be better if just some of them carried out their plan -- all of them together might terrify the townspeople, and once the people were alarmed, it would be impossible to get into the town, since the people's consent was required to enter the gates. Diabolus spoke up. 'It would be better if only a few of us made the assault, or even just one, and in my opinion, that should be me.' And they all agreed.

2. No, they shouldn't appear in their ragged, destitute appearance. Although Mansoul had dealt with invisible creatures in the spiritual realm, they had never seen anyone so hideous and repulsive before. Apollyon said, 'If even one of us appears to them as we are now, they will be horrified and put on their guard. Then we'll never get into the town.' Beelzebub added, 'That's sound advice. We should appear to them looking like common creatures, something familiar to them.' So what should they look like? Various suggestions were offered, and finally Lucifer said that Diabolus should assume the form of one of the animals under the stewardship of Mansoul. 'They'll never think to suspect one of their own animals of harming the town. In fact, how about appearing as the kind of animal Mansoul considers wiser than the rest?' This suggestion was applauded, and it was decided that the giant Diabolus should take on the form of a dragon, which was as familiar to the people of Mansoul as a bird is nowadays to any child.

3. No, they should not reveal their intentions to the people of Mansoul. If they did that, the people would never open the gates to them. In fact, that might make them appeal to the King for aid, and he would put a quick stop to all their plans. 'No,' said Legion, 'let's assault them with fake civility. Let's hide our intentions with all kinds of lies, flatteries, and misleading talk. Promise them things that will never happen, and lure them with hopes they'll never find. This is the way to win Mansoul and make them open their gates to us. In fact, they'll practically beg us to come in! They are simple and innocent people, all of them are sincere and candid. They don't know what it means to be assaulted with fraud, deception, and hypocrisy. They have never experienced lies and double-talk. If we're disguised, they'll never suspect our plans. They'll believe whatever we tell them, and fall for every one of our tricks. They'll trust all of our promises, especially if we pretend to love them and say that we only want what's best for them.' This seemed good to all of them, and they all readily agreed.

4. Yes, they should get some of the principle townspeople out of the way so that their plan would stand a better chance. They determined that the main

man to be removed was Captain Resistance. He was a great man, and the person that Diabolus and his companions feared more than the rest of town of Mansoul put together. But which of them should commit the murder? Tisiphone, one of the Furies of the Lake of Fire, was chosen to do it.

Now their counsel of war was over, and they got up to put their plan into action. They made themselves invisible -- all but Diabolus, who took on the shape of a dragon -- and marched towards the town of Mansoul.

They sat down at the Ear Gate, for that was the place where the people could hear everything going on outside the town in the same way that Eye Gate allowed them to see everything that went on. The companions laid an ambush for Captain Resistance within bow-shot of the gate. Then Diabolus, taking Ill-Pause with him to be his speaker, went to the gate and called out to the town of Mansoul. At this, some of the leading citizens of Mansoul came to see who was there -- Lord Innocent, Lord Will-be-Will, the Town Mayor, the Recorder, and Captain Resistance. Lord Will-be-Will demanded to know who he was, where he had come from, and why he had roused Mansoul with such an odd sound.

Diabolus, as gentle as a lamb, began to speak, saying, 'Gentlemen of this fine city, you can see that I'm one who doesn't come from far away, but I live near you. The King has obligated me to do homage to you and serve you to the best of my abilities. But first I must be upfront and share a concern with you. Please hear me out -- what I have to say is not for my own benefit, but yours. I've come to tell you how to free yourselves from a bondage you're unaware of, but that you're enslaved to nevertheless.' At this, the men of Mansoul were all ears. 'What's the matter? What is it?' they thought. Diabolus went on. 'I have something to say concerning your King and his laws, but it also affects you. I know that your King is great and powerful, but everything he has told you is neither true, nor advantageous to you.

'First, it is not true. The terrible consequence he has warned about will not happen, not even if you do the thing he has forbidden. Even if there is a danger, it's oppressive and enslaving to live under the threat of punishment for doing something as minor and insignificant as eating a little bit of fruit.

'And, second, as far as his laws, I must tell you that they are unreasonable, complicated, and extreme. They are unreasonable because the punishment is disproportionate to the crime; there's a vast difference between life and the bite of an apple, yet Shaddai requires that you pay for one with the other. It's also complicated because he says you may eat everything, but then he says you must not eat one. And, finally, it's extreme because the very fruit you're forbidden from eating -- if, in fact, it actually is forbidden -- will do something good for you that you don't know about. Consider the fruit, from the 'tree of the knowledge of good and evil.' Do you have that knowledge yet? Of course not. So how can you possibly know how good, how pleasant, how appealing wisdom is as long as you comply with your King's commandment? Why should his arbitrary rule keep you in blindness and ignorance? Why shouldn't you be enlightened and gain understanding?

'And lastly, inhabitants of Mansoul, I hate to break it to you, but you are not a free people. You are kept in bondage and slavery by a dreadful threat, with no reason given except that the King has said, 'This is the way I want it, so this is the way it's going to be.' Is it not tragic to think that the very thing you're forbidden to do might be the very thing that will profit you with both wisdom and honour? For then your understanding will be awakened and you'll be like gods. Since this is so,' he continued, 'how can you be under any greater bondage than you're under right now? You've been reduced to inferiors, burdened with inconveniences, which I have shown you. What greater bondage is there than being kept in blindness? Doesn't your own reason tell you that it's better to have eyes than not to have them? And isn't it better to have liberty than to be shut up in a dark, stinking cave?'

[Note -- You are kept in bondage and slavery: Diabolus holds out false liberty]

[Half-way point]

Even while Diabolus was speaking to Mansoul, Tisiphone shot Captain Resistance in the head as he was standing at the gate, and he fell over -- dead. The townspeople were shocked. He was the only trained soldier in the whole town, and now Mansoul felt completely vulnerable and unprotected. She didn't even have the heart to resist -- which is just what the devilish Diabolus wanted. And now Ill-pause, who had come to speak for Diabolus, delivered his speech.

'Gentlemen,' he began, 'my master is so glad to have a quiet and teachable audience, and we hope you won't reject our good advice. My master loves you so much. He knows that he is risking the anger of King Shaddai, but his concern for you makes it a sacrifice he's willing to take. Is there any need to provide proof for what he has said? The truth of it is self-evident -- the very name of the tree makes it clear. I'll only add this, with my lord's permission' (and here he made a very respectful bow to Diabolus), 'please consider his words. Look at the tree and its juicy fruit. Keep in mind that, at this point, you know very little -- but this fruit is the way for you to know more. If that's not reason enough for you to accept my lord's advice, then you're not the people I thought you were.'

The people did look at the tree, and they could see how appealing the fruit was. It was beautiful, and looked delicious. Of course they wanted to know more! So they did what Ill-pause suggested: they picked the fruit and ate it.

I should have mentioned before that while Ill-pause was making his speech, Lord Innocent sank down right where he was standing. Had he been shot, too? Or did fear, or the horrible breath of that treacherous Ill-pause cause him to lose consciousness? At any rate, he could not be revived, and died. Thus, two brave men died that day -- I call them brave because, as long as they were alive, they had been the beauty and glory of Mansoul, and now that they were gone, there was no longer any noble soul in Mansoul. All the people fell down and submitted their obedience to Diabolus. You shall hear how they ended up as his slaves and subjects.

[Note -- When disbelief of the truth of God's word takes root in the human mind, that is the end of man's innocence and righteousness forever.]

With Captain Resistance and Lord Innocent gone, the people acted like fools and set out to prove the giant's words. First they did what Ill-pause had advised: they looked, they considered, and they ate. They became drunk on that fruit, and, in their drunken state, they opened both Ear Gate and Eye Gate and let Diabolus with his horde of companions come streaming in. They completely forgot about good King Shaddai, his law, and the punishment he had warned them about if they broke his law.

Now that Diabolus was inside the town, he marched into the middle of the town square to complete his conquest. Since the people seemed to have some respect and admiration for him, he decided to strike while the iron was hot, and made this deceitful speech: 'Poor Mansoul! I have done you a great favour by enlightening your knowledge and increasing your liberty, but, you poor people! Now you'll need someone to defend you. As soon as King Shaddai hears what you have done, you can be sure that he'll rush here in alarm that you've broken his bonds and thrown off his leash. What will you do? Now that you've wised up, are you going to allow yourselves to lose your privileges and new-found liberty? What are you going to do?'

All the people said with one voice, 'You take charge of us and tell us what to do.' And Diabolus accepted their request and became the new king of Mansoul. Now that this was taken care of, the next thing was to take possession of the castle, which would make his conquest complete and give him control of the entire town. So off he headed for the castle -- the castle that King Shaddai had built in Mansoul for his own enjoyment and pleasure. Now it became a shelter and stronghold for the evil giant Diabolus.

Once the castle was in his possession, he made it his command post, strengthening and fortifying it with weapons and provisions to fend off King Shaddai or anyone he might send to try to gain the castle back.

But Diabolus still didn't feel quite secure, so he set out to revamp the town government by removing Shaddai's men and replacing them with his own staff. Lord Understanding, who had been the Mayor, was replaced, and Mr. Conscience was relieved of his job as Town Recorder.

[Note -- Once God's image of holiness is obliterated, and Satan, with all his horrid crew of lusts and vile affections, gains admittance, the understanding is perverted, and the affections are twisted.]

Although the Mayor was an understanding man, and had complied with the rest of the people to let in Diabolus, Diabolus didn't think it was a good idea to allow him to continue in his high position. He was a bit too perceptive. So Diabolus not only removed him from his office and authority, but he built a tall wall between the sun and Mr. Understandings house so that he dwelt in complete darkness. He might as well have been blind. On top of this, he was put under house arrest. So now, even if he wanted to help Mansoul, what could he do? How could he be of any use? Thus, as long as Mansoul was under the power and government of Diabolus -- and as long as Mansoul was under him, it obeyed him, even after the war to rescue Mansoul had started -- all that time, Mr. Understanding was more of a handicap to Mansoul than a help.

The Town Recorder, Mr. Conscience, had been well-versed in the King's law before the town was taken. He was also a man of courage, faithful to speak the truth on every occasion. His tongue was brave, and his mind full of good judgment. Of course, Diabolus couldn't tolerate such a person. Yes, the Recorder had consented to letting Diabolus into the town, but he was too smart to be deceived with schemes, lies, and tricks. It's true that his loyalty to King Shaddai had been compromised, but even though he accepted many of Diabolus's laws and benefits, his allegiance to Diabolus couldn't be counted on. Sometimes he would think about King Shaddai and a sense of dread would come over him about breaking his laws. When that happened, he would speak against Diabolus as forcefully as a lion. Sometimes he would have fits and speak out in front of the whole town. Naturally, Diabolus didn't get along with him.

[Note -- The biggest reason why such multitudes live and die in their sins is because they stifle the friendly checks and warnings of conscience.]

In fact, Diabolus feared the Town Recorder more than anyone else in the town because his words had a way of shaking up the townspeople. Since he wouldn't be wholly on the giant's side, Diabolus looked for ways to compromise and stain him -- to deaden his mind and harden his heart with pride. And he succeeded. Little by little, he drew the man into sin and wickedness. At first, only his conscience was defiled, but in time, he became so debased that he was almost unaware of sin. But that was as far as Diabolus could go, so he had to think of another plan. And he ended up persuading the townspeople that the Town Recorder was crazy and not to be taken seriously. To make this more believable, he encouraged his fits in order to prove that he was just a raving old lunatic.

[Note -- At first, only his conscience was defiled: the man is more corrupted than before]

By this and other means, he convinced Mansoul to disregard, neglect, and snub whatever the Town Recorder might say. One of the things Diabolus would do was to get the man in a lighthearted, joking mood and then make him negate and deny things he had said during one of his fits. This made him seem even more ridiculous, so that nobody even took him seriously any more. He no longer spoke freely for King Shaddai, but was inconsistent -- he would sometimes lash out, and sometimes be silent about the very same thing. Sometimes he seemed to be asleep, or even dead -- even when Mansoul was wholly given up to fun and entertained by the giant's antics.

In the beginning, Mansoul was frightened by the Recorder's thundering voice, and Diabolus would tell them not to let him worry them since the Recorder wasn't speaking out of love or concern for them, he just liked to hear his own voice. With those words, Diabolus would calm and pacify them. And, just to be sure, Diabolus would often say, 'Mansoul, do you realize that, in spite of Old Recorder's rantings about the anger of the King, you've heard nothing from Shaddai himself?' That liar and deceiver failed to tell them that the Town Recorder's outcries were the King's very voice calling to them. He would say, 'Shaddai doesn't care about your rebellion, and he's not going to bother coming all the way here to punish you for giving yourselves to me. He must know that, although you belonged to him once, now you're lawfully mine. He's left us to each other and washed his hands of us.

'Oh, Mansoul!' he would say, 'think of how I've given you the best that I have, and worked to provide everything in the world I could get for you! Besides, the rules and routines you have now bring you much more peace and contentment than the paradise you had before. You know for yourselves how you were once confined and stifled, but now I've expanded and broadened your liberty. I haven't laid any restraint on you. You have no rules, no dictates, no judgment from me to frighten you. I don't call any of you to account for your doings, except for that lunatic (you know who I mean). I've allowed each of you to live like a prince with as little control over you as you have over me.'

In this way Diabolus would hush up and sooth the town of Mansoul when the ex-Recorder would disturb them. You can imagine how these kinds of comments would set the whole town in a rage against the old gentleman. Sometimes they would get a mob mentality and want to destroy him. I've heard them say they wished he was a thousand miles away. His company, his words, the very sight of him, and the memory of how he threatened and condemned them, terrified and unsettled them.

[Note -- when the ex-Recorder would disturb them: pangs of conscience]

But in spite of their wishes and their discomfort, he was somehow preserved. Perhaps it was through the work and wisdom of King Shaddai. Besides, his house was as strong as a fortress, and was situated along the sturdy town walls and surrounded by a moat. If a mob came to threaten him, he could pull up the sluices and let in a flood of water that they couldn't cross.

[Note -- pull up the sluices: of fears]

Lord Will-be-Will was another aristocrat of the town of Mansoul. He was a property owner and as noble as any gentleman in the town. I think he also had some special privileges. He was a man of great strength, determination, and courage, and nobody could withstand him. I don't whether it's because of his pride in his estates or strength or what -- it must be pride of some kind -- but he refuses to be a slave in Mansoul. Instead, he has reduced himself and consented to be a petty governor with a small amount of authority under Diabolus. Imagine -- he, who used to be so headstrong! When Diabolus made his first speech at Ear Gate, this man was the first to consent to his words, agree to his suggestions, open the gate, and let him in. That's why Diabolus has a soft spot for him and created a position for him. When he saw this man's courage and power, he wanted to have him on his team to act in the most important matters.

[Lord Will-be-will: the will]

So Diabolus sent for him and shared the secret matter in his heart with him, but Lord Will-be-Will didn't need much persuasion. After all, he was initially willing to let Diabolus into the town, and he was just as willing to work for him.

When the tyrant saw how willing he was to serve him, and that his mind was leaning that way, he put him in charge of the castle, the town walls, and the gates of Mansoul. In fact, a clause was written into his contract that said that nothing could be done in Mansoul without his consent. So, Lord Will-be-Will became Diabolus's right hand man. And with that, Diabolus had complete control of the town of Mansoul. He also had Mr. Mind as his clerk. He spoke just like his master because they thought the same way and did almost the same things. And thus Mansoul was conquered and made to serve the desires and lusts of the will and the mind.

[Note -- the castle, the town walls, and the gates: the heart, the flesh, and the senses.]

Once Lord Will-be-Will had power in his own hands, he denied that he owed anything to his previous leader, King Shaddai. Then he took an oath and swore to be loyal to his new master, Diabolus. After he was settled into his new position with its privileges and promotions and prestige, he made all kinds of strange changes in Mansoul.

He became hateful to the Town Recorder. He refused to see him, or to listen to him. He would shut his eyes and stick his fingers in his ears any time he came near. And he couldn't bear any trace of Shaddai's laws anywhere in the town. For example, Mr. Mind, the clerk, had some old ripped up pages of the law in his house, but when Will-be-Will saw them, he threw them in the trash. It's true that the old Town Recorder has some of the laws at his house, but there's no way for Will-be-Will to get at them. He also said that the windows of the old Mayor's house let in too much light for Mansoul. He couldn't endure any light -- not even the light of a candle. Now, the only thing Will-be-Will liked was whatever pleased Diabolus, his master.

[Note -- He became hateful to the Town Recorder: the will, when it's in a carnal state, opposes the conscience
He couldn't endure any light: the will, in a corrupt state, prefers darkened understanding]

He liked to go through the streets bragging about Diabolus's brave nature, wise conduct, and great glory. He would wander all through the town talking up his distinguished master, and even make himself appear to be more humble and worthless than the worst citizens just to make his lord seem better. Whenever he was with these rascals, he would buddy up to them and pretend to be one of them. He did all kinds of damage and mischief on his own, without even being commanded.

Lord Will-be-Will had a deputy who worked under him; his name was Mr. Affection. His principles were corrupted. He was completely surrendered to physical pleasures, so they called him Disgusting-Affection. He fell in love with Mr. Mind's daughter, Vulgar-Appetite, and they got married and had several children: Sassy, Rude, and Arrogant were the boys, and the girls were Sneer-at-Truth, Provoke-God, and the youngest was Revenge. They all got married to townsmen and had naughty brats. But enough of that.

Chapter 2

Once the giant was firmly settled in the town of Mansoul and had set things up to his own liking, he began to deface the town. In the market place and on the castle gates there were images of the blessed King Shaddai. They were wrought in gold and so well created that they more closely resembled King Shaddai than anything else in the world. Diabolus commanded Mr. No-Truth to foully mutilate these and set up his own horrid and terrifying image in their place to mock the former King and further shame the town.

Diabolus also made a wreck of what was left of Shaddai's laws and statutes, which were the moral and ethical teachings in government documents and intuitive knowledge. He tried to desensitize Mansoul to the shock value of the worst behaviors. There was no good thing left in Mansoul that Diabolus and Will-be-Will didn't try to stamp out because their goal was to turn Mansoul into a senseless animal, like a sensual brutish swine, with the help of Mr. No-Truth.

After he destroyed Shaddai's orderly structure and just laws, he took the next step -- which was to alienate Mansoul from King Shaddai. He set up his own arrogant rules in all the places where Mansoul liked to relax and enjoy leisure time. These rules were intended to provide complete freedom without limits for the lusts of the flesh, the lusts of the eyes, and the pride of worldly life. These things are not of King Shaddai, but of this temporal life.

He encouraged and promoted lewdness with all kinds of ungodliness. He did even more than this to encourage wickedness in the town of Mansoul: he promised that, by following his commands, they would experience peace, contentment, joy, bliss -- and they would never have to answer for not obeying Shaddai's laws.

And now the town of Mansoul was completely under his control, to serve all of his whims, and the only thing ever seen or heard there was whatever tended to glorify Diabolus.

But now there was no Town Mayor or Recorder, and Diabolus feared that the people might complain that he had wronged them by depriving them of these leaders and decreasing their town's historical grandeur. So he hand-picked a new Town Mayor and Recorder of his own choosing, men who would serve him well.

His new Mayor was Lord Lustings, a man who had neither eyes nor ears. Whatever he did, whether on his own or for his job, he did without thinking, like a senseless animal. And what made him even more shameful was that he favoured evil over good. Mansoul couldn't see how unworthy Lord Lustings was herself, but observers looking on from the outside were grieved to see Mansoul's ruin.

[Note -- This paints a shocking but true picture of every man corrupted by the fall! Carnal man is mixture of devilish lusts and beastly and appetites. If we look around, we see selfish goals and twisted desires flooding the world. Most men have no higher purpose in life than the narrow limits of this worthless, fleeting, perishing world, and are therefore led captive by Satan at his will.]

The Recorder's name was Forget-Good, and he was a very sorry fellow. The only thing he could ever remember was mischief, and how to do it. He was naturally mean-spirited, and hurtful even to the very people living in Mansoul. The two of them, through their high position, corrupt actions, bad examples, and approval of evil did a lot of damage to the town and its citizens. We all know that when leaders are evil and corrupt themselves, they corrupt the whole region and country where they are.

[Note -- Ever since the fall, man's memory is so depraved that it can remember evil, but forgets that which is good, and the imagination works the same way.]

He also assigned his own men to be representatives and council members so that when the town needed governors and judges, they would have to pick from those men. The main ones were Mr. Incredulity, Mr. Haughty, Mr. Swearing, Mr. Adultery, Mr. Hard-Heart, Mr. Pitiless, Mr. Fury, Mr. No-Truth, Mr. Stand-to-Lies, Mr. False-Peace, Mr. Drunkenness, Mr. Cheating, Mr. Atheism -- thirteen in all. Mr. Incredulity was the oldest, and Mr. Atheism was the youngest.

Their relatives, the same sorts of men, were also elected to be common councilmen, bailiffs, sergeants, constables, and such -- too many to list by name.

After this was done, the giant Diabolus set out to build three indestructible strongholds in the town. He called the first one the Mainstay of Defiance. Its purpose was to command the whole town and keep it from knowing anything about its ancient King. The second was called Midnight

Safeguard, and its purpose was to keep Mansoul from knowing the truth about herself. The third was called Sweet-Sin Defense, and from here, Diabolus fortified Mansoul against any desire to do good. The first was built near Eye Gate to darken any light that might come in there. The second was built right up against the old castle to make it more blind, if that was possible. The third was built right in the center of the marketplace.

> *[Note -- Satan establishes his empire in the soul through a repulsion to divine instruction, blinded understanding, perverted will; and by a habit and delight in sin.]*

For governor of the first place, Diabolus chose Spite-God. He was a blasphemous wretch, and was among the mob that first approached Mansoul, and was, in fact, a native of Mansoul. The governor of Midnight Safeguard was Love-no-Light, and he was also among the mob that first approached Mansoul. And the governor of Sweet-Sin Defense was named Love-Flesh. He was as lewd as the other two, but not from the same place. This fellow could get more enjoyment from feeding on a lust than he ever did in the entire paradise of God.

And now Diabolus finally thought he was safe. He had taken Mansoul, he had shielded himself inside it, he had replaced the old officers with new ones, he had spoiled the images of King Shaddai and set up images of himself, he had destroyed the old law books and promoted his own arrogant lies, he had appointed his own magistrates and councilmen, he had built new strongholds and put his own men in charge of them -- and he had done all of this to make himself secure in case good King Shaddai or his son might come to attack him.

You might be wondering whether some word had reached King Shaddai to tell him that his Mansoul was lost, and that the renegade giant Diabolus had taken it for himself in rebellion against the King. Yes, he had heard about it; a messenger had related every detail.

First, how Diabolus had approached the simple and innocent people of Mansoul with craftiness, innuendo, lies, and deceit. He had treacherously murdered the valiant, noble Captain Resistance as he was standing at the gate with the rest of the townspeople. Lord Innocent had died, either from the toxic breath of Il-pause, or from grief at hearing his true and fair King Shaddai slandered by the mouth of the filthy Ill-pause. How Ill-pause had made a short speech to the townspeople for his master Diabolus, and the simple townspeople had believed every word of it, opened Ear Gate, and let Diabolus and his whole crew into Mansoul. The messenger told how Diabolus had treated the Mayor and Town Recorder and fired them. He also told how Lord Will-be-Will had turned into a real rebel and traitor, as well as his clerk, Mr. Mind, and the two of them wandered all over the town teaching the wicked ones their ways. He said that Will-be-Will had been given a high position with control over all the strong places in Mansoul, and Mr. Affection was his deputy in his rebellious affairs. 'Truly, this monster Will-be-Will has openly disowned his King Shaddai and tragically given his loyalty and promised his allegiance to Diabolus.'

'Besides all this,' added the messenger, 'the new leader, the rebellious tyrant over the once-famous but now perishing town of Mansoul has appointed his own Mayor and Recorder. He has made Lord Lustings his Mayor, and Mr. Forget-Good his Recorder -- two of the vilest people in the town.'

The faithful messenger told about the new representatives and council members, and Diabolus's three new strongholds in Mansoul. And, I almost forget to mention this -- the messenger told how Diabolus had armed Mansoul to help him resist King Shaddai if he came to try to reduce them to their former obedience.

The messenger didn't tell these things in private, but in open court -- the King, his son, the lords, Captains and nobles were all there to hear.

There was much sorrow and grief to think that the famous town of Mansoul had been taken. No one but the King and his son had foreseen this turn of events and they had a plan ready to relieve Mansoul, though they had not shared it with the others.

Yet they were still sad about Mansoul's misery, and they grieved along with everyone else. The King said it upset him to the heart, and his son was just as distressed. Their love and compassion for the famous town of Mansoul was clear to everyone. When the King was alone with his son, they discussed their pre-planned scheme, which was that since Mansoul would one day be lost, it should certainly be recovered again in a way that would win the King and his son eternal fame and glory. After this consultation, the son of Shaddai, a sweet and lovely person who always had compassion on those who were suffering, but had great enmity towards Diabolus because that's what he had been created for, and because Diabolus had tried to steal his crown and his dignity -- this son shook hands with his father and promised to do his bidding in order to recover Mansoul again, and he vowed not to go back on his promise. Their agreed plan was that, at a certain time they had both appointed, the son would take a journey to the country of Universe, and during his visit, he would make amends for the foolishness of Mansoul in a fair and honest way that would deliver Mansoul from Diabolus and his tyranny.

In addition, Emmanuel, the son, resolved that, at a convenient time, he would make war on Diabolus, even while the giant was in possession of Mansoul. He would use his strength to drive Diabolus out of his hold, out of his house, and he would re-take it for his own home.

Now that this was settled, the Chief Secretary was ordered to write down their determined plan and publish it throughout the country of Universe. Here is the gist of this document:

[Note -- write down their determined plan: the holy Scriptures, including prophecy]

'The son of King Shaddai is committed by covenant to his Father to bring his Mansoul back to him again. Through the power of his unmatched love, he will bring Mansoul to an even happier position than she had before Diabolus conquered her.'

This document was spread in several places, in spite of Diabolus's attempts to halt it, because he thought, 'now I'll be hindered, and my kingdom will be taken away from me.'

When the King's courtiers heard about their plan, they were amazed. They whispered amongst themselves, and then began to shout about it throughout the King's palace, in complete wonder at the glorious design that was on foot between the King and his son for the poor town of Mansoul. There was no part for the King's courtiers to play in this design, but they talked on and on about the King's love for Mansoul.

[Note -- they whispered amongst themselves: the angels]

The courtiers couldn't keep this news to themselves -- before the document was even finished, they came down and told about it throughout the country of Universe. The news finally reached Diabolus, and he was not happy. It troubled him to think about a plan against him. He turned it over it his mind and came up with a few ideas of his own.

First, this news should be kept from Mansoul if possible. He feared that if Mansoul knew that their former King Shaddai and his son, Prince Emmanuel, were planning something to help the town, Mansoul might revolt against Diabolus's government and return to their King.

In order to prevent this, he renewed his flattery towards Lord Will-be-Will and gave him a strict mission to keep watch over the town gates all day and all night, especially Ear Gate and Eye Gate. 'For I have heard about a plan,' Diabolus told him, 'to accuse us of treason and force Mansoul back into her old bondage again. I hope it's just a rumour,' he said, 'but don't let Mansoul catch wind of it, or they might be dejected. It can't be welcome news to you, and it certainly isn't to me. The best thing is to do everything we can to nip these rumours in the bud so they won't trouble our people. I want you to post strong guards at every gate. Question everyone who comes in to trade, and don't let them in unless they're favourable to our excellent government. Assign spies to walk up and down the streets of Mansoul, and grant them the authority to destroy anyone they find plotting against us, or chattering about what Shaddai and Emmanuel are planning.'

[Note -- keep watch over the town gates all day and all night: to keep the news from Mansoul]

Lord Will-be-Will was very willing to do this, and worked hard to keep anyone from entering the town who might leak the rumour to Mansoul.

Second, in order to strengthen the ties that kept Mansoul under his thumb, Diabolus wrote a dreadful oath whereby his people vowed never to desert him or his government, nor to betray him, nor to try to change his laws. Instead, they must confess him as their rightful king, stand by him, and defy anyone who might pretend any title or claim to the town of Mansoul. Diabolus didn't think Shaddai would have the power to absolve Mansoul from their death sentence and covenant with hell. And was Mansoul staggered or hesitant at this oath? Not at all. Those silly fools swallowed it without even chewing. Were they troubled? No. In fact, they even bragged about their bravery in vowing their loyalty to the giant, their false king, and swore that they wouldn't be fickle and forsake their lord for someone else. This is how Diabolus tightened his grip on Mansoul.

Third, Diabolus's doubt and jealousy compelled him to further strengthen his hold on Mansoul, so he came up with a plan to subvert Mansoul even further. He made Mr. Filth write up a a hateful, nasty, indecent decree and post it at the gates. This decree granted permission to all of Diabolus's faithful citizens to do whatever their lustful appetites prompted them to do, and no man was allowed to hinder them or attempt to stop them on pain of incurring the displeasure of their king.

[Note -- hateful, nasty, indecent decree: evil atheist pamphlets, and vulgar stories]

Here's why he did this:

1. So that the town of Mansoul would become weaker and weaker. In this way, even if news came that their redemption was being planned, they would be incapable of believing it, or of hoping, or consenting to the truth of it. Reason, after all, says that the bigger a sinner, the less cause there is to hope for mercy.

2. Perhaps if Prince Emmanuel saw the horrible, profane behaviour of Mansoul, he would change his mind about redeeming them. After all, Diabolus knew that Shaddai was holy, and so was his son. His own woeful experience confirmed that -- after all, it was his own sin that had gotten him cast down from the highest sphere. It seemed perfectly rational to conclude that sin would have the same result for Mansoul. But what if this wasn't enough? He had still another plan.

4. He would convince the people that Shaddai was gathering an army to come and overthrow and destroy the town of Mansoul. That should quell any rumours about Shaddai coming to deliver them. They might hear that Shaddai was coming, but instead of looking forward to being delivered, they would dread his coming. So he called the people into the market-place and gave this lying speech:

[Note -- Man in a sinful state will always speak negatively of holy things, resenting true religion as dull, melancholy thing that destroys everyone's fun.]

'Gentlemen, good friends, you are all my loyal subjects. You know how good I've always been to you, what liberty and privileges you've enjoyed under my government. My people, I've heard rumours abroad about trouble coming to Mansoul. I am sorry to have to report to you that my Lord Lucifer has sent me a post reporting that your old King Shaddai is raising an army to come against you and utterly destroy you. I've called you together, my people, to discuss what is to be done. For my part, I can take care of myself. If I wanted to, I could abandon you and flee to safety and leave you face this danger on your own, but my heart is so firmly devoted to you that I am willing to stand and fight with you, even if it means my destruction. What do you say, my people? Will you desert me now, or will you stand with your old friend?'

The people all cried out together, 'We will stand with you, and death to anyone who refuses to be faithful!'

Then Diabolus said, 'It's no use hoping for mercy from Shaddai, because the King doesn't know how to show mercy. He might sit down with us at first and give lip service to mercy so that he can more easily win you back and make himself the master of Mansoul again. Whatever he says, don't believe it. His lies are only to overcome us, and then, while we're wallowing in our blood, he'll make us the trophies of his ruthless victory. I propose that we resolve to resist him, and not to believe him on any account. His lies will be our undoing. Do we want to be flattered out of our very lives? I hope you understand enough about the basics of politics to prevent you from falling for that.

'But suppose he gets us to yield, and thus the lives of a few underlings are saved. What good will that do for the leaders of the town? How will that help those of you that I've put in positions of greatness as a reward for your faithfulness to me? Or, let's say he shows mercy to all of you. He will only return you to your former bondage, or worse -- and then what good will your lives be? Will you be able to enjoy pleasures as you do now? No! He will bind you with laws that restrain you and repress you so that you'll have to do what you hate. If you stick with me, I'll stick with you. It's better to die valiantly than to live like pathetic slaves. But even slavery is probably better than what he has in store for you. He wants blood! Every blast of his battle trumpet calls for your blood. Be afraid! I hear that he's headed this way. Get up, bear your weapons so that now, while there's still a chance that you might be able to retain your freedom, I can teach you how to fight. I even have armour for you, and it will protect you from head to foot. As long as you keep your armour on, he and his army can't harm you. Come to my castle, get some free armour, and dress yourselves for battle. For each of you, I have a helmet, breastplate, sword, and shield -- those will enable you to fight bravely.

> *[Note -- The weapons of rebellion with which the unsaved mind fights against God and its own happiness: a false and ill-founded security, hard-heartedness, scoffing at divine truths, profaneness, unbelief, and averseness to prayer. The greatest and most hurtful of these, because it is the source of the rest, is unbelief.]*

'1. My helmet is the hope that all will turn out for the best, no matter what kind of lives you live. This is what enabled those who led wicked lives to look forward smugly to eternal peace, so that they sinned all the more. This is a tried and true piece of armour. No arrow, no dart, no sword can pierce this head-piece. Keep it on your head, and you will ward off many a blow.

'2. My breastplate is made of iron. I forged it in my own country, and all my own soldiers are armed with one. In plain language, it's a hard heart -- a heart of iron, with no more feeling than a stone. If you keep this on, nothing will overwhelm you; mercy shall not win you over, and judgment won't scare you. This is a necessary piece of armour for all who hate Shaddai and want to fight him under my flag.

'3. My sword is a tongue that is fired by hell itself, and that is able to speak evil of Shaddai and his son and his people. This weapon has been tried and proven time and time again. Whoever has this weapon will keep it, and whoever makes use of it as I prompt him will never be conquered by my enemy.

'4. My shield is unbelief -- doubting or challenging the truth of any word about the judgment that Shaddai has appointed for wicked people. Make use of this shield. Shaddai has made many attempts to get through it, and it has sometimes been battered and dented, but those who have written about the wars of Prince Emmanuel against my servants have testified that the Prince was unable to do his work there because of their unbelief. To handle this weapon properly, don't believe what you hear just because it's true, no matter what it is or who says it. If someone speaks of judgment, don't listen. If they speak of mercy, ignore it. If Shaddai swears that he will relent and do good to Mansoul if she changes her mind, don't believe it. Question the truth of it. That's how to wield the shield correctly as my servants ought. Anyone who does anything else must not love me, and I count him as my enemy.

'5. The last piece of my excellent armour is a silent, prayerless spirit -- a spirit that refuses to ask for mercy. Wherever you find yourself, my Mansoul, be sure to make use of this. Why should you beg for mercy? If you want to be mine, don't ever do that! I know you are brave men, and I'm giving you fool-proof armour that cannot fail. Don't even think of crying to Shaddai for mercy! Besides all this, I also have a mace, stick of fire, arrows, and death -- these are all effective weapons.'

After he had outfitted his men with weapons and armour, he encouraged them with words like this: 'Remember that I am your rightful king. You have taken an oath and sworn to be loyal to me and true to my cause. Don't forget that. Be brave, be strong, men of Mansoul. Remember the kindness I've always shown you. I granted you blessings before you even asked: privileges, gifts, profits, and honours. In return, I expect your loyalty, my brave men. What better time to show it than now, when another king is trying to take my dominion into his own hands? One more thing, and then I'll be done. If we just stand strong and overcome this one battle, I am certain that in a little while, the world will be ours. When that day comes, my faithful people, I will make you kings, princes, and captains. What glorious times we'll have then!'

Now that Diabolus had armed and prepared his servants of Mansoul against their rightful King Shaddai, he doubled the guards at all the gates and hid himself in the castle, which was his stronghold. His servants wanted to show him how faithful and (supposedly) honourable they were, so they practiced with their weapons every day and taught each other feats of war. They also publicly defied their enemy and sang the praises of their tyrant. They boasted about how steadfast they would be if there ever was war between Shaddai and their king.

Chapter 3

Meanwhile, good King Shaddai was preparing to send his army to recover the town of Mansoul from the tyranny of their false king Diabolus. Rather than send them under the command of his son, he thought it might be good at first to send them by the hand of his servants, to test the waters and see if that might be enough to turn them back to obedience to their true King. This army consisted of over 40,000 soldiers, all faithful men who had been hand-picked from the King's court.

They arrived at Mansoul under the command of four powerful generals, each in charge of 10,000 soldiers. Their names were Captain Boanerges ("sons of thunder"), Captain Conviction, Captain Judgment, and Captain Execution. These were usually the leaders he sent to lead his armies in all of his wars, since they were strong, tough men who were fit to break through and hack their way with their swords, and their soldiers were just as worthy.

[Note -- Boanerges: sons of thunder, signifying powerful preaching of the gospel]

The King gave each Captain a banner to display the justice of his cause and his right to Mansoul.

Captain Boanerges was the head general. He had 10,000 soldiers under him; his lieutenant was Mr. Thunder, his banner was black, and his coat of arms was three burning thunderbolts.

The second general was Captain Conviction. He also had 10,000 men under him. His lieutenant was Mr. Sorrow. His banner was pale, and his coat of arms was an open law book with a flame coming out of it.

The third general was Captain Judgment and he also led 10,000 men. His lieutenant was Mr. Terror. His banner was red and his coat of arms was a burning fiery furnace.

The fourth general was Captain Execution and he also had 10,000 men. His lieutenant was Mr. Justice. His banner was also red, and his coat of arms was a fruitless tree with an axe lying near the roots.

These four Captains each commanded 10,000 men who were all loyal to King Shaddai and strong, disciplined fighters.

The King called them to battle by name and provided them with weapons suitable to their rank to make them ready to do his bidding.

After the King had mustered his troops (since he is the only one authorized to muster his host to battle), he gave the Captains their various orders in the hearing of all the soldiers and officers and commanded them to be faithful and to bravely follow through with their orders. Their mission was the same in form, but differed in details as far as location, so one example should suffice to demonstrate their orders.

'This is a Commission from the great Shaddai, King of Mansoul, to his trustworthy noble Captain, the Captain Boanerges, to make war on the town of Mansoul.

'You, Boanerges, my sturdy, great Captain over ten thousand of my valiant and faithful servants, go in my name with your army to the troubled town of Mansoul. When you arrive, offer them conditions of peace. Command them to throw off the yoke of that wicked tyrant Diabolus and return to me, their rightful King and Lord. Command them to remove themselves from all of his filth in the town, and then watch for genuine signs of obedience from them. If they submit to these conditions, then do everything in your power to set up a garrison for me in the town of Mansoul. Do not harm even the smallest of the native citizens of the town; treat them as if they were your friends or brothers because I love all of them dearly. Tell them that I will make time to pay them a visit, and let them know how merciful I am.

'But if they put up a resistance in spite of your summons and authority, if they stand up to you and rebel, then I command you to use all of your wits, power, strength, and force to bring them under by the strength of your hand. Fare you well.'

That was gist of all of their commissions; they were all more or less the same.

After each commander had received his orders and authority from the King, and the time and place of their rendezvous had been appointed, each commander appeared in full dress uniform. After one last rallying speech from King Shaddai, they began their march towards Mansoul. Captain Boanerges led the way, Captain Conviction and Captain Judgment made up the main body, and Captain Execution brought up the rear. Mansoul was quite a distance from King Shaddai's court, so the armies had a long way to go. They marched through many regions and countries without harming or abusing anyone, but leaving blessings wherever they went. The King provided for their needs from his own provisions.

After journeying for several days, they finally came within sight of Mansoul. When the Captains saw it, they wept at the condition of the town. They could see how far Mansoul had sunk under the will of Diabolus as they conformed to his ways and schemes.

The Captains came up to the town, marched to Ear Gate, and sat down there, where they could be heard. They pitched their tents and settled in, and then prepared to make their assault.

When the townsfolk saw the gallant company with their flying banners, weapons, orderly discipline, and shining armour, they came out of their houses and gazed at them in wonder. But that tricky old Diabolus feared that this sight might awe the people so that they would heed whatever they said and open the gates to the Captains. So he hurried down from the castle and herded the people into the market-place and delivered this deceitful speech to them:

[Note -- When the townsfolk saw the gallant company: the world are convinced by the well-ordered life of the godly]

'Gentlemen, you may be my faithful and beloved friends, but I must reprimand you a bit for this careless action of going out to stare at that great and mighty force who camped outside the town yesterday and are preparing to lay siege against Mansoul. Don't you know who they are, where they're from, and why they're here? They're the ones I warned you about long ago -- I told you they would come to destroy this town. This is the enemy I've prepared you to meet by giving you armour and pep talks. Instead of going out to stare at them, you should have raised an alarm so we could have taken up positions and been ready to receive them with defiance! That would have impressed me. But instead, your actions have made me a bit fearful -- just a bit -- that when we meet head to head, you'll turn coward and just give up. Why do you think I set up a watch and had you double the guards at the gates? Why have I worked to toughen you up and make your hearts as hard as flint? Was it to make you turn into a bunch of frightened women, or so you could go out and gape at your mortal enemies like a bunch of gullible babies? For shame! Get into military formation, beat the drums, gather together with your weapons, so that your enemies will know there are brave men in Mansoul to be reckoned with!

'No more reprimands -- but let me see no more of this kind of thing! From here on out, unless you have specific orders from me, I'd better not catch anyone even showing his head above the town walls. Do you hear me? If you do as I command you, I will take care of you and protect your honour and your safety. Farewell.'

But now the townspeople were strangely altered -- they were like men crazed with panic. They ran up and down the streets of Mansoul, crying, 'Help! Help! Those people who turn the world upside down have invaded our town!' They wouldn't stop crying out, their wits had left them because of their fear and they cried out even more, 'The enemy has come to destroy our peace and kill us!' Diabolus was pleased with this. 'Now the people of Mansoul are right where I want them. They're terrified and will do whatever I tell them to save themselves. Let's see Shaddai's men try to get control of Mansoul now!'

[Note -- The enemy has come to destroy our peace and kill us!: when sinners listen to Satan, they are moved to rage against godliness]

Before the third day, Captain Boanerges told the trumpeter to go to Ear Gate and summon Mansoul in the name of the great Shaddai to hear the proclamation that he was going to deliver in the King's name. The trumpeter's name was Pay-attention-to-what-you-hear. He went to Ear Gate and blew his trumpet to get the people's attention. But no one approached to listen or respond, because Diabolus had told the people not to. So the trumpeter went back to his Captain and reported what had happened. The Captain was grieved, and told the trumpeter to go rest in his tent.

[Note -- no one approached to listen or respond: they refuse to hear]

Captain Boanerges tried again later -- he sent the trumpeter back to Ear Gate to blow his trumpet for the people to come and hear, but it was just as before -- the people stayed away and would not respond, just as Diabolus had told them to.

So the Captains and their field officers held a council of war to consider what to do next in order to win back the town of Mansoul. After some discussion and debate about the specifics of their orders, they decided to try one last time to deliver their message. If the people still refused to listen, the trumpeter was to tell Mansoul that the soldiers would use whatever means they could to compel Mansoul to obey King Shaddai by force.

So Captain Boanerges commanded the trumpeter to go back to Ear Gate and command the people to listen to the King's message. The trumpeter went and gave a third summons to the people. He said that if they still refused to listen, the King's Captains would come and try to compel them to obey by force.

[Note -- Notice the long-suffering and patience of a merciful God!]

Then the governor, Will-be-Will, the defector who was mentioned before, stood up with the keeper of the gates. With fancy official-sounding words, he demanded to know who this trumpeter was, and why he was making such a racket at the gate and saying such outrageous things.

The trumpeter responded, 'I am servant to the noble Captain Boanerges, the general of King's armies. You and the whole town of Mansoul have rebelled against King Shaddai, and my Captain and I have a message for you. If you refuse to listen, you'll have to accept the consequences.'

[Note -- The trumpeters are the ministers of the gospel of peace proclaiming the glad tidings of salvation.]

Lord Will-be-Will said, 'I will pass the message on to my master, and I'll let you know his response.'

But the trumpeter said, 'Our message is not to the giant Diabolus. It's to the troubled town of Mansoul. We don't care what the giant's response is. We were sent to recover this town from his cruel tyranny, and to persuade it to submit to the excellent King Shaddai as it did before.'

Lord Will-be-Will said, 'I will pass your message on to the townspeople.'

'Do not deceive us,' said the trumpeter. 'That wouldn't deceive us as much as you'd be deceiving yourselves. If you do not submit to us peacefully, then we are resolved to make war on you and bring you under by force. To prove that I'm telling you the truth, this will be a sign to you: tomorrow, you shall see a black banner with an image of three burning thunder bolts set up on the hill as a message that we defy your false king, and as a token of our resolution to make you submit to your Lord and rightful King.'

So the Lord Will-be-Will came down from the wall, and the trumpeter went back to his camp. The Captains and their officers wanted to know if the people had listened, and what the result was. The trumpeter said, 'Lord Will-be-Will with the gate keeper came to the wall when they heard my trumpet. He asked me who I was and what I wanted, so I told him my message and by whose authority I brought it. He said he would tell the governor and the rest of Mansoul. And then I returned here.'

Captain Boanerges said, 'Let's wait in camp for awhile and see what these rebels will do.'

[Note -- Conviction does not always end in conversion; the cares of the world, or the deceitfulness of riches, conspire together to destroy the seed sown by God's word.]

When the appointed time came for Mansoul to hear Captain Boanerges and his army, the whole camp was commanded to stand with their weapons, ready to receive Mansoul with mercy if they would listen, but if they wouldn't, to force them to submit. The trumpets sounded to call them to arms. But when the people within Mansoul heard the trumpets sounding from the armies' camps, they thought the soldiers were going to storm the town. At first they were alarmed, but after they calmed down, they began to make preparations to defend themselves in case the army did attack.

Captain Boanerges told the trumpeter to summon Mansoul to listen to King Shaddai's message and give their answer.

The trumpeter blew his trumpet, and the people of Mansoul approached, but they reinforced Ear Gate against the army. Captain Boanerges asked to see the Town Mayor, which was then Lord Incredulity. He came to the wall, but when Captain Boanerges saw him, he cried out, 'You're not the Mayor! Where is Lord Understanding? I'd like to deliver my message directly to him.'

[Note -- Boanerges refuses to let his message be judged by Incredulity.]

Diabolus, who had also come to the gate, said, 'Mr. Captain, you have had the audacity to summon Mansoul four times to persuade her to submit to your King. He has no authority here, and this is not the time to dispute that. So I ask you -- what is the reason for this commotion? Do you even know what you're doing?'

Captain Boanerges, whose banner was the black one with three burning thunderbolts, took no notice of the giant. He addressed himself directly to the people of Mansoul. 'Know this, unhappy and rebellious Mansoul: the gracious, great King Shaddai, my Master, has sent me here with his official orders' (and, here, he showed them his commission) 'to bring you back to obedience to him. If you yield to my summons, he has commanded me to receive you as friends and brothers. But if you will not, if you hear the summons to submit and still refuse and rebel, we are to try to take you by force.'

Then Captain Conviction stepped forward. His banner was the one with the pale colors, and his coat of arms had the open law book with the flame coming out. He said, 'Listen, Mansoul! You were once famous for your innocence, but now you have degenerated into lies and deception. You've heard my brother, Captain Boanerges. You would be wise, and much happier, to submit and accept the conditions for peace and mercy when they're offered -- especially when the terms are offered by the one you've rebelled against, and who has the power to tear you to pieces. When King

Shaddai is angry, no one can stand before him. If you claim that you have not sinned or acted rebelliously against our King, then all of your evil actions since the day you cast off your service to him will be enough to testify against you. What else is it but rebellion for you to listen to the tyrant and accept him as your king? What else can it mean when you reject the laws of King Shaddai and obey Diabolus instead? What else can it mean when you take up arms to fight us, and shut your town gates against us, the faithful servants of your King? Accept my brother's invitation. Don't refuse his offer of mercy; make peace with your enemy quickly. Oh, Mansoul, don't allow yourselves to be kept from mercy and to suffer a thousand miseries because of the flattering lies of Diabolus. Perhaps his lies have convinced you that we're seeking our own profit in this mission, but we're only doing this because of our obedience to King Shaddai and our concern for your happiness.

'I say again, Mansoul -- is it not amazingly gracious for King Shaddai to humble himself so much as he does? He is reasoning with you through us with pleas and sweet persuasion to beg you to subject yourselves to him. Does he need you like you need him? No, of course not -- but he is merciful. He doesn't want his Mansoul to die; he wants you to return to him and live.'

Then Captain Judgment stepped forward. He was the one with the red banner, and burning fiery furnace as his coat of arms. He said, 'Oh, you people of Mansoul who have lived in rebellion and treason against King Shaddai for so long -- we have not come here to speak our own minds, or revenge our own quarrels. It is the King our Master who has sent us to persuade you to obey him. If you refuse to obey peacefully, then we have orders to compel you to submit. Don't let Diabolus make you think that King Shaddai doesn't have the power to bring you down and make you submit to him. Shaddai is the one who made everything. If he even touches the mountains, they smoke. Nor will the gates of his mercy stay open forever. The day that will bring his hot fire is coming; it is coming quickly, and will not sleep.

'Oh, Mansoul, does it seem trivial to you that our King is offering you mercy, and after you've provoked him so much? Yet, he is still holding out a golden scepter of peace to you and he is opening the gate of his friendship to you. Are you going to continue to provoke him? If so, then listen: his mercy won't be offered to you indefinitely. If you refuse to see him, his judgment will still be there. Believe him. Yes, because his wrath is real, beware! He can destroy you with a single stroke. If that happens, then no ransom can help you. Will he be tempted by your money? No, your gold and all your treasures won't make him change his mind, nor can you force him to relent, even if you bring all your strength against him. He has prepared his throne to sit as a judge. He will come with fire, and his chariots will come like a whirlwind to distribute his anger with fury, and deliver his rebukes with flames of fire. So listen up, Mansoul, or else, after you have earned judgment by being wicked, his justice and punishment will catch up with you.'

While Captain Judgment was saying these things, Diabolus was seen to tremble, but Captain Judgment just went on: 'O, unfortunate town of Mansoul, won't you open the gates and receive us, the deputies of your King, and the ones who would rejoice to see you live? Will your heart be able to take it, or can you remain strong, on the day he deals with you in judgment? Can you stand it if he forces you to drink the wine of anger that he has mixed for Diabolus and his servants? Think about it. Quickly, consider what you're doing.'

[Note -- mixed for Diabolus and his servants: Judgment without mercy is reserved for Satan and his demons; but justice and mercy are designed to work together to free sinners from ruin.]

[Half-way point]

Then the fourth Captain stepped forward -- noble Captain Execution -- and he said, 'Once, town of Mansoul, you were great, but now you're as barren as a tree with no fruit. Once you were the delight of the high ones, but now you're a den for Diabolus. Listen to me, too. My words are also from the great King Shaddai. Look -- the axe is right at the root of the trees. Every tree that doesn't bring forth good fruit is going to be chopped down and thrown into the fire.

'So far, Mansoul, you've been like a fruitless tree. You grow nothing but thorns and briars. Your poor fruit shows that you are not a good tree. Your grapes are all sour, and your berry clusters are bitter. You have rebelled against your King, and look -- we are like the axe sent by Shaddai. It's poised at the foot of the tree, ready to chop you down. What do you say? Will you turn back? Tell me now, before the first blow strikes -- will you turn back? Our axe has to be pointed in your direction before it can strike. It has to be facing you in a threatening stance before we strike to execute our punishment. Between these two actions, you can decide to repent -- but that's all the time you have. What are you going to do? Will you turn, or shall I attack? If I make my strike, you'll go down. I have orders to chop you down, and the only thing that can prevent me from carrying through with those orders is your repentance. If mercy doesn't prevent me from destroying you, what else are you fit for except to be cut down, thrown into the fire, and burned?

'Mansoul, patience and restraint won't last forever. They might be available for a year, or two, or three. But if you provoke your King with a three years' rebellion -- and your rebellion has already been going on for longer than that -- then what else can you expect him to say except, 'Cut it down'? Do you think these are merely idle threats, or that our King doesn't have the power to do what he says? Mansoul, you will discover that when sinners disregard or scoff at our King's words, there is not only threatening, but burning coals of fire.

'You have been like a deserted wasteland long enough, will you continue to be useless? It is your sin that has brought our army to your gates. Is this same army going to bring judgment and execution into your very town? You've been hearing what the Captains have said, but you still shut us out of your town. Speak up, Mansoul -- are you going to continue to resist us, or will you accept our conditions of peace?'

The town of Mansoul refused to listen to the brave speeches of the noble Captains. The words did give them something to think about, but not enough to make them open the gates. The town asked for some time to think about it and prepare an answer. The Captains said they would give them some time if they threw Ill-pause over the wall so they could punish him for his part in their rebellion, but if they wouldn't turn him over, they couldn't have any time. 'We know,' said the Captains, 'that as long as Ill-pause is within Mansoul, any attempts at logical reasoning will be confused, and nothing but mischief can be expected to result.'

[Note -- Ill-pause is well-named. Listening to corrupt and carnal reason is too often a means of preventing the soul from choosing Christ. Reason is not a good judge of these matters.]

Diabolus, who was also there, was reluctant to lose Ill-pause because he was his speaker; he wanted to answer right then for the town himself. But then he thought better of it, and commanded Lord Incredulity, his Mayor, to do it. He told him, 'My Lord Mayor, you give those renegades our answer, and speak up so that the whole town of Mansoul can hear and understand you.'

So, at Diabolus's command, Mr. Incredulity began and said, 'Gentlemen, you have disturbed our prince and meddled in our town of Mansoul by camping against it. We don't care where you came from, and we don't believe who you are. You claim to have authority from Shaddai, but we don't want to know by what right he commands you to come against us.

'By this supposed authority, you have also asked this town to desert her lord and to yield herself up to your king Shaddai for protection. You flatter her by claiming that if she submits, he'll overlook her past offenses.

'Furthermore, you have terrorized the town by threatening great and burning destruction to punish them if she doesn't do what you want her to.

'Now, Captains, wherever you come from, and however good your intentions may be, know that neither Diabolus, nor I, Incredulity his servant, nor the town of Mansoul, care about you, or your message, or the king that you claim sent you. We aren't afraid of his power, his strength, or his vengeance, and we will not yield at all to your summons.

[Note -- An accurate picture of unbelief.]

'As far as the war you threaten to make against us, we'll just have to defend ourselves as well as we can. Be warned that we are not without the means to defy you. To be brief, as I do not wish to be a bore, we take you to be some wandering renegade gang. You've shaken off any obedience to your own king, assembled yourselves as a motley band of troublemakers, and you're roving from place to place to see if your flatteries are skillful enough and your threats are fearful enough to make some silly town or country desert their place so you can take it over. But you won't get Mansoul!

'To conclude, we don't dread you, nor fear you, nor will we obey your summons. We will close our gates and lock you out. And we aren't going to let you linger here for long; our people are sensitive and your appearance disturbs them. So pick up your baggage and weapons and get out of here, or we'll attack you from the town walls.'

[Note -- walls: flesh]

Incredulity's speech was seconded by desperate Will-be-Will, who said, 'Gentlemen, we've heard your demands and threats and your summons. But we do not fear your armies, we won't listen to your threats. We will remain just as you found us. We command you to be gone within three days, or you'll know what it means to dare to rouse the lion Diabolus when he's asleep in his town of Mansoul.'

Forget-Good, who was the Town Recorder, added, 'Gentlemen, you see how our lords have used calm, gentle words to answer your rough, angry threats. I myself heard them give you permission to depart from here as peacefully as you came. Accept their kindness and leave. We could have come out here with force, and made you feel how sharp our swords are, but we are a peaceful, quiet people, and we don't want to hurt or trouble anyone.'

Then the people of the town shouted for joy, as if Diabolus and his companions had gotten some great gain from the enemy. They rang the bells, celebrated, and danced on the walls.

Diabolus went back to the castle, and the Lord Mayor and Recorder went to their office, but Lord Will-be-Will stayed to make sure the gates were locked with bolts and secured with extra guards. He also tried to get better security for Ear Gate, since that was where the King's forces seemed to want to approach. He promoted old Mr. Prejudice, an ill-tempered, surly fellow, to the rank of Captain and made him guard the gate with sixty men under him. These men were perfect for this job; they were called 'deaf' because they didn't listen to either the Captains or the soldiers.

When the Captains heard the responses of the town leaders, and realized they would not have the opportunity to be heard by the townspeople, and now that they knew Mansoul was determined to fight back against the King's army, they prepared to fight them and see what force would do. They positioned additional men at Ear Gate, knowing that they wouldn't be able to do much good unless they got through there. Then they stationed men in other positions and gave them the code word, which was, 'You must be born again.' Then they sounded the trumpet. Those inside the town answered back, both sides shouted, they met the attack with a counter-attack, and the battle began. The townspeople had positioned two big guns over Ear Gate, one called Pretentious, and the other called Violent. They put a lot of trust in these guns. They had been cast in the castle by Diabolus's founder, whose name was Mr. Puff-up, and they were dangerous. But the Captains were so diligent and attentive that, when they saw them, the bullets might sometimes whiz right by their ears, but they didn't hurt them. The townspeople greatly annoyed the camp of King Shaddai with these two guns, and that helped to secure the gate, but not much real damage was done by them, as you'll see.

The town of Mansoul also had a few handguns in it, and they used these, too, against the camp of Shaddai.

The soldiers from Shaddai's camp were just as courageous, and with just as much valour, they assaulted the town and Ear Gate. They realized that if they couldn't break through that gate, it would be useless to batter the wall. The King's Captains had several slings and a couple of battering rams. With these, they battered the houses and people in the town, and they tried to ram an opening through Ear Gate.

There were several skirmishes and lively fights in the army camp and in the town. The Captains made many attempts to break open or beat down the tower by Ear Gate and enter there, but the people of Mansoul defended it well with the help of the rage of Diabolus, the bravery of Will-be-Will, and the actions of old Incredulity, the Mayor, and Mr. Forget-Good, the Town Recorder. The battles of that summer seemed to take the most toll on the King's army. Mansoul seemed to be winning. So the Captains retreated to their camp for the winter. Was there a heavy loss to both sides? Read on and you'll see.

When the Captains had marched from Shaddai's court to Mansoul, they happened to cross paths with three young guys who wanted to be soldiers. These men appeared to be decent men of courage and skill. Their names were Mr. Tradition, Mr. Human-Wisdom, and Mr. Man's-Invention. These men approached the Captains and offered their services to King Shaddai. The Captains explained their mission and told them to not to join up too rashly, but the young men said they had already thought it through, and this mission was just the kind of thing they were seeking. In fact, when they heard the Captains were passing through, they had come specifically to meet them so they could enlist. Since Captain Boanerges could see that they were men of courage, he signed them up into his company, and they went with them to the war.

After the war had begun, during one of the most heated skirmishes, a company of Will-be-Will's soldiers went out from the town by a large back gate. They ended up at the rear of Captain Boanerges's company, where these three new recruits happened to be, and they captured them and took them prisoners. They dragged them into the town, and soon after they were there, the townspeople began to whisper that Will-be-Will's men had captured three important soldiers from King Shaddai's army. Finally, Diabolus heard about it in the castle.

[Note -- captured them and took them prisoners: this is what happens to all false followers who have any other foundation besides Christ Jesus.]

Diabolus sent for Will-be-Will to ask whether the report was true, and he said it was. Then the giant sent for the prisoners and demanded who they were, where they had come from, and what jobs they had done in Shaddai's army, and they told him. Then Diabolus sent them back to the prison. A few days later, he called them again and asked if they would be willing to fight for him instead, against their former Captains. They replied that they didn't live by religion, they just went wherever adventure took them. If Diabolus was willing to hire them, they were willing to fight for him. So

Diabolus sent them to serve under the command of Captain Anything, an active soldier in the town of Mansoul. He sent them with this note:

[Note -- sent them to serve under the command of Captain Anything: When the only true religion is discarded for tradition, human reason, or man's invention, man will be ready to go along with whatever is trendy, and utterly ruin their souls.]

'Captain Anything, my friend -- these three men want to serve me in the war, and I don't know of a better leader to have charge of them than you. Receive them into your company in my name, and make use of them in the battles against Shaddai and his soldiers. Farewell.'

So Captain Anything added them to his forces. He made two of them sergeants, but he made Mr. Man's-Invention his flag bearer.

Meanwhile, King Shaddai's soldiers did some damage to the town. They beat in the roof of the Town Mayor's house, exposing it more than ever. They hit Will-be-Will with their sling and almost killed him, but he recovered. With a single shot, they killed six legislators: Mr. Swearing, Mr. Adultery, Mr. Fury, Mr. Stand-to-Lies, Mr. Drunkenness, and Mr. Cheating.

They also removed the two guns mounted on the tower by Ear Gate and threw them to the ground. I mentioned that the King's soldiers had settled to their camp for the winter. From there they were able to harass the townspeople with clamorous warnings, and this was so effective that Mansoul was constantly troubled. She could no longer sleep as peacefully, or go about her revelries happily as before. There were so many urgent, disturbing alarms, one after another, first at one gate, and then at another, and then at all the gates at the same time, that there was no peace. The alarms were so frequent, and they happened during the longest nights and coldest weather, so the season was completely unpleasant -- a winter like none they had ever seen before. Sometimes trumpets would blare, and sometimes stones would be flung into the town. Sometimes ten thousand of the King's soldiers would run around the town at midnight, shouting and crying for battle. Sometimes citizens in the town would be wounded, and their cries would distress the rest of the town, which was beginning to deteriorate. The King's soldiers harassed the town so much that Diabolus, their king, had little rest.

I was told that new ideas and conflicting thoughts started to enter the minds of the people. Some would say, 'we can't live like this.' Others would answer, 'this won't last forever.' Then a third person would suggest, 'let's return to King Shaddai and put an end to these troubles.' And a fourth would say fearfully, 'I'm not sure he would take us back now.' And Mr. Conscience, who was once their Town Recorder, had started talking out loud again, and his words sounded to the people like great claps of thunder. His voice was as terrifying as the noise of the soldiers and shouts of the Captains.

And things had started to be scarce in Mansoul. The things her soul lusted after seemed to be harder to find. The beautiful things she had enjoyed were marred and burnt. Old, wrinkled skin and reminders of the shadow of death were everywhere. Oh, how Mansoul would have loved some peace and contentment, even if it came with meager living conditions!

In the dead of winter, the Captains sent the trumpeter with a summons to the town of Mansoul to submit to the great King Shaddai. They did this not once, or twice, but three times, hoping that at some point, Mansoul might be inclined to surrender and only needed an invitation to do so. In fact, as far as I could tell, the town would have surrendered if it hadn't been for old Incredulity's opposition and Will-be-Will's fickleness. Diabolus also started to bristle with annoyance, so Mansoul was undecided about yielding, which meant that they still lived under a state of distress with these bewildering fears.

[Note -- In the dead of winter: The condition of the soul in its natural state is compared to winter.]

I just said that the King's army sent the trumpeter three times to Mansoul to ask her to submit.

The first time, the trumpeter brought words of peace. He told them that the noble Captains pitied the misery of the poor town of Mansoul, and were troubled to see them resisting their own deliverance. If Mansoul would simply humble herself and return, all of her previous rebellions and flagrant treasons would be forgiven by their merciful King, and forgotten. He begged them not to stand in the way of their own help and lose everything. Then he went back to camp.

The second time, he spoke a bit more roughly. After sounding the trumpet, he said that their continued rebellion was irritating and angering the Captains, and they were resolving to conquer Mansoul or kill them and line their bones up along the walls.

The third time, he dealt with them even more roughly. He said that since they had been so unbelievably disrespectful, he didn't know whether the Captains were inclined to show them mercy or judgment. 'All I know,' he said, 'is that they commanded me to tell you to open the gates to them.' And then he went back to camp.

These summons, especially the last two, distressed the town so much that they called a meeting. The result of that meeting was to send Lord Will-be-Will to Ear Gate with a trumpet to call the Captains for a conference. The Captains came with their weapons and armies. The townspeople said they had heard their summons and considered it. They said they would come to an agreement with them and King Shaddai upon certain terms and conditions that their prince told them to specify. If they agreed, then they would become one with them. These were the terms:

> *[Note -- would become one with them: religion while holding onto one's old lusts and inordinate affections, cannot be. Old things must pass away. Christ can have no union with Satan.]*

1. That King Shaddai would allow those of their company, such as their Mayor, and Mr. Forget-Good, and Will-be-Will, to continue as governors of the town, castle and gates.

2. No one serving under Diabolus should be fired or lose the freedom that he now enjoyed in the town of Mansoul.

3. The people of Mansoul should enjoy the rights and privileges that had been granted to them under their lord and defender, king Diabolus.

4. No new laws, officers, or judges should have any power over them unless they consented.

'These are our conditions of peace,' they said; 'upon these terms, we will submit to your King.'

When the Captains heard this weak and lame offer with its bold demands, Captain Boanerges responded with this speech:

'Inhabitants of Mansoul, when I heard your trumpet calling us to discuss terms of peace, I was sincerely glad. When you said you were willing to submit yourselves to our Lord and King, I was even more glad. But then, when I heard your silly provisions and ridiculous complaints, you laid the stumbling block of your own foolishness in front of yourselves. Then my gladness was turned to sorrow, and my hopes that you would return languished into swooning fears.

'I suspect that old Ill-pause, the ancient enemy of Mansoul, drew up those proposals you presented us with. They don't deserve to be taken seriously by anyone who claims allegiance to King Shaddai. Therefore, with the highest contempt, we refuse and reject your terms and consider them great sins.

'But, Mansoul, if you will only surrender yourselves to us -- or, rather to our King, and if you will trust him to make whatever terms he sees fit (and I think you will find those terms very beneficial to you), then we will receive you and be at peace with you. But if you don't want to trust yourselves in the hands of King Shaddai, then things are right where they were before, and we know what we need to do next.'

Then the Mayor, old Mr. Incredulity, cried out and said, 'What kind of idiot who is out of reach of his enemy would be so foolish as to hand his own weapons over into the power of who knows who? For my own part, I will never give in to such an unlimited proposal. Do we have any idea what your king is like? I've heard that he lashes out in anger if one of his subjects steps even an inch out of line. And others say that he requires more of them than they could ever do. It seems wise to me, Mansoul, to be extremely cautious what you do here. Once you yield, you're under the power of someone else, and you're no longer your own. To surrender yourselves to some unknown and unlimited power is the greatest insanity in the world. Surrender with no terms? Once you're his, how do you know which of you he'll kill, and which of you he'll allow to live? Or maybe he'll kill us all and send some other people from his own country to live here in this town.'

[Note -- old Mr. Incredulity, cried out and said: unbelief never says anything useful, but always speaks mischievously.]

This speech of the Town Mayor's undid everything, and completely ruined any hopes for an agreement. So the Captains went back to their trenches and tents, and the Mayor went back to the castle and his prince.

Chapter 4

Diabolus had been waiting for the Mayor to come back and tell him what had been decided. When he came into the state room, Diabolus greeted him with, 'Welcome, my lord! How did it go?' And Mr. Incredulity bowed low and said, 'The Captains said such and such, and I said such and such.' Diabolus was glad to hear the report and said, 'Mr. Mayor, my faithful servant, I have tested your loyalty many times and always found you to be trustworthy. I promise you, if we get through this, I'll promote you to a place of honour, something much better than the position of Mayor. I'll make you my Deputy -- second only to me. You'll rule over nations. You'll bind them so they won't be able to resist. None of our servants will walk at liberty except those who are willing to be your slaves.'

And the Mayor left as if he had gained a great favour. He went to his home with a bounce in his step, looking forward with ambitious hopes to the day when he should achieve greatness.

But now, although Diabolus and the Mayor were on the same page, the Mayor's rejection to the Captains put Mansoul into a mutiny. While the Mayor, Mr. Incredulity, was telling Diabolus what had been said, the previous Mayor -- that is, Mr. Understanding -- and the previous Town Recorder -- Mr. Conscience -- found out what had happened at Ear Gate. They hadn't been allowed to be there themselves, for fear they would have joined the Captains, but they heard what had been going on and they were concerned. Now they got some of the townspeople together and began to bring them to reason about the logic of the Captains' demands, and the negative consequences that would follow the refusal of Mr. Incredulity, especially his lack of respect to the Captains, and the way he insinuated that they were disloyal traitors. 'What else could he have meant when he said he wouldn't yield to their propositions, and then suggested that the Captains would destroy us when they had previously sent word that they wanted to show us mercy?' The multitude now saw the mischief that Mr. Incredulity had done, and they dispersed into groups through the town. They began to murmur, and then to talk openly, and finally they were going all over town shouting, 'Oh, those brave Captains! I wish we were under the government of the Captains, and their King Shaddai!'

[Note -- they heard what had been going on and they were concerned: conviction begins to distress Mansoul]

When the Town Mayor heard that Mansoul was in an uproar, he came down to appease the people, and hoped to soften their anger by smiling and speaking cheerfully with them. But as soon as they saw him, they rushed at him and would have harmed him if he hadn't made a mad dash back into his house. They then attacked his house and would have pulled it down around him, but his house was too sturdy, and they couldn't tear it down. So he took some courage and addressed them through a window:

'Gentlemen, why are you so upset?'

Then Mr. Understanding said, 'It's because you and your master have not done as you should have to Shaddai's Captains. You were faulty in three ways. First, you wouldn't let me and Mr. Conscience be there to hear what was said. Second, you demanded terms and conditions that could never be agreed to unless you meant for Shaddai to be king in name only so that Mansoul could still be allowed to live in all the obscenity and arrogance he wanted and keep Diabolus as the real king. And third, after the Captains stated their conditions, and would have received us with mercy, you undid everything with your obnoxious, untimely, and improper speech.'

[Note -- Unbelief throws insurmountable obstacles in the way to prevent poor sinners from coming to Christ.]

When old Mr. Incredulity heard this, he cried out, 'Treason! Treason! Pick up your weapons, trusty friends of Diabolus!'

Mr. Understanding: 'Sir, think what you want about my words, but I'm certain that Captains from such a high lord as their King deserved better treatment from you.'

Old Mr. Incredulity said, 'I was speaking for my prince, for his government, and to quiet the people. Your unlawful actions have made them mutiny against us!'

Then Mr. Conscience said, 'You shouldn't criticize what Mr. Understanding said. It's obvious that he spoke the truth, and that you're an enemy to Mansoul. Your rude and combative words have been damaging, have grieved the Captains, and have harmed Mansoul. If you had accepted the terms, the sound of trumpets and alarm of war would have ceased by now. But those sounds continue, all because of your lack of wisdom.'

Old Mr. Incredulity said, 'I'll tell Diabolus what you have said, and he'll have an answer for you. Meanwhile, I'm looking out for the best interests of this town, and I don't need any advice from you.'

Mr. Understanding: 'Sir, you and your prince are both foreigners here. You're not natives of Mansoul. It's possible that after you've made things worse here, and realized that your only chance of safety is to flee from here, you might abandon us and leave us to fend for ourselves. Or else you might set us on fire, walk out by the light of the flames, and leave us here in the smoking ruins.'

Mr. Incredulity: 'You forget that you have a governor, and you should be respectful like a good subject. When my lord hears about what has happened as a result of your words, he'll see that you are punished.'

While these gentlemen were arguing, down came Lord Will-be-Will, Mr. Prejudice, Ill-pause, and some of the newly promoted councilmen and legislators, and asked for the cause of the disturbance and commotion. Everyone began to speak at the same time, so that nothing could be understood. Then all was quiet, and crafty Mr. Incredulity began to speak. 'My lord,' he said, 'these are a couple of bad-tempered gentlemen. Their bad dispositions have caused them to take the advice of Mr. Discontent and gather these people against me today. They have also tried to make the people rebel against our prince.'

[Note -- When Satan senses that he is losing his influence because of the Holy Spirit's work in the heart, he sends unbelief and fears sprung out of a guilty conscience to oppose God's work. But in vain!]

All of those who were faithful to Diabolus stood up and proclaimed that all of this was true.

When those who sided with Mr. Understanding and Mr. Conscience saw that things were likely to go badly, since all the force and power was on the side of Mr. Incredulity, they stepped forward to help. So there was a large crowd on both sides. Those siding with Mr. Incredulity would have had the two gentlemen thrown into jail, but those on the other side wouldn't have it. Then they started to cheer for their sides: Diabolus's servants cheered for Mr. Incredulity, Forget-Good, the newly appointed councilmen, and Diabolus. The other group cheered just as loudly for King Shaddai, his Captains, his laws, their mercy, and their terms and conditions. This bickering went on for awhile, and evolved into actual fighting and brawling on both sides. Mr. Conscience was knocked down twice by a Diabolian named Mr. Be-numbing. Mr. Understanding was almost killed by a rifle, except that the shot missed him. On the other side, Mr. Rash-head had his head punched by Mr. Mind, Lord Will-be-Will's servant. And Mr. Prejudice was kicked and tumbled in the dirt. He had recently been made captain over some of Diabolus's soldiers, which was detrimental to the town, but now some of Mr. Understanding's group had cracked his head. Mr. Anything took an active part in the fighting, but both sides fought against him because he was loyal to no one. He had one of his legs broken, but the guy who did it wished it had been his neck. There were more injuries than that. It was odd to see Lord Will-be-Will standing by indifferently. He didn't seem to prefer either side more than the other, but it was noticed that he smiled when he saw Mr. Prejudice tumbled and thrown down into the dirt. And when Mr. Anything came hobbling towards him, he pretended not to see him.

[Note -- cracked his head: 'The carnal mind is enmity against God.' But the Holy Spirit destroys the enmity, roots out prejudice, and enlightens the understanding.]

After the brawl was over, Diabolus had Mr. Understanding and Mr. Conscience thrown into jail for being the ringleaders of the intense riot in Mansoul. So the town settled back down quietly. The prisoners were treated badly; in fact, Diabolus considered having them executed, but that wouldn't have helped his cause, as the war was practically at all their gates.

The Captains, when they had gone back to their camp, called for a council of war to decide what to do next. Some wanted to go and take the town, but most thought it would be best to give the people another chance to answer the summons to yield. It seemed like the town was more inclined to submit now than they had been before. 'And if,' they said, 'while some are softened and leaning towards yielding, we treat them roughly by attacking, we'll make them bitter and likely to shut down altogether.' This sounded reasonable to all of them, so they told the trumpeter what to say, and sent him back to the town. A few hours later, he made his way towards Ear Gate and blew his trumpet. Those within hearing distance came to see what he wanted, and he made this speech:

'Oh, hard-hearted, disgraceful town of Mansoul! How long will you prize your sinful, depraved childishness, you fools? How long will you delight in your contempt? Do you still reject our offers of peace and deliverance? Do you still refuse King Shaddai's merciful proposal, and trust the lies and deceptions of Diabolus? Do you think after Shaddai has conquered you, that your memories of how you carried yourself towards him will bring you comfort and peace, or that your tangled speeches will make him cringe in fear like a grasshopper? Is Shaddai making these offers because he's afraid of you? Do you think you're stronger than he is? Look at the sky -- how high do think those stars are? Are you strong enough to lasso the sun and make it stop setting, or make the moon cease giving off its light? Can you count the stars, or stop the rain from falling? Can you command the waters of the sea to come and water your fields? Can you locate every person who's proud, and humble him to his face privately? Yet these are just some of the things that our King, in whose name we come, can do. He sent us to bring you under his authority. Therefore, I summon you in his name to yield yourselves up to his Captains.'

[Note -- Loving and practicing sin is the vilest drudgery, and the service of Satan is the most cruel tyranny. And it doesn't pay very good wages, either!]

At this speech, the people of Mansoul seemed to be stupefied. They didn't know how to respond. So Diabolus came forward to give them an answer himself. He directed his speech to the people of Mansoul.

'My faithful subjects,' he began, 'if this trumpeter is correct about the greatness of his king, then the terror of him will always keep you in bondage. You'll have to sneak around him to do anything. Can you bear to think of such intense power even when it's so far away? And if it's unsettling to think of when it's at a distance, what will you do when you're in its presence? I am your prince, well-known to you, and you can manipulate me as if I was a puny little grasshopper. Think about what's in your best interest, and remember the freedom I've given you.

'Even more, if everything this man said is true, why are all of his subjects enslaved wherever his Captains go? No one in the universe is as unhappy as his subjects; they're completely trampled over.

'Think about it, Mansoul -- I wish you were as unwilling to leave me as I am to leave you. But the ball is in your court. You already have liberty, if you know how to use it. You have a king, too -- do you know how to love and obey him?'

At this speech, the town of Mansoul hardened their hearts even more against King Shaddai's Captains. The idea of his greatness did discourage them, and thoughts of his holiness reduced them to despair.

So, after some brief deliberation, some men on Diabolus's side sent back a message for the trumpeter to bring back to his Captains. They said that they were determined to stay loyal to their king, and they would never yield to Shaddai. It was useless to give them any more summons because they would rather die than yield. Things appeared to be hopeless, and Mansoul seemed completely unreachable, but the Captains knew what their Lord was capable of, and they couldn't be discouraged that easily. In fact, they sent another summons, more harsh and severe this time. But the more summons they sent to reconcile them to King Shaddai, the farther away they seemed to be pushed. They kept calling to them, and the people kept refusing, even though they were only calling them be at peace with the Most High.

Since that wasn't working, they resolved to try something else. The Captains gathered together to discuss their options for delivering the town from Diabolus. One said one thing, and one said something else. Captain Conviction said, 'Brothers, this is what I think.

'First, we should keep flinging stones into the town to keep them on their toes, and not stop alarming them day or night. That might help to subdue their bold spirit. Even a lion can be tamed through continual exasperation.

'Then, while that's going on, we should work together to write up a letter to King Shaddai. After we've informed him of the condition of Mansoul and affairs here, and begged his pardon for not succeeding in his mission, we can ask for his help. Maybe he'll send in more forces with a brave, well-spoken Captain to lead them. That way, King Shaddai won't lose the advantage we've already gained for him, and he might even complete his conquest.'

All the Captains agreed to this plan. They wrote up a letter that said this:

'Most gracious and glorious King, Lord of the best world, and builder of Mansoul: Dreaded Sovereign, at your command, we have put our lives in jeopardy, and, as you asked, threatened war upon the famous town of Mansoul. When we first approached the town, we obeyed our orders and offered conditions of peace. But, great King, they didn't take us seriously, and refused to listen to our reproaches. They wanted to close the gates and shut us out. They loaded their guns, attacked us, and did whatever damage they could to us, but we kept hounding them with alarm after alarm, returning whatever retribution was fair, and we've done some of our own damage to the town.

'Diabolus, Incredulity, and Will-be-Will are the ringleaders against us. Currently, we're camped at our winter headquarters, but we're still continuing to harass them to keep them in distress.

'At one time, we think that if we had had just one solid friend within the town who could have seconded our summons, the people might have yielded as they ought, but there were nothing but enemies within, and no one to speak to the people on behalf of our King. So, although we've done the best we could, Mansoul still lives in a state of rebellion against you.

'Please, King of kings, pardon us for our lack of success in conquering Mansoul. We ask that you would send more forces to help subdue Mansoul, and a man to lead them whom the town might both love and fear.

'We don't speak like this because we don't want to continue the war -- in fact, we're willing to lay down our very lives for the cause -- we request this only so that the town of Mansoul may be won for you. We ask you to act quickly, so that once they are subdued, we can put your other gracious plans into effect. Amen.'

This letter was signed, sealed, and carried with all haste to the King by the hand of that good man, Mr. Love-to-Mansoul.

When this letter had come to the King's palace, it was delivered to none other than the King's son. He unsealed it and read it. He liked what it said and even added a few comments of his own before carrying it by his own hand to the King.

The King was glad to see the letter, but even more so when he saw how his son had agreed with its contents. He was glad to think that his Captains were so hearty in their work, and so determined, that they had already made some headway in conquering the town.

So the King called his son, Prince Emmanuel, and his son said, 'Here I am, Father.' His Father said, 'You know the condition of Mansoul as well as I do, and what we've determined to do about it, and what you have done to redeem her. So, my son, prepare yourself for war, for I'm sending you to my camp outside of Mansoul. There, you will prosper, and prevail, and conquer the town of Mansoul.'

The King's son said, 'Your law is in my heart; I am happy to do your will. This is the day we have longed for, and the work I've waited to do for a long time. So provide me with what you think I'll need, and I will go and deliver the perishing town of Mansoul from Diabolus and his power. My heart has often been distressed over the poor town of Mansoul, but now my heart is glad and rejoicing.'

And, at that, he leaped for joy, saying, 'In my heart, I haven't thought any price was too much for Mansoul. The day of vengeance for you is in my heart, Mansoul, and I am so glad that you, my Father, have made me Captain of their salvation! Now I can plague those who have been a plague to my town of Mansoul, and I can deliver her from them.'

After saying this to his Father, the news flew around the King's court. All the courtiers could talk about was what Emmanuel was going to do for the famous town of Mansoul. They were excited, too, about the Prince's plan. They were so stirred with this project, and with the justness of the war, that the highest lords and greatest associates in the kingdom wished they could serve in the Prince's army to help him recover the troubled town of Mansoul for King Shaddai.

[Half-way point]

It was decided that a few should go on ahead to carry a message to the camp, letting them know that the Prince himself was coming to recover Mansoul, and he was bringing an army that was so strong, and so invincible, that he couldn't be resisted. Even the high ones at court were ready to run like stewards to bring this news to the camp! When the Captains found out that the King was sending his son, Prince Emmanuel, and that the Prince was delighted to be sent on this errand, they were so pleased that they gave a shout that shook the earth all around. That shout echoed from the mountains, and made Diabolus tremble and shake.

Mansoul itself wasn't concerned at all about any of this; the people were distracted with their own pleasures and lusts. But Diabolus was concerned! He had his spies everywhere, bringing him intelligence about all kinds of things. They told him what was being planned against him at the King's court, and that Prince Emmanuel was on his way with an army to invade him. There wasn't anyone in the court or, indeed, in the entire kingdom that Diabolus feared more than Prince Emmanuel. If you remember, Diabolus had already felt his power once before, and this made him more afraid.

And now the Prince was ready to march forth towards Mansoul. He brought five noble Captains and their forces with him:

1. The first was the noble Captain Belief. His banner was red and carried by Mr. Promise, and his coat of arms was a holy lamb and golden shield. He had an army of 10,000 men.

2. The second was faithful Captain Good-Hope. His banner was blue, his standard-bearer was Mr. Expectation, and his coat of arms had three golden anchors. He also had 10,000 soldiers.

3. The third was fearless Captain Charity. His standard bearer was Mr. Pitiful, his banner was green, and his coat of arms was a bosom embracing three little orphans. He also had 10,000 soldiers.

4. The fourth was daring Captain Innocent. His standard bearer was Mr. Harmless, his banner was white, and his coat of arms was three golden doves. He also had 10,000 soldiers.

5. The fifth was loyal and beloved Captain Patience. His standard bearer was Mr. Long-Suffering, his banner was black, and his coat of arms was a golden heart pierced with three arrows. He also had 10,000 soldiers.

Prince Emmanuel began his march with these five Captains. Captain Belief led the way, and Captain Patience brought up the rear. The other three made up the main body, and Prince Emmanuel rode in his chariot at the head of the group.

They began their march with trumpets sounding, armour shining, and their banners waving in the wind. The Prince had golden armour that shone like the sun. All the Captains had armour of steel that glittered like the stars. There were also some men from King Shaddai's court who rode along because of their love for the King, and the joy they felt in seeing Mansoul's deliverance.

When Prince Emmanuel had gone to recover the town of Mansoul, his Father had commanded him to take fifty-four battering rams and twelve slings. All of these were made with pure gold, and they were carried with the army along with their armour as they went along to Mansoul.

[Note -- fifty-four battering rams, and twelve slings: the 66 books of the Bible. Christ is the sum and substance of the Bible.]

When they were a couple of miles from the town, the Captains met them and apprised them of the situation, and then they traveled together to the camp. When the other soldiers saw that they had new forces to help them, they gave such a shout that the walls of the town shook, giving Diabolus another fright. The new forces surrounded the town so that no matter which way the people looked, Mansoul saw forces, power, and siege mounds lying against them on every side. Mansoul was situated between two mountains -- Mount Gracious was on one side of the town, and Mount Justice was on the other. There were also several natural banks and fields, such as Plain-Truth Hill and No-Sin Banks, where they set up slings against the town. Four slings were set up on Mount Gracious, and four on Mount Justice, and the rest were placed in various places around the town. The five biggest battering rams were placed on Mount Hearken to help break open Ear Gate.

[Note -- The Lord must first work on the ear and heart so that it can receive the work of salvation.]

When the people within the town saw the multitude of soldiers, rams, and slings set against them, and the shining armour, and waving banners, they were forced to re-think their position. They had been confident that they were sufficiently protected, but now they weren't so sure.

At this point, Prince Emmanuel hung out a white flag with three golden doves on it between the slings on Mount Gracious for two reasons:

1. To demonstrate that he would still be gracious to them if they returned to him.

2. To remove any excuse they might make for destroying them if they continued in their rebellion.

The white flag was hung out for two days to give the town time to consider, but they didn't even acknowledge it.

So the Prince commanded that the red banner of Captain Judgment with the fiery furnace be hung on Mount Justice. This banner waved in the wind for several days, but the townspeople didn't acknowledge that flag, either.

Then the Prince commanded his men to hang out the black banner of defiance with the three burning thunderbolts on it. But Mansoul was as unconcerned as ever. When the Prince saw that neither mercy, nor threats, nor judgment could touch the heart of Mansoul, he was very sorry and said, 'their strange behavior must be the result of their ignorance of what war is like rather than from any secret defiance of us or disgust at their own lives. Or if they do know about war in general, they don't know the kind of wars that I wage against my enemy Diabolus.'

So he sent a message to Mansoul explaining what the banners meant -- and that they were being given a choice between grace and mercy, or threats and judgment. During all this time, the people had kept their gates locked and bolted, with twice as many guards as usual. Diabolus kept them encouraged with rousing talks to continue their resistance.

[Note -- This is an accurate image of natural man -- he hardens his heart and refuses to hear, while the enemy uses various temptations and distractions to keep him in spiritual blindness.]

So this is the answer the townspeople gave to the Prince:

'Great Sir, your messenger has asked us whether we would accept your mercy or fall by your justice, but we are bound by our town laws and traditions, and we are unable to give you any certain answer. It is a violation of our law and against our king's command to make peace or war without his consent. But this is what we will do: we will ask our king to come down to the wall and do what he thinks is suitable, and in our best interests.'

When the good Prince heard this answer and saw the slavery and bondage of the people, and how content they were to continue under the oppression of the tyrant Diabolus, he was grieved to the heart. Every time he saw a sign that they were satisfied to remain enslaved to the giant, his heart would ache.

When the people carried all of this news to Diabolus and told him that the Prince was waiting by Mouth Gate for his answer, he acted proud and insolent, but in his heart, he was afraid.

He said, 'I'll go down to the gates myself and give him the most fitting answer.' So he went to the gate and prepared to speak, but using language that the people wouldn't understand. Here's the gist of his response:

'Great Emmanuel, Lord of all the world, I know you -- you're the son of the great Shaddai. Why have you come to torment me and cast me out of my rightful town? You know very well that Mansoul is mine for two reasons:

'1. It is mine by right of conquest. I won it fair and square. What right do you have to take my lawful prey, or to rescue my rightful captive?

'2. Mansoul is also mine because they have willingly subjected themselves to me. They opened their gates to me voluntarily, they swore loyalty to me, chose me to be their king, and gave me their castle. In fact, they've put their entire town under my power.

[Note -- castle: man's heart]

'In addition, the town of Mansoul has denied you -- they have rejected your law, your name, your image, and everything that is yours, and in their place, they have accepted and set up my own law, my name, my image, and everything that is mine. Ask your Captains -- they'll tell you that, in answer to your summons, the people have shown love and loyalty to me, but only arrogance, aversion, neglect, and scorn to you. You call yourself the Just One and claim to be holy, and you shouldn't do anything wicked. So go away, and leave what's rightfully mine alone.'

[Note -- The devil first tempts, then accuses, and finally torments all who live and die in his service.]

This speech was made in Diabolus's own language. He has the ability to speak to every man in his own language -- how else could he tempt them the way he does? -- but he does have a language of his own. It's the language of the foul, black pit.

So the poor people of Mansoul didn't know what he was saying, nor did they see him crouching and cringing when he was in the presence of their Prince Emmanuel.

[Note -- The devil is unable to even stand in the presence of Emmanuel.]

All this time, they assumed he had a power and force that couldn't be resisted. Even while he was making his case before the Prince, begging to be able to keep Mansoul and not have it taken from him by force, the people of Mansoul were bragging about his courage, saying, 'Is there anyone strong enough to make war against him?'

When this false prince had finished his speech, Emmanuel the Golden Prince stood up and gave the following speech:

'You deceiver! In my Father's name, and in my own name, and for the good of this poor town of Mansoul, I have something to say to you. You pretend to have a lawful right to the pitiable town of Mansoul, when it's obvious to everyone in my Father's court that everything you've gotten from Mansoul has been through treachery and lies. You deny my Father, you oppose the law, and thus you deceive the people of Mansoul. You act like the people have chosen you as their king and captain, but that's only because you cheated and deceived them. If lying, scheming, wicked deviousness, and all kinds of appalling hypocrisy will pass for fairness and rightness in my Father's court (and, after all, it's in that court that you'll be tried), then and only then will I admit that you have made a lawful conquest. Any thief, tyrant, or devil can make that kind of conquest! But I can demonstrate, Diabolus, that in all your pretences of conquering Mansoul, you have nothing truthful to say. Do you think my Father has fallen for your lies? What do you have to say about deliberately twisting the intent of the law? Was it a good thing for you to prey on the innocence and gullibility of Mansoul? You fooled them by promising them they would be happy living in sin and transgressing against my Father, when you know very well from your own experience that such actions will destroy them. You have also added to your crimes by defacing my Father's image out of spite, which did intolerable damage to the town of Mansoul.

'Not only that, but, as if these were just trivial things to you, you have not only cheated and wrecked Mansoul, but by your lies and phony position of superiority, you have turned them against their own deliverers. You have incited them against my Father's Captains and provoked them to fight against the very ones who are trying to set them free. You have done all of these things and more, even while you know they're wrong, in contempt of my Father and his law -- and you have done all of this for the purpose of making my Father displeased forever with the poor town of Mansoul. Therefore, I have come to avenge the wrong you have done to my Father, and to deal with the blasphemies you've used to make poor Mansoul blaspheme his name. You, prince of the underworld, are to blame, and I will make you pay for that.

'As for myself, Diabolus, I come against you by lawful authority to use my own power to pry Mansoul out of your burning fingers. This town of Mansoul is mine, Diabolus, and it's mine by lawful right. Anyone who searches the authentic, ancient records will see that this is true. I will make a case for my right to Mansoul, and confound you to your face.

'First, my Father built Mansoul himself and modified it with his own hands. The palace that's in the middle of town is also something he built for his own pleasure. Therefore, the town of Mansoul belongs to my Father. He has the best right to it, and no one can truthfully deny it.

'Second, you liar, Mansoul belongs to me because:

'1. I am my Father's heir, his firstborn. Thus, I have come against you to defend my own rightful property and recover my rightful inheritance from out of your hand.

'2. Furthermore, beyond inheriting Mansoul, my Father has gifted it to me. It was his, and he gave it to me. I never offended him so that he changed his mind and gave it to you instead. And I have never been bankrupt and needed to sell my beloved Mansoul. Mansoul is my passion, my delight, and the joy of my heart.

'3. Mansoul is also mine because I paid for it. I bought it for myself. So I have inherited it, been given it, and purchased it. By any lawful right, Mansoul belongs to me. You are a usurper, a tyrant and a traitor to claim that it's yours. The reason I purchased Mansoul is this: Mansoul had trespassed against my Father. My Father had told them that if ever they trespassed against him, they would die. It is more possible for heaven and earth to pass away than it is for my Father to break his word. So, when Mansoul sinned after believing your lie, I stepped in and offered to become a surety to my Father -- my body for theirs, my soul for theirs, in order to make amends for Mansoul's transgressions, and my Father accepted that. So, when the appointed time came, I gave body for body, soul for soul, life for life, blood for blood. In that way, I redeemed and bought my beloved Mansoul.

'4. I don't do anything halfway. My Father's law and justice, which were both compromised by sin, are now both satisfied, and very content that Mansoul should be rescued from you.

'5. I did not come out here to fight you on my own, but because my Father commanded me to. He told me, 'Go down and deliver Mansoul."

'So, know this, you deceiving liar, and let it also be known to the town of Mansoul -- I have not come here on my own without my Father.

'And now,' said Prince Emmanuel, 'I have something to say to the town of Mansoul.' But as soon as the confused town heard that he wanted to talk to them, the leaders locked and guarded the gates and would not permit any of the people to listen. But the Prince spoke anyway. 'Poor unhappy town of Mansoul. I can't help but have pity and compassion for you. You have accepted Diabolus as your king, and put yourselves in the service of that tyrant rather than your supreme Lord. You've opened your gates to him, but locked me out. You consider everything he says, but you refuse to even hear me. He brought you to destruction, yet you're happy to receive both him and your own ruin; I come bringing you salvation, and you ignore me. With blasphemous hands, you have taken your very selves and everything within you that belongs to me, and given it all to my adversary, who is my Father's greatest enemy. You have bowed and subjected yourselves to him, and sworn to be his. Poor Mansoul! What should I do to you? Should I save you, or destroy you? Should I attack you and grind you into dust, or make you a token of my richest grace? Listen, town of Mansoul -- listen to me and you shall live. I am merciful, Mansoul, and you will discover that I am just that. Don't shut me out of your gates.

'Oh, Mansoul, my orders are not to hurt you, nor do I want to hurt you. Why do you flee from me, your friend, and stick so close to your enemy? It is good for you to be sorry for your sin, but I don't want you to despair of life. I didn't bring this troop of soldiers to hurt you, but to deliver you from your bondage and make you obey me.

'My orders are to make war against Diabolus your king and all of his companions, because he's like a strong, armed man trying to take your house, and I want him out. I need to divide his spoils, take his armour, cast him out of his fortress, and make it a home for myself. And Diabolus will realize this when I lead him out in chains, and you will rejoice to see it.

'If I were to exert my strength, I could make him leave you and flee right now. But I have something else in mind for him, so that everyone can see how just and fair it is for me to make war against him. He has taken you by fraud, and keeps you through violence and deceit, but I will expose him to the whole world.

'Everything I'm saying is the truth. I am strong enough to save you, Mansoul, and I will deliver you out of his power.'

He made this speech directly to Mansoul, but Mansoul wouldn't have any of it. The people shut Ear Gate up tight, barricaded and bolted it, set a guard there, and told all the people not to use that gate. They did all of this because Diabolus had enchanted them to shut out their rightful Lord and Prince. So no one from the Prince's army was able to enter the town.

Chapter 5

When Emmanuel saw how entangled Mansoul was with sin and how they despised his words, he called his army to be ready at an appointed time. The only lawful way to get into Mansoul was through the gates, and since Ear Gate was the most important gate, he commanded his Captains and soldiers to bring their battering rams and slings there and to Eye Gate so they could take the town.

When Emmanuel had made everything ready for battle against Diabolus, he sent a message again to Mansoul to ask if they would yield peaceably, or whether they were determined to make him use his strength? The town called a council of war with Diabolus and resolved upon certain propositions to offer Emmanuel, and if he would accept them, they would agree to yield. But who should deliver their propositions? There was an old man, a companion of Diabolus, named Mr. Loath-to-stoop. He was stiff in a certain way, and did errands for Diabolus, so they sent their message by him. At the appointed time, he went to the camp and met with Emmanuel and his Captains. After a Diabolian ceremony, he said, 'Great sir, I want everyone to know what a good-natured man my prince is. He has sent me to tell you how willing he is to deliver half of the town of Mansoul to you rather than go to war. Will your Mightiness accept this generous proposal?'

Prince Emmanuel said, 'The whole town was given to me, and purchased by me. I am not willing to lose even half of it.'

[Note -- An 'almost Christian' might as well be an infidel. We cannot serve two masters.]

Then Mr. Loath-to-stoop said, 'Sir, my master says he would be satisfied for you to be lord of all in name if you would allow him to possess just a part.'

Emmanuel answered, 'But the whole thing is mine -- not just in name only. I insist on being the sole lord and possessor of all of Mansoul, or not at all.'

Mr. Loath-to-stoop said again, 'Look how far my master is willing to compromise! He says that he will be satisfied if you just give him some small, secluded place in Mansoul where he can live and not bother anyone -- and you can have all the rest of it.'

Emmanuel said, 'Everything the Father gave me shall be mine, and of everything he has given me, I will not lose anything, not even a hair or a hoof. I will not grant your master the least corner of Mansoul to live in; I insist on having it all to myself.'

Mr. Loath-to-stoop went even further. 'Sir, what if my master resigns the entire town to you, with the small caveat that you would allow him to visit once in a while, for old time's sake, and he could be entertained like a traveller for a couple of days, or a week, or a month or so? Couldn't this small favor be granted?'

'No,' said Emmanuel. 'He visited David as a traveller once, and even though he didn't stay long, that visit almost cost David his soul. I will not consent to allow him any rights there.'

Then Mr. Loath-to-stoop said, 'Sir, you're very stubborn. How about this? Suppose my master yields the whole thing to you, as you have requested, but his friends may have permission to trade in the town and enjoy their current homes? Will you grant just that, sir?'

'No,' said Emmanuel. 'That is against my Father's will. All Diabolians that are there currently, or that shall ever be found in Mansoul in the future, hereby forfeit not only their property and liberty, but their lives as well.'

Mr. Loath-to-stoop continued. 'But sir, can't my master maintain an acquaintance with Mansoul by letters, news, and chance opportunities -- as long as he delivers the town all up to you?'

'No,' answered Emmanuel. 'Absolutely not. Any friendship, acquaintance, or even contact that is maintained in any way will have a tendency to corrupt Mansoul, or separate his affections from me, and will endanger their peace with my Father.'

Mr. Loath-to-stoop still kept on, 'But sir, my master has many dear friends in Mansoul. Can't he give them some kind of token gift to remind them of the fondness he had for them, so that Mansoul might look at these remembrances and think of their old friend who was once their king, and the merry times they had together during the time they lived happily together?'

'No,' said Emmanuel. 'If Mansoul comes to be mine, I will not allow even the least scrap or shred of Diabolus to be left behind, and no gifts to remind them of the horrible communion there once was between them.'

'I have one more proposition, and then my mission will be complete. What if, after my master has left Mansoul, there is some important business to be done that only my master is able to do? Might he be sent for in such a case? Might he even be permitted to meet in one of Mansoul's villages with the individual involved to discuss the matter?'

That was the last of the ensnaring proposals that Mr. Loath-to-stoop requested on behalf of Diabolus, but Emmanuel wouldn't grant even that. He said, 'When your master is gone, there won't be any matter that can happen in Mansoul that can't be solved by my Father. It would be a great insult to my Father's wisdom and skill to allow anyone to go seeking Diabolus's advice when they're supposed to let their requests be made known by prayer and supplication to my Father. Besides, that would leave a door open for Diabolus to plot, plan, and execute treasonable schemes. That would grieve my Father and me, and result in the destruction of Mansoul.'

After Mr. Loath-to-stoop had heard this answer, he departed to report back to his master. He told Diabolus everything -- how Emmanuel refused to allow him any kind of access, or anything to do with Mansoul by any means once he was out. When Diabolus and Mansoul heard this, they both agreed to try their best to keep Emmanuel out. They sent Ill-pause to pass that message on to the Prince and his Captains. Ill-pause climbed to the top of Ear Gate and called out to the camp, and when he had their attention, he said, 'My master commands me to bid your Prince Emmanuel and tell him that Mansoul and her king are determined to stand together, and fall together. It is useless for your Prince to think Mansoul will ever he his unless he can take her by force.' This was passed on to Prince Emmanuel, and he said, 'Then I'll have to try the power of my sword. After all the rebellions and rejections that Mansoul has made against me, I refuse to take my weapons and leave. I am determined to conquer Mansoul and deliver her from the power of her enemy.' He commanded Captain Boanerges, Captain Conviction, Captain Judgment, and Captain Execution to march right up to Ear Gate with their trumpets blowing, banners flying, and shouts of battle ringing in the air. He wanted Captain Belief to join them. He commanded Captain Good-Hope and Captain Charity to set up in formation at Eye Gate, and said that everyone else should position themselves in strategic spots around the town. Everything was done as he commanded.

He said that the code word would be 'Emmanuel.' Then an alarm was sounded, battering rams were carried, stones were flung over the town walls from the slings, and the battle began. Diabolus himself was in charge of the townspeople during the war. He had men at every gate. Townspeople themselves fighting at the gates made the resistance all the more offensive and atrocious to Emmanuel. The battle went on for several days, and it was a sight worth seeing to watch how King Shaddai's Captains handled themselves in this war.

All of the Captains fought fiercely. Captain Boanerges made three brutal assaults, one right after the other, upon Ear Gate so that her very posts shook. Captain Conviction worked with him, and when they saw the gate about to give way, they commanded the battering rams to be used against it. Captain Conviction went up close to the gate and was driven back, receiving three wounds in his mouth. The volunteer soldiers made their rounds encouraging the Captains.

[Note -- volunteer soldiers: angels.]
[The Captains are evangelists preaching the word.]

To reward the bravery of these two Captains, the Prince called them to his pavilion for rest and refreshment, and Captain Conviction's wounds were taken care of. The Prince gave them each a gold chain and told them to be of good courage.

Captain Good-Hope and Captain Charity fought just as bravely. They did so well at Eye Gate that they almost broke it open. They and the rest of the Captains were also rewarded for their heroism.

During the battle, several of Diabolus's officers were killed, and some townspeople were wounded. Captain Boasting was one of the officers who died. He thought that nobody would be able to upset the posts at Ear Gate, or shake the heart of Diabolus. Captain Secure was also slain. He used to brag that even the blind and lame could protect the gates from Prince Emmanuel's army. Captain Conviction cut his head in two with his double-handed sword; that's how he got the three wounds in his mouth.

Captain Bragman had been in charge of a group of those who threw deadly torches and arrows at Emmanuel's army. Captain Good-Hope gave him a mortal wound in the heart at Eye Gate.

Mr. Feeling wasn't a captain, but he played a great role in inciting Mansoul to rebellion. One of Captain Boanerges's soldiers wounded him in the eye. Captain Boanerges himself would have killed him if he hadn't made a sudden retreat.

Lord Will-be-Will was never so dismayed in all his life. He wasn't able to play his usual role, and his leg was wounded so that he limped afterwards when he patrolled the wall.

There were many soldiers who were killed, maimed, or wounded within the town. When the people saw the posts of Ear Gate shaking, Eye Gate practically broken in, and their captains slain, many of them lost heart, and some were also hit with stones from the enemies' slings.

One was Mr. Love-no-Good; he was one of the companions of Diabolus. He received a mortal wound in the town and died shortly afterwards.

Mr. Ill-pause received a serious wound in the head; some say his skull was cracked and caused brain injury. I have noticed that he was never able to do as much mischief to Mansoul after that. Old Mr. Prejudice and Mr. Anything fled.

When the battle was over, the Prince commanded that the white banner should be flown again on Mount Gracious to show that he still had grace for the distressed town of Mansoul.

Diabolus saw the white flag, and he knew it wasn't meant for him but for Mansoul. So he plotted until he came up with another scheme. He contrived to see if he could get Emmanuel to end his siege and leave if he promised that Mansoul would reform. So after the sun had gone down one evening, he called Emmanuel to meet him at the gate and said,

'Since you make it appear by your white flag that you're wholly disposed to have peace and order, I thought it was appropriate to let you know that we're ready to accept the terms you want to impose.

'I know you're given to reverence and pleased with holiness; in fact, I know that your whole purpose in making this war against Mansoul is to make it a holy place to live. So then, call off your forces, and I'll transform Mansoul to your preference.

'I will withdraw all acts of hostility against you, and I'll agree to be your deputy. Then instead of working against you, I'll put my services to work under you in Mansoul. In particular:

> *[Note -- Many, when under the conviction of sin, try in vain keep the law to assuage their guilt and earn salvation, but the law can't save us; only the Spirit can do that.]*

'1. I will persuade Mansoul to receive you as their Lord. They'll be more willing to do that once they realize that I'm your deputy and working for you.

'2. I'll show them where they've been wrong, and explain to them that transgression gets in the way of experiencing real life.

'3. I'll show them the holy law that they must conform to, including those laws that they have broken.

'4. I will emphasize the necessity for them to reform in order to conform to your law.

[Note -- Relying on outward reformation, a mere form of godliness, is dangerous. Beware of self-righteousness that persuades sinners that they are too holy to need Christ.]

'5. To make sure that none of these things fails, I will set up my own team of administrators at my own cost, and I will also deliver lectures to Mansoul.

'6. As a token of our subjection, we will send you whatever taxes and gifts you think are appropriate every year.'

Then Emmanuel said to him, 'You deceiver! Your ways are completely inconsistent and shifting. You have changed and rechanged so often, trying to find some way that you might still be able to keep possession of my Mansoul, even though, as I have already declared to you, I am the rightful heir and owner of her! You have made a number of proposals already, and this one is no better than any of the others. Since you weren't able to deceive me when you showed your true loathsome self, now you think you'll have better luck by transforming yourself into an angel of light, or a minister of righteousness.

'But note this, Diabolus: nothing you put forward should even be acknowledged because you do nothing but deceive. You have no conscience before God, nor love for the town of Mansoul, so why should these proposals of yours amount to anything but sinful tricks and treachery? Anyone who is willing to say anything for the purpose of destroying those who believe him should be abandoned, and no notice should be taken of anything they say. If righteousness is so precious to you, how is that you were so wicked not so long ago? But this is neither here nor there.

'You talk about reforming Mansoul and, you say that if I let you, you'll be in charge of that reformation, yet you know very well that no matter how skilled man can be at keeping the law, it won't be enough to take away the curse from Mansoul. It will be no better than nothing! Because once a law is broken by Mansoul for which a curse is pronounced on her by God, there is no amount of obeying the law after that point that can deliver her.

Not to mention that a real reformation is unlikely when the devil is the one correcting her vices! You know as well as I do that everything you've said concerning this is nothing but dishonesty and deceit, and that you have no other card to play. Many recognize you when they see your horns and tail, but not many recognize you when you're all in white and full of light. But you will not trick my Mansoul that way, Diabolus, because I still love my Mansoul.

'Besides, I haven't come to give Mansoul a set of works to live by. If I did that, I'd be just like you. But I have come so that by me and what I have done and will do for Mansoul, they may be reconciled to my Father, even though their sins have provoked him to anger, and even though they can't earn mercy by obeying the law.

'You talk about subjecting this town to make them do good, when none of them wants to do good under your influence. My Father sent me here to possess the town myself, and to use my own power to guide them into conforming to what pleases him. So I will possess it myself. I will expel you and throw you out. I will set up my own banner in the middle of them. I will also govern them with new laws, new officers, new motives, and new ways. Yes, I will pull this whole town down and rebuild it, and it will be as if the old corrupted town never existed, and then it will be the glory of the universe.'

[Half-way point]

When Diabolus realized that his trickery hadn't worked, he was disconcerted and taken aback. But since he had within him a fountain of wickedness, rage, and hatred against Shaddai and his son, he merely strengthened his resolve to fight against Prince Emmanuel. So there was another battle before it was all over. There were fatal blows given by both sides, and the advantage switched from one side to the other as both fought to make himself master of Mansoul.

Diabolus withdrew behind the wall to encourage his forces within Mansoul, and Emmanuel returned to the camp. So they both tried to put themselves in a better position in their own ways.

Diabolus became more desperate to keep Mansoul in his own hands, and more determined to do whatever mischief he could to the Prince's army, and even to the town of Mansoul itself! After all, it wasn't the happiness of the silly town that he cared about; he was more interested in utterly ruining it and overthrowing it, as must be obvious by now. So he commanded his officers that when it looked like victory was hopeless, they should do whatever pillaging and destruction they could, even ripping apart men, women, and children. 'We should completely demolish the place and leave it a ruinous heap,' he said, 'rather than leave it fit for Emmanuel to live in.'

Emmanuel knew that the next battle would be the final one to decide the war. He commanded his officers and soldiers to be brave and prove themselves true fighters against Diabolus and all his companions -- but to be kind, merciful, and patient with the native citizens of Mansoul. 'Try to steer the worst of the fighting towards Diabolus and his men,' he said.

When the day for battle had arrived, the command was given and the Prince's orders were carried out. The Captains fought bravely and focused their assault on Ear Gate and Eye Gate, just like before. Now their code word was, 'Mansoul has been won!' And Diabolus made resistance as cruelly as he could with his army within Mansoul.

After a few distinguished assaults by the Prince and his noble Captains, Ear Gate was broken open! The bars and bolts that had been used to keep the Prince locked out were smashed into a thousand pieces. Then the Prince's trumpets sounded, the Captains gave a great shout, the town shook, and Diabolus ran and hid in his fortress. Once the Prince had burst through the gate, he set his throne in it, and set his banner up on one of the hills where his army had stationed their slings -- the hill was called Mount Hear-well. The Prince stationed himself there -- right by the gate. He commanded his army to continue using their golden slings, especially against the castle, because that's where Diabolus was hidden.

[Note -- golden slings: God's promises brought home to the heart by the Spirit of God.]

From Ear Gate, the street went straight to the house of the Recorder, Mr. Conscience -- it had been built like this even before Diabolus took the town. Right next door to his house was the castle that Diabolus had made his troublesome den. So the Captains used their slings to clear that street in order to get to the heart of the town. Then Prince Emmanuel commanded Captain Boanerges, Captain Conviction, and Captain Judgment to march right up to the Recorder's gate. In the most fierce, warlike manner they could, they entered through the gate, marched down the street with their banners flying, and came right up to the Recorder's house. They had brought their battering rams to open the castle gates, but the Recorder's house was as strong as the castle. When they got to the house, they demanded entrance. Mr. Conscience wasn't yet sure what their intention was, so he kept his gates shut during this entire battle. When there was no response, Captain Boanerges gave the gate one good strike with the battering ram that made the gentleman inside tremble, and made his house shake and totter. Mr. Recorder finally came to the gates and asked, with quivering lips, who was there. Captain Boanerges answered, 'We are King

Shaddai and his son's great Captains, and we demand your house for the use of our noble prince.' And the battering ram struck the gate again. The old gentleman trembled and didn't dare refuse. When he opened the gate, the King's three Captains marched in. The Recorder's house was conveniently close to the castle, strongly fortified, large and roomy, and also faced the castle where Diabolus was now hiding because he was afraid to come out of his den. The Captains were very indifferent with Mr. Conscience the Recorder, so that he didn't know what to make of all this, and didn't know how it all would end. News flew fast that the Recorder's house was in the hands of the enemy and was now the seat of the war. As soon as this was known, the townspeople were alarmed. Rumor followed rumor, and in a little time, the entire town was convinced that the Prince was plotting their destruction. Eyewitnesses saw the Captains treating the Recorder coldly, and the Recorder trembling. They watched the Captains occupying the rooms, and saw the battering rams banging at the castle gate to beat it down, so of course they were paralyzed with fear. The Recorder himself, when anyone asked him what was going on, made things worse by telling them that death and destruction were all Mansoul had to look forward to.

[Note -- The Recorder is the conscience. The conscience of the unconverted man is in a profound state of lethargy; some cannot be roused except by the thundering terrors of the law.]

'After all,' he said, 'you know very well that we have been traitors and despised the victorious Prince Emmanuel. He has forced his way through our gates, and even Diabolus is fleeing from him. You can see that he's made my house his fortress against the castle. I know I have sinned myself by keeping quiet when I should have spoken, and twisting justice when I should have fairly executed it. It's true, I have suffered greatly at the hand of Diabolus for wanting to uphold the laws of King Shaddai, but what good will that do me? How can I make up for the rebellion and treason I have participated in? I dread how all of this will end!'

[Note -- Conviction comes first, though it does not always end in conversion; the conscience must first be struck with a sense of guilt before it will sue for mercy. But when it does, Christ pours the oil of forgiveness and the wine of his grace into the wounded spirit.]

While the brave Captains were busy in the house of the Recorder, Captain Execution was just as busy elsewhere in the town, securing the back streets and town walls. He also hunted down Lord Will-be-will; he pursued him relentlessly so that he had no rest and even his own men abandoned him. Captain Execution wounded three of his men; one was old Mr. Prejudice, who had been wounded in the initial mutiny. Lord Will-be-will had put him in charge of Ear Gate, and Captain Execution wounded him there. Another man named Mr. Backward-to-all-but-nothing was put in charge of the two guns that had been mounted above Ear Gate, and he was also wounded by Captain Execution. And vile Mr. Treacherous, a trusted captain of Will-be-will's, was also wounded.

Captain Execution also slaughtered many of Will-be-will's soldiers, killing many strong, rugged men, and wounded others who had been skillful and active for Diabolus. But these were all Diabolians. Of the natives of Mansoul, not one person was hurt.

The other Captains performed equally brave feats of war. Captain Good-Hope and Captain Charity fought valiantly at Eye Gate. Captain Good-Hope slew the gate-keeper, Captain Blindfold, who had been in charge of a thousand men who fought cruelly with maces. Those soldiers were also chased, and all of them were either killed, wounded, or fled and buried their heads in corners.

[Note -- Captain Blindfold: the minds of carnal men are blind to the things that relate to their true peace -- until Christ enlightens them.]

Mr. Ill-pause was also at that gate. He was an old man with a beard that reached down to his belt, and Captain Good-Hope killed him.

Dead Diabolians lay in every corner, but there were still too many left alive in Mansoul.

The old Recorder, Mr. Conscience, and the old Mayor, Mr. Understanding, with some of the other leaders of the town who knew that their own fate would depend on what happened with Mansoul, met together to consult. They agreed to write up a petition and send it to Prince Emmanuel while he was sitting in the gate of Mansoul. In this petition, the old leaders of the currently deplorable town confessed their sin and said they were sorry they had offended his princely Majesty, and begged him to spare their lives.

The Prince gave no response to this petition, so the leaders were more troubled than ever. Meanwhile, the Captains who were in the Recorder's house were using the battering rams against the castle to beat the gates down. After some time and labour, the gate called Impregnable was broken into splinters so that the Prince's army were able to force their way in to where Diabolus was hiding. When this news was carried to Prince Emmanuel, trumpets were sounded throughout his camp to celebrate that the war was near an end and Mansoul was close to being set free.

The Prince himself rose and, with some of his fittest men, marched down the street to the Recorder's house.

The Prince was clad in gold armour, and he marched with his banner flying before him, but his expression was reserved so that the people couldn't tell whether he was angry or compassionate. The townspeople came to their doors to see him, and they were struck with the glory and dignity of his bearing, but also a little taken aback by his reserve. He communicated through his actions and works rather than with words or smiles. But poor Mansoul did what anyone in their situation is apt to do: they interpreted his bearing and reserve the same way Joseph's brothers did, and read the exact opposite of what he meant. 'After all,' they thought, 'if Prince Emmanuel loved us, he would show it in his looks or words, but he's not showing anything. So he must hate us, which means he's going to kill us and make our town a ruin.' They realized that they had violated his Father's law, and rejected him to ally themselves with his enemy, Diabolus. And, what's more, they knew that Prince Emmanuel knew it. They perceived him to be a divine angelic being of God with the ability of knowing everything that was done anywhere in the world, and this made them view their situation as miserable, and made them convinced that he intended to destroy them.

'And what better time than now to destroy us,' they thought, 'when he has us right where he wants us?' And they couldn't restrain themselves from cringing, bowing, and licking the dust of his feet as he passed. They wished with all their might that he would become their Prince, Captain, and Protector. They commented to one another about his handsomeness, and how he excelled all the great ones of the world in glory and valour. But, poor things, they bounced from one extreme to the other between wistful admiration and utter terror.

As the Prince approached the castle gates, he commanded Diabolus to come down and surrender to him. How the beast hated to appear before him! He hesitated, shrank, and cringed -- but he had to come. At the Prince's command, he was bound in chains to be reserved for the judgment appointed for him. Diabolus begged him not to send him into the deep pit, but to allow him to leave Mansoul in peace.

But Emmanuel led him in chains into the market-place and, in front of the entire town of Mansoul, tore from him the armour he loved to boast about. This was one of the Prince's ceremonies of triumph over his enemy, and while this was going on, trumpets were blowing, the Captains were shouting, and their soldiers were singing for joy.

Then Mansoul was invited to witness the beginning of Emmanuel's triumph over the beast in whom they had trusted and boasted before, when he had won them with flattery.

After Diabolus was exposed and disgraced in the eyes of Mansoul and Emmanuel's troops, the Prince commanded that he be bound to his chariot wheels with chains. Then, leaving Captain Boanerges and Captain Conviction to guard the castle in case Diabolus's followers made any attempt to put up a resistance and take it back, the Prince rode all around the town in triumph, and out through Eye Gate, and on into his camp.

What a shout went up in Emmanuel's camp when they saw the tyrant bound by the Prince to his chariot wheels!

And they said, 'Emmanuel has led captivity captive; he has ruined empires and powers. He has made Diabolus submit to the power of his sword, and made him the object of mockery!'

The volunteer soldiers and others who had come to see the battle shouted with a great voice and sang so enthusiastically that those in the town opened their windows to see what the glorious cheering was all about.

The townspeople didn't know whether to rejoice or despair. They weren't sure what would happen to themselves, but the rejoicing seemed so promising that their eyes, hearts and minds were absorbed as they observed Emmanuel's orders being carried out.

When Prince Emmanuel had finished this part of his triumph over his enemy Diabolus, he told him, in the midst of his contempt and shame, that he would no longer be the possessor of Mansoul. Diabolus left Emmanuel's presence to seek rest in parched places in a salt wasteland, but he found no rest.

Chapter 6

Meanwhile, Captain Boanerges and Captain Conviction were quartered in Mr. Conscience's house. They were both very majestic, and had faces as bold as lions, and powerful voices of authority. Now that Diabolus was gone, the townspeople turned their attention to these noble Captains. But the Captains were carrying themselves with a detached air of foreboding and authority, as they had been instructed to do. So they kept the townspeople in a state of intimidation and dread, not knowing what was in store for them. They had no rest, or peace, or hope.

[Note -- The terrifying alarms of some awakened sinners are nudges of the Holy Spirit, intended to bring them to a realization of their misery and danger through sin, so that they will seek Christ.]

The Prince didn't come into the town; he stayed in his royal tent in his camp with his Father's army. A bit later, he called for Captain Boanerges to summon all the people of Mansoul into the castle yard, and while they watched, put Mr. Understanding, Mr. Conscience, and Lord Will-be-Will under arrest and guarded them until he was ready to let them know what he wanted to be done with them. This made the people even more apprehensive. They were sure the town would be destroyed now. What kind of death was in store for them? They were afraid that Emmanuel would command them to be thrown into the pit, the same place Diabolus was so afraid of -- and they knew they deserved it. The idea of dying in public disgrace by the hand of a Prince who was so good and holy also distressed them severely. In addition, they were troubled for the three men who had been arrested -- these men were their guides and administrators; if they were put to death, their execution would surely signify the beginning of Mansoul's punishment and ruin. So they wrote up a petition and asked Mr. Would-live to deliver it to Prince Emmanuel. This is what the petition said:

'To the great and wonderful Ruler, defeater of Diabolus and conqueror of our town. We miserable inhabitants of the afflicted town of Mansoul humbly beg that we would find favour in your sight. Please don't remember our former transgressions, or the sins of our leaders, but spare us according to your great mercy. Please let us live and not die! We are willing to be your servants and to put our dependence on you. Amen.'

So the petition was sent, and the Prince took it from the hand of Mr. Would-live -- but sent him away without a word. This response was unsettling to the people of Mansoul, but what other options did they have besides petitioning or death? So they sent another petition much like the first one.

But who should deliver this one? They wondered if perhaps the Prince had been offended by something in the manner of Mr. Would-live, so they decided to ask Captain Conviction. But he said he didn't dare petition the Prince on behalf of traitors, nor was he willing to appear as the allies of rebels. 'And yet,' he said, 'our Prince is good. What if you sent it by a native of Mansoul with a rope around his neck, pleading for nothing but mercy?'

They procrastinated as long as they dared, and longer than was good, but finally, fearing to wait any longer, they thought they would send Mr. Desires-awake. He lived in a poor hovel and came at his neighbour's request. They told him what needed to be done, and what the petition said, and asked him to deliver it to the Prince.

Mr. Desires-awake said, 'why shouldn't I do whatever I can to save such a famous town as Mansoul from the destruction they deserve?' So they put the petition in his hand, told him what to say and how to act with the Prince, and wished him luck. He went to the Prince's pavilion and asked to speak to his Majesty. Prince Emmanuel came out of his tent to see him. Mr. Desires-awake fell flat on the ground on his face and cried out, 'Oh, please let Mansoul live!' and handed over the petition. Prince Emmanuel read it, and then turned around and wept, but then recovered himself and turned back to the man, who was still crying at his feet. The Prince said, 'Go back to Mansoul while I consider your request.'

The people of Mansoul were filled with guilt and feared that their petition might be rejected. They were extremely anxious to know how the Prince would respond to their petition. At last they saw their messenger returning. They asked him how it had gone, what Emmanuel had said, and what would happen with their petition. But he said he didn't want to say anything until he had seen Mr. Understanding, Mr. Conscience, and Lord Will-be-will. So he went to the prison where they were being held, and the entire town flocked after him to see what he was going to say. At the prison, Mr. Understanding looked white as a sheet, and Mr. Conscience was trembling in apprehension. 'Tell us, good sir --' they said, 'what did the great Prince say to you?' Mr. Desires-awake said, 'When I saw the Prince, I fell at his feet and gave him the petition. Because of his greatness and glory, I didn't dare stand on my two feet. As he took the petition, I cried out, "Please let Mansoul live!" Then he turned away from me for a little bit, and finally told me to go back to Mansoul while he considered our request.' The messenger added, 'The Prince is so beautiful and glorious, that anyone who sees him has to both love him and fear him. I personally can't do anything else. But I don't know what the end result of this petition will be.'

At this answer, nobody knew what to say, neither the men in the prison, nor the townspeople who had followed the messenger. They didn't know what to make of the Prince's response. When most of the people had gone their way, the three prisoners discussed Emmanuel's words. Mr. Understanding said it didn't sound altogether harsh, but Will-be-Will said it didn't sound promising to him, and Mr. Conscience said it sounded like certain death. The townspeople who were still left couldn't hear everything they said, but they caught enough of what was said to be of all three different opinions. Everything was in confusion.

These people went back to Mansoul spreading all three possibilities, one crying one thing, and another saying the opposite, and both swore theirs was the right interpretation. After all, they reasoned, they had heard it with their own ears. So one swore they were all going to be killed, and someone else swore they were going be saved, a third person said the Prince didn't care about Mansoul, and a fourth said that the prisoners were going to be executed. And everyone insisted that his version was the only right one and the others were wrong. And those hearing all of this had no idea who was right among all the voices. So it was a long, sad night spent in puzzlement and uncertainty.

As far as I could tell, most of this tumult originated from Mr. Conscience when he said that it sounded to him like the Prince was going to put them to death. This is what fired the town and had them in such fright. In previous times, Mansoul had considered Mr. Conscience as a prophet, so his words carried more weight, and this had them terrified.

And now Mansoul began to realize the cost of their stubborn rebellion and illegal resistance against the Prince. They began to feel swallowed up and engulfed by guilt and fear. And, as the leaders were so involved in the rebellion, they felt a larger measure of the effects of guilt and fear.

But after the initial panic subsided, and the prisoners had recovered themselves a little, they began to take heart and to consider a third petition to the Prince to beg for life. So they composed yet another petition, which said this:

[Note -- Pray without ceasing; persist in prayer.]

'Prince Emmanuel, great Lord of all worlds and Master of mercy -- we, your poor, wretched, miserable, dying town of Mansoul, confess that we have sinned against you and your Father. We are no longer worthy to be called your Mansoul. We deserve to be thrown into the pit. If you kill us, we are aware that it's only what we deserve. If you condemn us to the pit, we acknowledge that you are righteous and fair in doing that. Whatever you do to us, we have no right to complain. But please let mercy reign, and let your mercy extend far enough to reach us! Please let mercy take hold of us and free us from our transgressions, and we'll sing about your mercy and your judgment forever after that! Amen.'

But who should deliver this petition? Some suggested the man who delivered the first one, but others thought not. Some suggested sending an old man in the town named Mr. Good-Deed. That was his name, but not his nature or personality. The Recorder, Mr. Conscience, didn't like that idea. 'We need mercy right now,' he said, 'and sending our plea by a man named Good-Deed seems to oppose the petition itself. Why should we have Mr. Good-Deed carry our message, when our petition is a plea for mercy?

[Note -- We must approach the throne of grace, not through our righteousness, but through the righteousness of Jesus, our mediator, because it's not by our works, but by his mercy that we are saved.]

'Besides,' he continued, 'if the Prince asks him his name -- and you know he will -- and Mr. Good-Deed tells him, then the Prince will say, "What? Is old Good-Deed still alive in Mansoul? Then let Good-Deed save Mansoul from her distress." And if he says that, we're lost for sure. Even if we had a thousand Good-Deeds, that couldn't save us.'

Everyone thought this sounded logical, so they decided to send Mr. Desires-awake again, and he readily agreed. They warned him not to say or do anything, or even show any kind of attitude, that might offend the Prince. 'As far as we can tell, if you cause even the least offense, we will probably be utterly destroyed,' they said.

Mr. Desires-awake asked to bring Mr. Wet-eyes with him. Mr. Wet-eyes was a close neighbour of Mr. Desires-awake, a poor man with a broken spirit, but a man who could convey the right tone when delivering a petition. They all said it was fine for him to go along, too. So they prepared for their mission. Mr. Desires-awake put a rope around his neck, and Mr. Wet-eyes went wringing his hands together. In this manner, they went to the Prince's tent.

[Note -- Desires-awake and Wet-eyes: a humble and a contrite spirit.]

In the back of their minds, they wondered whether coming a third time would begin to be an annoying bother to the Prince. So when they came to the opening of his tent, they began by apologizing for themselves, and for coming and troubling him so often. They said that they hadn't come today because they enjoyed being a nuisance, or because they loved hearing themselves talk, but because it was necessary to come to his Majesty. They said they simply couldn't rest night or day because of their transgressions against King Shaddai and his son Emmanuel. They also wondered whether some misbehaviour of the last visit of Mr. Desires-awake had offended the Prince, and perhaps that was why he had returned from such a merciful Prince so sadly empty-handed. Then Mr. Desires-awake fell prostrate on the ground like he had the first time and said, 'Oh, please let Mansoul live!' And then he delivered the petition. The Prince read the petition, and, just like before, he turned away for a while. When he returned, he demanded of the petitioner, who was still lying on the ground, what his name was, and what position he held in Mansoul that the town should have sent him on such an errand. And the man answered, 'Oh, please don't be angry, my Lord! Why do you inquire about someone as worthless as I am, who might as well be dead? Pass by, I beg of you, and take no notice of who I am. There is too great a difference between your high dignity and my insignificance. The town of Mansoul must have had their own reasons for sending me, but I'm sure it wasn't because of any special favour your Majesty had for me. Speaking for myself, I don't hold much value in myself, so why should anyone care about me? Yet, I would still rather live than die, and I would rather that my townsmen live, too. Both they and I are guilty of major violations, and that's why they sent me. I come on their behalf to beg you for mercy. Please choose to show us mercy, but don't ask about us minions. We're too inconsequential to be worth your notice.'

Then the Prince asked, 'And who is this friend of yours who has accompanied you on such an important matter?' Mr. Desires-awake told him that he was a poor neighbour of his, and one of his closest friends. 'His name, if it please your Majesty, is Wet-eyes, and he lives with me in the town of Mansoul. There are many in Mansoul who are nobodies and not worth distinguishing, but I hope you aren't offended that I brought him with me.'

Then Mr. Wet-eyes fell on his face to the ground and apologized for coming:

'My Lord,' he said, 'I don't know what I am myself, or whether my name suits me or not, especially when I hear that I was given my name because Mr. Repentance was my father. Good men sometimes have bad children, and sincere men sometimes have offspring who are hypocrites. My mother called me Wet-eyes from the time I was a baby, but I don't know whether that was because of having water on the brain, or having a soft heart. I can recognize selfish motivations in my own tears, and filthiness at the bottom of my prayers. But I pray,' -- and all this time he was weeping -- 'please don't hold our transgressions against us, or be offended because we, your messengers, are so unqualified. Please be merciful and overlook the sin of Mansoul. Don't hold back your grace.'

> *[Note -- Even our best service to God is mixed with sin because we're human. This awareness should keep us humble.]*

The Prince bid them to rise, and they got up and stood, trembling, before him. He said to them:

'The town of Mansoul has severely rebelled against my Father. They rejected him for their King, and chose instead a liar, a murderer, and a renegade slave to lead them. Diabolus, your false prince, who you esteemed so much, rebelled against my Father and myself back at our court. He wanted to be prince and king himself. But we knew about his plot and were able to stop it. To punish him for his wickedness, he was bound in chains and removed to the pit along with his evil companions. So he offered himself to you, and you welcomed him.

'This has been highly offensive to my Father for a long time. My Father sent you a powerful army to subdue you to obedience. But you remember how you treated those Captains and their men. You rebelled against them, locked the gates against them, and gave them battle. You fought for Diabolus against my own men! So they asked my Father for reinforcements and I came with my troops to subdue you. But you treated me as badly as you treated my Captains. You stood against me with hostility, shut your gates to keep me out, refused to listen to me, and resisted as long as you could. But now I have conquered you. When you had the least little hope of prevailing against me, you had no thought of crying for mercy. Why didn't you come to me when my white flag of mercy was set up, beckoning you? You didn't ask for mercy, either, when I set up my red flag of justice, or my black banner of execution. Only now that I've conquered your precious Diabolus are you coming to seek my favour, but why didn't you help me to fight off your mighty enemy? Nevertheless, I will consider your petition, and I will respond in the way that best reflects my glory.

'Go back and tell Captain Boanerges and Captain Conviction to bring their three prisoners to me at my camp tomorrow, and tell Captain Judgment and Captain Execution to stay in the castle. You yourselves, watch your step and keep everything calm in Mansoul until you hear more from me.' Then he turned away from them and went back into his royal pavilion.

So the petitioners began their trip back to Mansoul. But they hadn't gone very far when they began to conclude that the Prince didn't intend to show them any mercy. They were on their way to the prison where the three captives were, but their minds were so discouraged about Mansoul's future that they weren't sure they'd be able to deliver their message from the Prince.

They finally arrived at the gates of the town. The townspeople were waiting anxiously to hear what answer was made to their petition. 'What news from the Prince? What did Emmanuel say?' they asked eagerly. But, just like before, they said they wouldn't say anything until they spoke with the prisoners. So they went to the prison with a multitude following them, as before. When they came to the prison, they delivered the first part of their message -- the part about how Mansoul had demonstrated their disloyalty by choosing Diabolus as their king, fighting for him, taking his suggestions, allowing him to rule them -- while despising the Prince and his men. This made the prisoners look pale. The messengers went on and said, 'The Prince said he would consider your petition and respond in the way that best reflects his glory.' And here, Mr. Wet-eyes gave a great sigh. All the people were discouraged and didn't know what to say. They were gripped with dread and fear. Certain death seemed to be hanging over them. There was a man among them of note, a clever, frugal man with considerable property, whose name was Mr. Inquisitive. He asked, 'Is that all he said?' 'Well, no,' Mr. Desires-awake answered. 'I thought as much,' said Mr. Inquisitive. 'What else did he say?' They paused, unsure how much to say. Finally it came out: 'He told us to have Captain Boanerges and Captain Conviction bring the three prisoners to the camp tomorrow, and Captain Judgment and Captain Execution are to hold down the castle until we get further word.' They also mentioned how the Prince had turned away from them and retreated into his pavilion as soon as he had said these things.

This was distressing news! The last part especially, about the prisoners being brought to the Prince in his camp, made them melt with fear. All three prisoners wailed loud enough to be heard in heaven. Mr. Recorder said, 'this is just what I was afraid would happen.' Then they each prepared to die, concluding that the next day would be their last. The town concluded that the same fate awaited them. Therefore, all of Mansoul spent the night in mourning. When the time came for the prisoners to be brought to the camp, they were dressed in mourning clothes, and had ropes around their necks. Half the town showed up in mourning clothes to bid them goodbye, reflecting that perhaps the Prince might see them, be stirred with compassion, and relent. Meanwhile, the town busy-bodies ran up and down the streets in groups, some wailing and crying in grief, and others proclaiming that everything would be fine! They were utterly distracting to the rest of the town.

Captain Boanerges and a guard led the prisoners, who were bound in chains, and Captain Conviction followed with another guard. The guards carried bright banners, but the prisoners were dejected and depressed.

The prisoners, in mourning clothes, had put ropes around their necks, and kept striking themselves on the chest with their fists. They didn't dare look up towards heaven, but kept their heads down. When they arrived at the camp and were in the midst of the Prince's army, the glorious sight of that army made them feel even more afflicted. They cried out, 'We are so wretched and unhappy!' Their chains added to the noise by clanking, and made the scene even more lamentable.

When they came to the door of the Prince's pavilion, they fell down on their faces on the ground. The Prince was told that his prisoners had arrived. He ascended an official throne and sent for them. They came in, trembling before him, and covering their faces in their shame. When they got near the throne, they threw themselves down before him. The Prince told Captain Boanerges, 'Bid the prisoners to stand up.' So they rose up, trembling. He asked them, 'Are you the men who used to be the servants of King Shaddai?' They said, "yes, Lord, we are.' 'Are you the men who allowed yourselves to be corrupted and defiled by that abominable beast, Diabolus?' They said, 'We did more than simply allow it; we chose it of our own free wills.' The Prince asked further, 'If his tyranny had continued, would you have been content to live under it until you died?' 'Yes,' they said, ' because his ways were satisfying to our flesh, and we had become foreigners to anything better.' Then the Prince asked, 'When I brought my forces against this town, did you wholeheartedly wish that I might not have victory over you?' 'Yes, Lord,' they admitted. 'What punishment do you think you deserve under my hand for these sins, and all the other ways you have violated my laws?' They all said, 'We deserve death, Lord. We don't deserve anything more.' He asked if they had anything to say about why they should die, why they thought they deserved to die, why a death sentence should not be passed on them. They answered, 'You are fair and just, Lord. We have nothing to say. We know we deserve to die. We know we have sinned.' 'Why are those ropes around your necks?' asked the Prince. The prisoners said, 'they are to make it easier for you to tie us to the place of execution if you do not choose to show mercy.' The Prince asked whether all of Mansoul was in this same state of confession. 'All the native citizens are, Lord. As far as the Diabolians who came with the tyrant, we don't know about them.'

[Note -- ropes: sins; natives: God-given powers of the soul; Diabolians: corruptions and lusts.]

The Prince commanded that a herald should be sent throughout the camp of Emmanuel, to sound with a trumpet and proclaim that the Prince, the son of King Shaddai, had achieved a perfect conquest and complete victory over Mansoul, and that the prisoners should follow behind agreeing by shouting 'Amen!' And this was done, just as he commanded. Shortly after this, the music in the higher region began to sound melodious, and the Captains in the camp began shouting, the soldiers started singing triumph songs to the Prince, and colourful banners were flown in the breeze. Signs of great joy were everywhere -- everywhere, that is, except in the hearts of the people of Mansoul.

The Prince called for the prisoners to come and stand before him again. They came and stood, trembling. And he said to them, 'The sins, violations, and wicked deeds that you and the whole town of Mansoul have done against my Father and me -- my Father has given me the command and authority to forgive the town of Mansoul, and I do forgive you.' Then he gave them a parchment sealed with seven seals. When it was opened, it turned out to be a comprehensive and general pardon, with an article commanding the Town Mayor, Lord Will-be-will, and Mr. Recorder to proclaim it throughout the whole town of Mansoul by dawn the following day!

In addition, the Prince removed their mourning clothes and gave them 'beauty for ashes, the oil of joy for mourning, and garments of praise for their spirit of heaviness.'

Then he gave each of them three jewels of gold and precious stones. He took the ropes off their necks and put gold chains there, and put golden rings on their fingers. When the prisoners heard the Prince's gracious words and saw all the kind things being done to them, they almost fainted away. The grace, the goodness, the pardon were so sudden, so glorious, and so big that they staggered under it. Lord Will-be-will began to swoon, but the Prince stepped in, put his everlasting arms under him, embraced him, kissed him, and told him to cheer up, because everything would be done according to his word. He also kissed, hugged, and smiled upon the other two, saying, 'Receive these as further proofs of my love, favour, and compassions towards you. Mr. Recorder, I assign you to tell the town of Mansoul what you have seen and heard here today.'

Then their chains were broken into pieces right in front of them and thrown into the air. They fell down at the feet of the Prince and kissed his feet and let their tears fall on them, crying out with a loud voice, 'Blessed be the glory of the Lord!' They were sent home to tell Mansoul what the Prince had done. He sent someone with a flute and drum to go before them playing music all the way to the town. Then what they hadn't even imagined was fulfilled, and they were allowed to possess what they had never dreamed of.

[Note -- chains were broken: their guilt]

The Prince commanded Captain Belief and some of his officers to march with the three noble men of Mansoul with flying banners. He told Captain Belief that when the Recorder read the general pardon to the townspeople, he and his ten thousand soldiers should march in with his banners at Eye Gate, and on up the street to the castle gates, and take possession of the castle in the name of the Prince. And then he should tell Captain Judgment and Captain Execution to leave the castle and return to the camp.

[Note -- When faith and pardon come together, Judgment and Execution leave the heart.]

So now the town of Mansoul was delivered from their fear of the first four Captains and their forces.

Chapter 7

While the three prisoners were at the camp with the Prince, the townspeople were waiting with heavy hearts for news of their deaths. Their minds were distracted with grief and fear, and they kept stealing glances over the wall to see if there was any news. At last they saw some people coming towards the town. Who could it be? When they realized that it was the three prisoners, they were surprised and bewildered, especially when they saw the happy manner and honor in which they were being escorted home. The prisoners had gone to the camp wearing black mourning clothes, but they were coming back dressed in white. They had gone with ropes around their necks, but they were returning with gold chains. They had gone expecting death, but they were coming back with assurance of life. They had gone with heavy hearts, but they were coming back to the sound of the flute and drum. As soon as they came to Eye Gate, the poor staggering people of Mansoul dared to give a shout -- and it was such a shout that the Captains accompanying them were startled! And who could blame them? It was if their dead friends had come back to life again. They had expected nothing but execution and death, but look! Joy and gladness, comfort and consolation, and such merry music that it could have cheered the sickest heart.

When the three men came through the town gates, they were greeted with, 'Welcome back! Blessed is the Prince who spared you!' and 'We see that it went well for you, but what's going to happen to Mansoul?' The Recorder and Mayor answered, 'Oh, we have such good news! Such joy for poor Mansoul!' And there was another shout. Then they asked for more specifics about what happened at the camp, what message they had from Emmanuel, and everything the Prince had done for them. Hearing these details made Mansoul marvel at the wisdom and grace of Prince Emmanuel. Then the three said they had a paper to read for the whole town of Mansoul, and the Recorder gave them a preview of what it said: 'Pardon! It's a pardon for Mansoul! You'll hear more about it tomorrow!' And he summoned all of Mansoul to meet together in the market-place on the following day to hear the general pardon.

Imagine what a turn, what a change, what a transformation this made in the mood of Mansoul! No one slept that night because of their excitement and joy. In every house there was merriment and music, singing and rejoicing. Chattering about Mansoul's happiness was all they wanted to do, and they sang songs similar to, 'Yay, we'll have even more of this joy when the sun rises! More joy tomorrow!' And one person would say, 'Who could have guessed yesterday that today would have turned out like this? Who would ever have thought that the prisoners who left us in mourning clothes would have returned with gold chains? Those prisoners thought the Prince would be their judge, and he acquitted them! Not because they were innocent, but because the Prince is merciful, and he sent them home to the music of the flute and drum. Is this the way princes normally behave? Do they normally show this kind of favour to traitors? No! This is unique to King Shaddai and his son, Prince Emmanuel!'

In the morning, the Mayor, Will-be-Will, and the Town Recorder came down to the market-place at the time the Prince had appointed. The townspeople were already there, waiting for them. The three freed captives came dressed in the white clothes the Prince had dressed them in the previous day, and their glory lighted the whole street. They went to the farther end of the market-place, to Mouth Gate, because that was the usual place to read public notices. They came in their white clothes, led by their flute players. By this time, the people were intensely eager to know the rest of the matter.

The Recorder stood on a platform and motioned for silence, and then he read the pardon out loud. When he came to the words, 'The merciful and gracious Lord who forgives sins, violations, and wicked deeds, forgives the town of Mansoul for all of their various blasphemies and sins --' the people couldn't help leaping for joy. The pardon had been addressed to each person in Mansoul by name, and the seals had made it look very official and imposing.

[Note -- to each person in Mansoul by name: the names of believers are written in heaven.]

When the Recorder had finished reading the pardon, the townspeople climbed up to the tops of the walls and danced and skipped up there for pure joy, and they bowed again and again towards the camp where the Prince's pavilion was, and shouted joyously, 'May Emmanuel live forever!' Then some young men were commanded to ring the bells in celebration, so the bells rang, the people sang, and there was music in every house in Mansoul.

As commanded by the Prince the previous day, after the pardon was read, all the trumpets in the camp were blown, all the banners were flown on Mount Justice, and all the Captains and soldiers in dress uniform shouted for joy outside the town. Captain Belief, who was in town in the castle, couldn't remain silent; he appeared at the top of the fortress blowing a trumpet to the people of Mansoul and to the soldiers in the camp!

So that is how Prince Emmanuel recovered the town of Mansoul from the force and power of the tyrant Diabolus.

~ . ~ . ~ . ~ . ~ . ~ . ~ .

After these joyful ceremonies, the Prince commanded his Captains and soldiers to show Mansoul some fighting tactics, so they did. The town of Mansoul was amazed at their feats of war -- their agility, dexterity, and bravery!

They marched, they opened up in formation, closed and wheeled, and displayed two dozen other marching formations. It delighted the townspeople. They also showed their impressive skill at handling weapons.

When this was over, the whole town of Mansoul came out to the camp and each person thanked the Prince and praised him for his overwhelming courtesy. They begged him, bowing in the humblest way, to come to Mansoul with his men and live there forever. He said, 'Peace be unto you.' The people came near him and touched the top of his golden scepter, and said, 'I wish you and your Captains and troops would come and live in Mansoul forever! I wish your battering rams and slings would stay in Mansoul to help protect us. We have plenty of room for you and all of your men, and room for all of your weapons and armour. Please come, and you can be our King and Captain forever. Yes, come and govern however you want, and put your Captains and soldiers in positions as governors and rulers, and we'll be your servants and follow your laws.'

They begged him to consider it. 'After all,' they said, 'now that you've bestowed your grace on us, if you were to leave us now, our town would die. Now that you've done so much good for us, and shown us so much mercy, if you leave, our joy will disappear, and our enemies will come back with more rage than ever. We beg of you, as our delight and the protector of our town, accept our invitation -- come and live with us and let us be your people. For all we know, there may still be Diabolians lurking in Mansoul, and if you leave us, they'll betray us into the hands of Diabolus again. They may have plans against us even now! We dread falling into his horrible hands again. Please come and live in the palace in our town, and your soldiers can take the best houses we have.'

> *[Note -- This fear of losing the Lord's presence is a good sign.]*

The Prince said, 'If I do come to your town, will you allow me to do even more that I want to do against our mutual enemies? Will you help me in that?'

They answered honestly, 'We can't say for sure what we'll do. We never thought we'd be such traitors, but we were. So what can we say? We aren't trustworthy. Just come and live in our castle, and make our town your stronghold. Set your noble Captains and brave soldiers over us. Conquer us with your love, and overcome us with your grace. Stay with us, and let it always be like the morning when we heard your pardon. We'll do whatever you say, and follow your ways, and obey your word.

'And one last thing -- we don't know the depth of your wisdom, sir. Who would have imagined that so much joy could come out of those bitter trials we had? We could never have foreseen that! But, Lord, let the light of your knowledge go first, and then let love come after. Take us by the hand and lead us with your guidance, and do whatever you think is best for us. Come to Mansoul and do whatever you please. Please come live in Mansoul, do whatever you want there, just keep us from sinning, and make us useful servants to your Majesty.'

Then the Prince said, 'Go back to your homes in peace. I will do this much: I will take down my tent and come with my forces to Eye Gate tomorrow, and march into Mansoul. I'll take possession of your castle and set my soldiers in charge over you. In fact, I'll do things in you that have never been done in any nation, country or kingdom in the world.'

Then the people of Mansoul gave a terrific shout, and returned peacefully to their homes. They told their friends and families about the good things the Prince had promised them. 'Tomorrow,' they said, 'he will march into our town and make his home there, he and his men, right in our town of Mansoul.'

Then the people went out to gather branches and flowers to decorate the streets for the Prince. They made garlands and other beautiful ornaments to show how happy they were to receive Prince Emmanuel into Mansoul. They spread greenery all the way from Eye Gate to the castle where the Prince was going to live. They prepared the best music they could afford to play in front of the palace.

At the appointed time, the Prince made his approach to Mansoul. The gates were all opened wide to welcome him. All the elders and leaders met him at the gate to greet him with a thousand welcomes. And he and all his servants entered Mansoul, while the people of Mansoul danced before him to the castle gates. He was wearing golden armour and riding in his royal chariot. Trumpets were sounding around him, banners were flying, his own ten thousand soldiers marched along, and the elders of Mansoul danced before him. The walls around the town were filled with people who had climbed up to view the approach of the blessed Prince and his royal army. The windows, balconies, and roofs of the houses were filled with all sorts of people to view their town being filled with goodness.

When the Prince had come as far into the town as the Recorder's house, he commanded someone to go ahead to Captain Belief to see whether the castle had been prepared to entertain his royal presence, since that job had been tasked to him. And the answer was that the castle was ready. Then Captain Belief was told to come out to meet the Prince and conduct him into the castle. And the Prince spent that night in the castle with his mighty Captains and soldiers, and the town of Mansoul was overjoyed.

The next concern was where the Captains and soldiers should stay -- not because nobody wanted soldiers quartered in his house, but because everyone wanted to fill his house with the Prince's soldiers! Their regard for the Prince was so great that they grieved that their houses weren't large enough to lodge his entire army! They considered it an honor to wait upon them, and fetch and carry for them like butlers.

This is what they finally settled on:

1. Captain Innocency would stay at Mr. Reason's house.

2. Captain Patience would stay with Mr. Mind, who was formerly Will-be-will's clerk during the recent rebellion.

3. Captain Charity would quarter at Mr. Affection's house.

4. Captain Good-Hope would stay at the home of Mayor (Mr. Understanding). The Recorder requested that Captain Boanerges, Captain Conviction and all their men might stay in his house because the Prince had ordered that, if ever there was an attack, he should be the one to sound the alarm and alert Mansoul.

5. Captain Judgment and Captain Execution and their men stayed with Lord Will-be-will, since the Prince made him governor of Mansoul to help them, as he had done before the tyrant Diabolus had caused all the damage. The help of these Captains would be invaluable.

6. Captain Belief and his men remained quartered in the castle, and the rest of the men were spread out throughout the rest of the town. So all the Prince's men had places to stay in Mansoul.

The old men and leaders of the town couldn't get enough of the Prince. All that he said, what he did, his manner, everything about him was so appealing, so enchanting, and so desirable to them. So they begged him that, even though he lived in the castle (and they hoped he would live there forever), he might visit the streets and homes and citizens frequently, 'because, your Majesty, your presence, your glances, your smiles, your words are the very life and strength of the town of Mansoul.'

In addition, they requested that they might have easy, uninterrupted, continual access to him so that they could watch and learn about his doings, and the strength of the castle and his royal mansion. In order to grant their request, the Prince commanded that the castle gates should always remain open.

Any time he spoke, the people hushed to listen. When he walked, they loved to follow him wherever he went.

One time Emanuel gave a feast at his castle for the whole town. On the day of the banquet, he served all kinds of unusual and exotic foods -- food that didn't grow anywhere in Mansoul, or even in that universe. In fact, it was food from his Father's court. Dish after dish was set before them, and they were invited to eat as much as they wanted. And every time something new was set before them, they whispered, 'what is it?' because it was so unlike anything they were familiar with, and they had no idea what to call it. They also drank wine that had been transformed from water, and they had a great time with him. All during the feast there was music playing. They ate angels' food, and had honey from a rock. So Mansoul tried food from the King's court, and had as much of it as they could eat.

The musicians themselves weren't from Mansoul; they were the King's court musicians playing songs from the royal palace.

After the feast was over, Emmanuel entertained the townspeople with some curious puzzles and mysteries written by his Father's Secretary at the King's dictation. These puzzles were about King Shaddai himself, and his son, and the wars and doings of Mansoul.

[Note -- puzzles and mysteries: The holy Scriptures.]

Emmanuel explained some of these riddles himself, and the people were awed and enlightened. They understood what they had never grasped before about wonders they could never have even imagined could have been explained with familiar words. As the puzzles were unraveled before them, it was if their eyes were opened. They could see that these things were allegories, like a portrait of Emmanuel himself. When they saw the pieces fit together as if in a picture, they saw that it bore a good likeness to the Prince himself. Emmanuel couldn't help saying, 'Yes! this is the lamb, this is the sacrifice, this is the rock, this is the red cow, this is the door, this is the way!'

You can only imagine how this entertainment amused the town of Mansoul. They were transported with delight, they were overcome with wonder as they heard and understood and reflected on Emmanuel's puzzles and he opened mysteries to them. When they were back in their homes, they couldn't stop singing about him and all the things he did. They were so taken with the Prince that they sang about him in their sleep!

Then the Prince thought it would be good to remodel the town of Mansoul and make it more to his liking as well as benefit the productivity and security of the now-flourishing town itself. He provided means to protect against insurrections within the town, and invasions from abroad. That's how much he cared about Mansoul.

[Note -- Newly saved Mansoul must be remodeled.]

He had the slings he brought with him permanently mounted -- some on the castle walls, some on the town's towers. He also added new defense towers to Mansoul. He invented a machine to hurl grenades from the castle out through Mouth Gate. This catapult never missed its target and could not be resisted. Because of the wonders it could do, there was no name worthy of it. Captain Belief was put in charge of its maintenance and management in case of war.

The Emmanuel put Will-be-will in charge of the gates, walls, and towers. He also put him in charge of the militia with special instructions to withstand any revolts and riots that might happen against King Shaddai to disturb the peace and calmness of Mansoul. If Will-be-will found any Diabolians lurking anywhere in Mansoul, he was to apprehend him and confine him until he could be brought to a legal trial.

Then he called Mr. Understanding who had been the Mayor until Diabolus replaced him, and gave him his old job back again -- and gave him the position for life. He told him to build a palace near Eye Gate for defense. He also commanded him to read from the 'Revelation of Mysteries' every day of his life so that he would know how to perform his duties properly.

He gave Mr. Knowledge the job of Town Recorder -- not out any slight to Mr. Conscience whose job it had been, but because he had another job for him which he would explain later.

He had the images of Diabolus taken down, beaten into powder, and cast out to the wind outside the town wall. Then the image of King Shaddai was set back up, along with an image of the Prince, but crafted even more skillfully than before, since he and his Father had come to Mansoul in more grace and mercy than before. He also wanted his name engraved at the front of the town in highest quality gold for the honour of Mansoul.

Then the Prince gave orders that three Diabolians were to be apprehended: Mr. Incredulity and Mr. Lustings, who had been Mayors under Diabolus, and Mr. Forget-Good, who had been the Recorder. Others who had been council members and legislators were to be kept under guard of the now brave and noble Will-be-will.

These others were Mr. Atheism, Mr. Hard-heart, Mr. False-Peace, Mr. No-truth, Mr. Pitiless, Mr. Haughty, and their friends. They were to be watched closely by Mr. True-Man. Mr. True-Man was one of the men who came with the Prince from King Shaddai's court.

After this, the Prince commanded that the three strongholds Diabolus had built should be torn down and demolished. This took awhile because the places were so huge, and all the bricks, timber, metal, and rubbish had to be carried outside the town.

When this had been done, the Prince commanded that the Mayor and legislators of Mansoul should bring to trial and execute the imprisoned Diabolians under the supervision of Mr. True-Man, their jailer.

Chapter 8

On the day of the trial, Mr. True-Man brought the prisoners to the court room. They were all chained together, according to the custom of Mansoul. They were presented before the Mayor, the Recorder, and the rest of the court officials, and then the jury was picked and the witnesses sworn in. The jurors were Mr. Belief, Mr. True-Heart, Mr. Upright, Mr. Hate-Bad, Mr. Love-God, Mr. See-Truth, Mr. Heavenly-Mind, Mr. Moderate, Mr. Thankful, Mr. Good-Work, Mr. Zeal-for-God, and Mr. Humble. The witnesses were Mr. Know-All, Mr. Tell-True, and Mr. Hate-lies. If another witness was needed, Will-be-will was also available along with his clerk.

The prisoners were brought to the front. Mr. Do-Right, the town clerk, said, 'Bring Atheism forward, jailer.' When that was done, the town clerk said, 'Mr. Atheism, hold up your right hand. You are hereby accused, as an intruder in Mansoul, of treacherously and ignorantly teaching that there is no God, so nobody needs to pay any attention to religion. In doing this, you have trespassed against the person and the honour of the King, and acted against the peace and safety of the town of Mansoul. How do plead? Are you guilty, or not guilty?'

Atheism responded, 'Not guilty.'

The courier asked for the witnesses -- Mr. Know-All, Mr. Tell-True, and Mr. Hate-lies -- to be brought in.

So they appeared before the court.

The clerk said, 'You are all called on as witnesses for King Shaddai. Take a look at the prisoner. Do you recognize him?'

Mr. Know-All said, 'Yes, your Honour, we know him. His name is Atheism. He has been a corrupting influence in Mansoul for many years.'

Clerk: 'Are you sure you know him?'

Mr. Know-All: 'Know him? Oh, yes! I've been in his company more times than I can count. He is a Diabolian, and the son of a Diabolian. In fact, I knew his father and grandfather before him.'

Clerk: 'He has been charged with teaching that there is no God, so nobody needs to pay any attention to religion. As the King's witness, what do you say to this? Is he guilty?'

Mr. Know-All: 'Your Honour, he and I were once in Villain's Lane together, and he spoke enthusiastically about lots of opinions. I heard him say that, for his part, he didn't believe there was a God. But he said he could pretend he believed, and act religious when he needed to.'

Clerk: 'Are you sure you heard him say that?'

Mr. Know-All: "Yes, your Honour, I can swear it on oath, I heard him say that.'

Then the clerk said, 'Mr. Tell-True, what do you say to the King's judges about the prisoner at the front of the court room?'

Mr. Tell-True: 'Your Honour, I used to be a great friend of his, I regret to say. I often heard him say, sometimes very forcefully, that he didn't believe there was any God, or angel, or spirit.'

Clerk: 'Where did you hear him say so?'

Mr. Tell-True: 'In Blackmouth Lane and Blasphemer's Row, and many other places, too.'

Clerk: 'Do you know much about him?'

Mr. Tell-True: 'I know he's a Diabolian, the son of a Diabolian, and a person who's terrible enough to deny the existence of a deity. His father's name was Never-be-good, and Atheism wasn't his only child. That's all I have to say.'

Clerk: 'Mr. Hate-lies, look at the prisoner -- do you know him?'

Mr. Hate-lies: 'Yes, your Honour. This man Atheism is one of the most vile wretches I've ever been around, or been associated with in my life. I myself have heard him say there's no God. I've heard him say there's no future world to come, no sin, no punishment after this life, and, even worse, I've heard him say that it's just as good to go to a brothel as to a church service!'

Clerk: 'Where did you hear him say these things?'

Mr. Hate-lies: 'In Drunkard's Row, right at Rascal-Lane's End, in the house where Mr. Impiety lived.'

Clerk: 'Set him aside by the jailer, and bring up Mr. Lustings. Mr. Lustings, you, an intruder in the town of Mansoul, are hereby charged with traitorishly teaching, by practice and filthy words, that it is proper and useful for a man to give in to his physical desires, and you, for your part, have never denied, nor will never deny yourself any sinful pleasure as long as your name is Lustings. Do you plead guilty or not guilty?'

Mr. Lustings said, 'Sir, I am a man from a privileged family, and I've always been used to an abundance of pleasures and leisure activities. I have never been looked down on for my ways, and I've always been left to follow my passions as if it were my only law. It seems strange to me to be called into question for that. In fact, I'm not the only one who does this -- almost all people love and approve of this kind of lifestyle, whether they do it openly and blatantly, or in secret.'

Clerk: 'Sir, we are not interested in the social status of your family, although someone with such connections ought to have known better. This court is only concerned with your plea: do you plead guilty, or not?'

Mr. Lustings: 'Not guilty.'

Clerk: 'Courier, call on the witnesses to step forward.'

Courier: 'Gentlemen, witnesses for the King, come forward and present your testimony against the accused.'

Clerk: 'Mr. Know-all, look at the prisoner. Do you know him?'

Mr. Know-all: 'Yes, your Honour. I know him.'

Clerk: 'What is his name?'

Mr. Know-all: 'His name is Mr. Lustings. He's the son of Mr. Beastly, and he was born in Flesh Street. His mother was Evil-Passion's daughter. I know the whole family.'

Clerk: 'You have heard the charge against him, what do you have to say? Is he guilty of what he has been accused of?'

Mr. Know-all: 'Your honour, as he said, he comes from a privileged family -- and he has the privilege of being a thousand times times greater in wickedness.'

Clerk: 'But what do you know about his specific actions, and especially with reference to his guilt?'

Mr. Know-all: 'I know he swears, lies, and dishonours the Sabbath. I know he commits adultery, and is a shameful person. I know he's guilty of all kinds of evils. I know him to be a thoroughly disgusting man.'

Clerk: 'And where did he commit his wicked actions? Was in some dark, hidden corner, or blatantly out in the open?'

Mr. Know-all: 'It was all over town, your Honour.'

Clerk: 'Come to the front, Mr. Tell-True; what can you say about the prisoner?'

Mr. Tell-True: 'Your Honour, I can corroborate what the first witness said. It is all true, and a great deal more besides.'

Clerk: 'Mr. Lustings, do you hear what these gentlemen say?'

Mr. Lustings: 'It has always been my opinion that the happiest life a person could live was to indulge in whatever he wanted, and to deny himself nothing he desired in the world. I have been sincere about following this opinion, and I have lived by this passionately for my entire life. Nor was I ever stingy; having found this to be the best kind of life, I have shared and recommended this lifestyle to others.'

The Court said, 'We've heard enough to convict him. Set him aside, jailer, and bring Mr. Incredulity to the front.'

Mr. Incredulity was brought forward.

Clerk: 'Mr. Incredulity, as an intruder in the town of Mansoul, you are hereby charged with illegal and wicked wrongdoing. When you were an officer in the town of Mansoul, you were put in charge of forces fighting against King Shaddai and his Captains when they demanded possession of Mansoul. You defied the King's armies, and with Diabolus as your captain, you incited and encouraged the people of Mansoul to repel and resist the King's forces. How do you plead? Guilty, or not guilty?'

Mr. Incredulity said, 'I don't recognize Shaddai. I am loyal to my old prince. I considered it to be my obligation to be true to my duty and to do my best to persuade the people of Mansoul to resist strangers to their town, and to encourage the people to fight against them. I still maintain that opinion, and will not change my mind just because you are currently in power.'

Then the Court said, 'As you can see, this man is hardened and irredeemable. He intends to sustain his villainies by using substantial words, and he plans to continue his rebellion with brazen tenacity. Therefore, Mr. Jailer, set him aside, and bring Mr. Forget-Good to the front.'

Forget-Good was brought forward.

Clerk: 'Mr. Forget-Good, you are hereby charged, as an intruder in the town of Mansoul, of crimes because, when you were in charge of the affairs of Mansoul, you neglected to act in their best interests and, instead, joined with the tyrant Diabolus against King Shaddai and his Captains to dishonour the King, violate his law, and endanger the town of Mansoul. How do you plead? Guilty, or not guilty?'

Mr. Forget-Good said, 'Your Honour, for the several charges against me, I ask that you would not hold them against me, but attribute them to my age and forgetfulness, and rather than consider my crimes as carelessness of mind, count them as momentary insanity. I hope thereby to be excused from punishment even though I am guilty.'

The Court said, 'Oh, come now, Mr. Forget-Good -- your forgetfulness wasn't just a weakness of age. It was deliberate, and because you hated to keep virtuous things in your mind. You had no problem remembering what was wicked, but you couldn't bear to think of anything good. You're using age and forgetfulness as an excuse to twist this court's opinion, and as a cloak for your villainy. Let's hear what the witnesses have to say against the prisoner. Is he guilty, or not?'

Mr. Hate-lies: 'Your Honour, I have heard Mr. Forget-Good say that he could never bear to think about goodness for even fifteen minutes.'

Clerk: 'Where did you hear him say this?'

Mr. Hate-lies: 'In All-Base Lane, at a house next door to the sign with the picture of the conscience seared with a hot iron.'

Clerk: 'Mr. Know-All, do you have anything to say against the prisoner?'

Mr. Know-All: 'Your Honour, I know this man very well. He is a Diabolian, the son of a Diabolian named Love-Nothing. I have often heard him say that he considered good thoughts the most tedious things in the world.'

Clerk: 'Where did you hear him say this?'

Mr. Know-All: 'In Flesh Lane, across the street from the church.'

Then the Clerk said, 'Mr. Tell-True, please contribute your evidence concerning the prisoner and his charges for this honourable court.'

Mr. Tell-True: 'I have frequently heard him say that he would rather think about the vilest, most disgusting thing imaginable than anything contained in the Holy Scriptures.'

Clerk: 'Where did he say such disturbing words?'

Mr. Tell-True: 'Where? In lots of places -- especially in Nauseous Street, in the home of Mr. Shameless, and in Filth Lane, at the sign of the Reprobate, next door to Mr. Descent-into-the-pit.'

Court: 'Gentlemen, you have heard the charges, Mr. Forget-Good's plea, and the testimony of the witnesses. Jailer, bring Mr. Hard-Heart forward.'

He was brought forward.

Clerk: 'Mr. Hard-Heart, you, an intruder to the town of Mansoul, are hereby charged with fiercely and wickedly taking possession of Mansoul with no remorse or pangs of conscience. Furthermore, you kept Mansoul from remorse and sorrow over their evils during the whole time they were backslidden and rebelling against King Shaddai. How do you plead? Guilty or not guilty?'

Mr. Hard-Heart: 'Your Honour, I've never known what remorse or sorrow meant in my whole life. I am rock hard and impenetrable. I don't care about any person, and I can't be touched by any person's grief. Mansoul's cries and sobs can't even enter my heart. No matter who I harm, no matter who I wrong, it might sound like mourning to others, but it sounds like music to me.'

Court: 'You can see the man is unquestionably a Diabolian, and his own words have convicted him. Take him away, jailer, and bring Mr. False-Peace forward.'

False-Peace came forward.

'Mr. False-Peace, you, an intruder to the town of Mansoul, are hereby charged with wickedly and satanically bringing Mansoul to a false, unsupported, and dangerous sense of peace and security. You not only brought her there, but you kept her and held her there in a state of backsliding and rebellion. This has caused dishonour to King Shaddai, violations of his law, and great damage to the town of Mansoul. How do you plead? Guilty or not guilty?'

Mr. False-Peace said, 'Gentlemen, and all of you who have been appointed to judge me, I acknowledge that my name is Mr. Peace, but I utterly deny that my name is Mr. False-Peace. If you question anyone who knows me well, or the midwife who delivered me, or the ladies who were at my christening, any of them will tell you that my name is not False-Peace; it's just Peace. And Peace is not only my true name, it's also my defining characteristic. I have always been a person who loves a quiet life. And since that's what I love, why shouldn't everyone else love that, too? Therefore, any time I ever saw someone upset with an unsettled mind, I tried to help as much as I could. I can give you many examples of my mild temper.

'1. When Mansoul first rejected the ways of Shaddai, and some of them began to have troubled consciences because of what they had done, I was saddened to see them so distressed, and I sought whatever means I could to soothe and calm them.

'2. In the old days, during the time and culture of Sodom, if anything happened to interfere with those who were enjoying the local customs, I worked hard to quiet their thoughts so they could go on with their pleasures undisturbed.

'3. More recently, during the wars between Shaddai and Diabolus, if I ever saw Mansoul panicked about destruction, I would do everything in my power to alleviate their terror. You can see that I've always had an easy, agreeable disposition, and isn't that the very definition of a peace-maker? And peace-makers are commendable and praiseworthy, aren't they? So you gentlemen who are known for justice and fairness -- doesn't a man like me deserve freedom, as well as restitution from those who have accused me and been the cause of my being treated so inhumanely?'

The clerk said, 'Courier, make a statement.'

Courier: 'Your Honour, since the prisoner denies that his name is not the one mentioned in the charges, the Court calls upon anyone who can provide the correct name of the prisoner, since he declares his innocence.'

Two men entered the court and asked for permission to tell what they knew about the prisoner. They were Mr. Search-Truth and Mr. Vouch-Truth. The Court asked whether they knew the prisoner.

Mr. Search-Truth began, 'Sir, I --'

Court: 'Wait; you need to be sworn in first.'

This was done, and he proceeded.

Mr. Search-Truth: 'Your Honour, I have known this man since we were children, and I can verify that his name is False-Peace. His father was Mr. Flatterer, and his mother was Mrs. Soothe-Up. He was born shortly after they were married and they named him False-Peace. We used to play together as children, although I was a little older. When his mother used to call him in, she would cry out, 'False-Peace, get in here right now and don't make me have to come and fetch you.' I knew him when he was still a nursing toddler. I was still pretty young then myself, but I can still remember his mother sitting on her front porch with him, playing with him and saying, 'My little False-Peace! My precious darling little False-Peace!' or, 'Mama's naughty little sweetie, False-Peace!' The local gossips know this is true, even if he has the nerve to deny it right here in a legal court.'

Then Mr. Vouch-Truth was sworn in to tell what he knew.

Mr. Vouch-Truth: 'Your Honour, everything that Mr. Search-Truth said is accurate. His name is False-Peace, and he is the son of Mr. Flatterer and Mrs. Soothe-Up. In the past, I have known him to get angry when anyone called him anything else but False-Peace; he used to consider anything else an insulting nickname used to mock him. But that was when Mr. False-Peace was an important man -- back in the days when the Diabolians were in charge of Mansoul.'

Court: 'Gentlemen, you've heard what these two witnesses have said under oath. Mr. False-Peace, you have denied that your name is Mr. False-Peace, but these two men have sworn that it is. As far as your accusation, you have misrepresented the charges. You have not been charged with evil-doing because you are a man of peace, or because you are a peace-maker. You have been charged with wickedly and satanically bringing Mansoul to a false, unsupported, and dangerous sense of peace and security as well as keeping her and holding her there in a state of backsliding and rebellion. All you have done on your behalf is to deny your name, but we have witnesses who can prove that you are the man. I must remind you that the kind of peace you brag about is not naturally found existing side by side with truth and holiness. Your brand of peace has no foundation; it rests on a lie and, as King Shaddai has said, it is both deceitful and accursed. Therefore, your plea makes you more culpable of guilt. But you shall have a fair trial. We will call witnesses to testify as to the facts. Let's see what they have to say.'

Clerk: 'Mr. Know-All, what can you say against the prisoner?'

Mr. Know-All: 'Your Honour, for a long time, this man has made it his business to keep Mansoul in a state of tranquil composure in the midst of her lewdness, filthiness, and uproar. I have heard him say, 'Come now, let's leave trouble behind; let's live a quiet, peaceful life even if it has no foundation."

Clerk: 'Mr. Hate-lies, what do you have to say?'

Mr. Hate-lies: 'Your Honour, I have heard the prisoner say that peace combined with sin is preferable to distress combined with truth.'

Clerk: 'Where did you hear him say this?'

Mr. Hate-lies: 'I heard him say it in Folly-yard, at Mr. Simple's house next door to Self-deceiver. I've known him to say it there at least twenty times.'

Clerk: 'We don't need any more witnesses; this evidence is sufficient. Set him aside, Mr. Jailer, and bring Mr. No-Truth forward. Mr. No-Truth, you, an intruder in the town of Mansoul, are charged with deliberately defacing and destroying any remainders of the law and every image of King Shaddai from after her backsliding with Diabolus, the spiteful tyrant. This has dishonoured King Shaddai and threatened to utterly ruin the town of Mansoul. How do you plead? Guilty, or not guilty?'

Mr. No-Truth: 'Not guilty, your Honour.'

Witnesses were called to testify, starting with Mr. Know-All.

Mr. Know-All: 'Your Honour, this man was there during the tearing down of King Shaddai's image. In fact, he pulled it down with his own hands. I myself saw him do it. He did it at the command of Diabolus. This man, Mr. No-Truth, went beyond that -- he also set up the horned statue of Diabolus in the same place. Not only that, but at the bidding of Diabolus, he ripped, tore, and burned any shred or scrap of King Shaddai's laws, even within the town of Mansoul itself.'

Clerk: 'Who else saw him do these things?'

Mr Hate-lies: 'I did, your Honour, and so did many others. This was not done secretly out of sight; it was done in public, where everyone could see. He chose to do it openly because he was so elated about doing it.'

Clerk: 'Mr. No-Truth, how could you be brazen enough to plead not guilty when you are so obviously guilty about doing all of this wickedness?'

Mr. No-Truth: 'Your Honour, I had to say something, and since my name is, after all, No-Truth, that's how I speak. It has gained me advantages in the past, and it's all I know how to do. With a bit more luck, it might have worked and gotten me off this time, too.'

Clerk: 'Set him aside, Mr. Jailer, and bring Mr. Pitiless forward. Mr Pitiless, you, an intruder in the town of Mansoul, are charged with treacherously and wickedly cutting off any sign of compassion. You refused to allow poor Mansoul to soothe her own misery when she backslid and left her rightful King. Instead, you evaded and turned her mind away from the regretful thoughts that should have led her to repentance. How do you plead? Guilty, or not guilty?'

Mr Pitiless: 'I am not guilty of lacking pity. All I did was try to cheer up Mansoul. My name isn't actually Pitiless, it's Cheer-Up. I couldn't bear to see Mansoul downcast and unhappy. Is that so wrong?'

Clerk: 'What! You deny your own name and claim to be Cheer-Up? Call the witnesses. Let's hear what they have to say.'

Mr. Know-All: 'Your Honour, his name really is Mr. Pitiless. That's how he's always signed his name. But these Diabolians love to use fake names. Mr. Covetousness calls himself Good-Stewardship or something similar, Mr. Pride, when he needs to, calls himself Mr. Neat or Mr. Handsome or the like. They all do that.'

Clerk: 'Mr. Tell-True, what do you say?'

Mr. Tell-True: 'His name is Pitiless, your Honour. I have known him since childhood, and he's always done what the charges accuse him of. He's part of a whole group of Diabolians who are ignorant about the danger of eternal, so anyone who thinks seriously about avoiding hell seems melancholy to them.'

Clerk: 'Bring Mr. Haughty forward, Mr. Jailer. Mr. Haughty, you, an intruder in the town of Mansoul, are charged with treacherously and villainously teaching the town of Mansoul to respond insolently and arrogantly when King Shaddai's captains summoned them. You also coached Mansoul to speak contemptuously and slanderously about their King. In addition, you encouraged Mansoul to take up arms against the King and his son with your words and example. How do you plead? Guilty, or not guilty?'

Mr. Haughty: 'Gentlemen, I have always been a man of courage and valour. I'm not used to hanging my head down in humiliation even when I'm under the greatest disgrace. I've never liked to see people cower when someone opposes them, even if their adversaries are ten times stronger than they are. I have never taken any notice of who my enemy was, or why he was against me. It was enough for me to carry it bravely, fight like a man, and win.'

Court: 'Mr. Haughty, you are not being charged for being valiant or brave in times of distress. You are being charged with using your pretended courage to entice the town of Mansoul into acts of rebellion against King Shaddai and his son. That is the crime you are accused of.'

Mr. Haughty did not answer.

Now that the court had heard from all the prisoners, they asked the jurors for their verdict.

'Gentlemen of the jury, you have seen these men, heard their charges, their pleas, and the witnesses who have testified against them. All that remains is for you to withdraw to the jury room and consider together what verdict to bring against them for the King, and then bring your verdict to us.'

So the jury, consisting of Mr. Belief, Mr. True-Heart, Mr. Upright, Mr. Hate-bad, Mr. Love-God, Mr. See-Truth, Mr. Heavenly-Mind, Mr. Moderate, Mr. Thankful, Mr. Humble, Mr. Good-Work, and Mr. Zeal-for-God, withdrew to do their work. Once they were in the jury room, they began discussing how they should decide.

Mr. Belief, who was the foreman, said, 'Gentlemen, I personally believe that all of the prisoners deserve the death penalty.' 'Agreed,' said Mr. True-Heart, 'that's just what I think.' Mr. Hate-Bad said, 'thank goodness those evil men have been caught!' 'That's for sure!' exclaimed Mr. Love-God, 'this is one of the happiest days of my life!' Mr. See-Truth said, 'If we recommend the death penalty, even King Shaddai will support our verdict.' 'I have no doubt that's the right verdict,' said Mr. Heavenly-Mind, 'Mansoul will be much improved when beasts like that are removed from the town!' Mr. Moderate said, 'I don't like to pass judgment rashly, but the crimes of these prisoners are so heinous, and the evidence is so credible, that a person would have to be blind not to see that they deserve death.' Mr. Thankful said, 'I'm so grateful those traitors are in custody!' 'I join all of you esteemed men,' said Mr. Humble. 'I'm happy to agree,' said Mr. Good-Work. The true-hearted, passionate man, Mr. Zeal-for-God exclaimed, 'Get rid of them! They have been a plague to us all and tried to destroy Mansoul!'

Since they were all agreed, they went back into the Courtroom.

Clerk: 'Gentlemen of the jury, raise your hand when I call your name: Mr. Belief, Mr. True-Heart, Mr. Upright, Mr. Hate-Bad, Mr. Love-God, Mr. See-Truth, Mr. Heavenly-mind, Mr. Moderate, Mr. Thankful, Mr. Humble, Mr. Good-Work, and Mr. Zeal-for-God. Good and faithful men, let's hear your verdict: are you all agreed?'

Jury: 'Yes, your Honour.'

Clerk: 'Who is going to speak for all of you?'

Jury: 'Our foreman, Mr. Belief.'

Clerk: 'Gentlemen of the jury, you have been appointed to this task for King Shaddai to serve in a matter of life and death. You have heard the trials of these prisoners; what do you say? Are they guilty of the charges brought against them, or are they not guilty?'

Mr. Belief: 'Guilty, your Honour.'

Clerk: 'Remove your prisoners from this courtroom, Mr. Jailer.'

That was in the morning; by afternoon, they had formally received the sentence of death according to the law.

So the jailer put them all in maximum security until their execution the following morning.

But between the time of the sentence and the time of the execution, one of the convicts, Mr. Incredulity, broke out of prison and escaped. He got far away from the town of Mansoul and lay in hiding until he could find another opportunity to harm Mansoul as vengeance for what they had done to him.

Chapter 9

When the jailer, Mr. True-man, realized that he had lost one of his prisoners, he was disconcerted because Incredulity was the worst of the lot. He immediately told the Mayor, Mr. Recorder, and Lord Will-be-will and got a warrant to search through the entire town. A thorough search was made, but there was so sign of the prisoner anywhere.

The only thing they could figure was that Mr. Incredulity had lurked around the outside of the town for a while, and had been glimpsed by various citizens as he escaped out of Mansoul. A couple of people had seen him outside the walls crossing the plain swiftly. Mr. Did-see said he had seen him ranging all over dry waste places looking for Diabolus, and they had finally made contact near Hell-gate Hill. But now he was long gone, and it was too late to apprehend him.

Mr. Incredulity had quite a sorrowful tale to tell Diabolus about the lamentable change Prince Emmanuel had made in the town of Mansoul.

He told how, after a few delays, Emmanuel had granted a general pardon to Mansoul, and they had invited him into the town and given him the castle. He told how the town had quartered the soldiers and celebrated with song and dance. 'But the worst of it,' he said, 'is that he pulled down your statue, my prince, and set up his own. And Will-be-Will, that traitor, who I never guessed would turn against us, is now in as great favour with Emmanuel as he was with you! And on top of all this, that Will-be-will received a special commission to seek out and execute all and any Diabolians he can find in Mansoul. He has already taken eight of your most trusted servants and thrown them in jail. Even worse, I am grieved to have to tell you that they've all been tried, condemned, and are probably all dead by now. I would have been the ninth, but, as you see, I made my escape.'

When Diabolus heard this, he let out a yell of rage and cried bitter tears. He swore he would have his revenge on Mansoul for this. He and Mr. Incredulity discussed possible plans to get the town of Mansoul back again.

Back in Mansoul, the day had come for the prisoners to be executed. They were brought to the cross, where executions took place, in the most solemn manner. The Prince had said that executions must be done first-hand by the townspeople. 'That way,' he had said, 'I'll be able to see your faithfulness in keeping my word and obeying my commands now that you have been redeemed, and I'll be able to bless you. Evidence of your sincerity pleases me. Therefore, Mansoul should personally lay their hands on the Diabolians who are to be executed.'

So the people of Mansoul killed them according to the command of their Prince. When the prisoners were brought to the cross, they made it unbelievably difficult for Mansoul. The prisoners knew they were going to die, and they had an unrelenting hatred towards Mansoul. When they got to the cross, they took courage and put up a resistance. The men had to call for help from the Captains and soldiers. King Shaddai had a Secretary in the town who loved the people of Mansoul, and he was also there at the execution. When he heard the men of Mansoul calling for help with the struggling unruliness of the prisoners, he got up and lent them a helping hand. So they crucified those troublesome Diabolians who had been such a plague and an offense to Mansoul.

After this valiant and necessary work was done, the Prince came down to see the people of Mansoul, to pay them a visit, give them words of comfort, and encourage them in such work. He told them that by this act of obedience, he had proved them and now he knew they truly loved him, obeyed his laws, and respected his honour. He also said that, so their town wouldn't be weakened by the loss of nine men, he would promote one of their own people to the rank of Captain, and that Captain would rule over a thousand people for the benefit of the now-flourishing Mansoul.

He called over a man named Mr. Waiting and said, 'Go quickly to the castle and ask for a man named Mr. Experience who serves Captain Belief. Tell him to come see me.' So the messenger went and did as he was commanded. The young gentleman, Mr. Experience, was watching Captain Belief train his soldiers in the castle yard. Mr. Waiting told him, 'Sir, the Prince would like to see you.' So he brought him to Emmanuel and he bowed before him. Everyone in town knew Mr. Experience, because he had been born and raised in Mansoul. They knew he was a man of good conduct, bravery, and he was wise and prudent. He was also handsome, well-spoken, and successful at everything he did.

The townspeople were overjoyed to find out that the Prince had been so impressed with Mr. Experience that he was promoting him and giving him command of a group of men.

They all bowed before Emmanuel and shouted, 'Let Prince Emmanuel live forever!' Then the Prince said to Mr. Experience, 'I have decided to promote you to a place of trust and honour in my town of Mansoul.' And the young man bowed and worshiped. 'I am making you a Captain over a thousand men in my beloved town of Mansoul.' And the new Captain said, 'Let the King live forever!' The Prince ordered the King's Secretary to draw up a commission making Captain Experience a leader over a thousand men. 'Then bring it to me so I can add my royal seal,' said the Prince. And it was done.

As soon as the new Captain had his commission, he blew his trumpet to call forth anyone who wanted to volunteer to be in his troop of 1000 men. Lots of young men answered the call. In fact, the most important town leaders sent their own sons to enlist under his command. So Captain Experience came under command and was a benefit to Mansoul. Mr. Skillful was his lieutenant, and Mr. Memory was his trumpeter. He had too many under-officers to list. His banner was white, to signify the town of

Mansoul. His coat of arms was a dead lion and a dead bear. So the Prince went back to his royal palace in Mansoul.

Then the leaders of Mansoul -- the Mayor, the Recorder, and Will-be-will, went to congratulate him and personally thank him for his love, care, and kind compassion that he showed to his ever-obliging town of Mansoul. After a time of delightful communion, the townsmen went back to their own homes.

Emmanuel also scheduled a day to renew their charter -- a day when he would enlarge their property and assess any necessary repairs so that Mansoul's burden would be a little lighter. They hadn't asked him to do this, it was his own noble idea. He looked at their old charter, and set it aside, saying, 'Now the thing that's old and decaying is ready to vanish away. The town of Mansoul will have another one -- a newer, better charter that will be more steady and solid.' This is the gist of what it said:

[Note -- renew their charter: he does this by allowing us to see more of himself and his blessings.]

'Emmanuel, Prince of Peace and Lover of Mansoul. In the name of my Father and my own indulgence, I give, grant, and bequeath the following to my beloved town of Mansoul:

'First: free, thorough, and eternal forgiveness of all wrongs, injuries, and offenses they have done against me, my father, their neighbours, or themselves.

'Second: I give them the holy law and my testament, with everything it contains, to comfort and console them forever.

'Third: I am giving Mansoul some of the same grace and goodness that are in my Father's heart and mine.

'Fourth: I freely give Mansoul the world and everything in it for their good. They shall have whatever power and authority they need in order to use the world for their own comfort and to bring honour and glory to me and my Father. I grant them permission to make use of plants and animals to help with their work, and to kill them for the benefit of the town, and I grant this permission over things that are here now as well as things that will be here in the future. Only my Mansoul has this privilege; no other town or country has this privilege.

'Fifth: I give them permission and free access to call on me anywhere in my palace at any time of year in order to let me know their needs and desires. I promise that I will listen to their grievances and try to remedy them.

'Sixth: I give Mansoul complete authority and power to seek out, capture, enslave, and destroy any and all Diabolians that are found straggling in or around Mansoul.

'Seventh: Mansoul is not obligated to share these excellent privileges with strangers or foreigners or their descendants. All of these grants, privileges, and immunities are for the original natives of Mansoul and their legitimate offspring.

'But all Diabolians, no matter what their rank or where they're from, are excluded from any share of these grants, privileges, and immunities.'

The new charter had even more bountiful provisions than those included here! The leaders of Mansoul took it to the market-place, and Mr. Recorder read it to all the people. Then it was taken to the castle and the Prince had the words of the charter engraved in gold letters on the castle doors so that when the people walked by, they could see and read what a blessed freedom their Prince had bestowed on them. Then their joy would be increased, and their love for their Prince would be renewed.

What joy and comfort filled the hearts of the people of Mansoul! They rang the town bells, the musicians played, the people danced, the Captains shouted, the banners were flown, and the silver trumpets were blown. The evil Diabolians weren't so happy, though -- they just wanted to hide their heads. They looked withered and pale, like people who are near death.

After this, the Prince sent for the leaders of Mansoul to discuss an idea for a teaching ministry he wanted to establish among them. This would be a project to instruct them about things that concerned their present state, and their future.

'Unless you have teachers and guides,' he said, 'you won't know the will of my Father. And if you don't know what he wants, how can you obey?'

The leaders of Mansoul brought this idea to the people, and they loved the idea. In fact, they loved anything the Prince proposed. They begged the Prince to establish this teaching ministry so they could know King Shaddai's laws, judgments, statutes and commands and be certified in good, decent things. So the Prince said he would establish two teachers among them: one would be from his Father's court, and the other would be someone who was a native of Mansoul.

'The one who is coming from my Father's court,' he said, 'has no less quality and dignity then my Father or myself. He is my Father's Lord Chief Secretary, the one in charge of all of my Father's laws. He understands hidden things and knows about profound truths as well as my Father and I. In fact, he's one with us in essence, and he loves Mansoul and is as loyal and concerned about her welfare as we are.

[Note -- Lord Chief Secretary: the Spirit of all wisdom, truth, and grace, influencing the conscience.]

'This is the one who will be your main teacher,' said the Prince. 'He's the only one who can teach you clearly in all spiritual and supernatural things. He is the only one who knows how things are done at my Father's court, and he can show what my Father's heart is like regarding all things, all situations, all the time about Mansoul. Just as nobody knows what's within a man better than his own spirit, so nobody knows my Father's heart better than his great Secretary. No one can better inform you how and what to do in order to keep yourselves in the love of my Father. He will bring lost things to your remembrance, and tell you about things to come. You must love him and esteem him more than your other teacher because of the dignity of who he is, and his excellent teaching. He will also help you make and create petitions to ask for my Father to help you. My Father wants you to love this teacher, respect him, and be careful not to grieve him.

'This person has a way of putting things that makes them seem alive and persuasive, and he has a way of getting it into your heart. He can make seers out of you, and tell you what will happen in the future. You must seek his help when you send petitions to my Father. You must not let anything enter Mansoul without his advice, lest you disgust and grieve this noble teacher.

'I'll say it again -- don't do anything that might grieve or disappoint this person. If you do, he might fight against you, and if he ever takes up arms against you, that would be more distressing for you than if my Father sent twelve legions of troops to declare war against you.

'But if you listen to him, love him, devote yourself to his teaching, and seek to be in communication with him -- then you'll find him ten times better than owning the whole world. He will spread the Father's love in your hearts, and Mansoul will be the wisest and most blessed people in the world.'

Then the Prince called Mr. Conscience (the Recorder) by name, and told him that since he was skilled in the law and had experience governing Mansoul, and could properly inform them of the Father's will regarding routine and domestic affairs, that he would make him a teacher to instruct Mansoul in all the laws, statutes, and judgments of the town. The Prince added, 'You must limit yourself to teaching about moral virtues and temporal duties. Do not presume to try to reveal the spiritual, supernatural mysteries of my Father's heart. No man knows about them; only my Father's Secretary can reveal them.

'You are native to the town of Mansoul, but the Secretary is native to my Father's court. You have knowledge of the laws and customs of the town of Mansoul, but the Secretary has knowledge about the things and the will of my Father.

'Although I have made you a teacher and junior preacher in the town, Mr. Conscience, you will be a student and learner of the Secretary's just like everyone else.'

[Note -- Conscience must be in subordination to the all-wise Spirit of God.]

'When it comes to spiritual, supernatural things, go to him for information and knowledge. Although man has a spirit, the Secretary's inspiration must give that spirit understanding. So, Mr. Conscience, remain modest and humble -- and never forget the Diabolians who didn't obey their primary trust, but left their rightful places to try and raise themselves higher. They're now prisoners in the pit. Therefore, be content with your position.

'I have made you a governor on earth over the specific things I mentioned. Use whatever power is needed to teach Mansoul -- even whips and punishments if they won't willingly do what you tell them to.

'And since you are old, Mr. Conscience, and weakened from many abuses, I give you permission to go to my fountain any time you wish and drink as much as you'd like of the grape juice that runs freely from the spout. That will help to drive out of your heart and stomach any impure, disgusting, and detrimental attitudes within you. It will also help keep your eyes clear, and strengthen your memory to receive and retain what the Secretary teaches you.'

[Note -- drink as much as you'd like: We continually need to apply Christ's atoning blood.]

When the Prince had established Mr. Conscience in his new position as teacher and junior preacher, Emmanuel spoke to the townspeople.

'Look how much love and care I have for you,' said the Prince to Mansoul. 'In addition to everything I've given you, I've added this additional mercy: a noble Secretary to teach you high, sublime mysteries, and this gentleman' (pointing at Mr. Conscience) 'to teach you about physical and domestic things. He is allowed to tell you about things he has heard and learned from the Secretary, but he must not presume to pretend to reveal those high mysteries himself. The ability to open them and divide them into manageable pieces and explain them to Mansoul only lies in the authority and skill of the Secretary himself. Mr. Conscience may talk about them, and so may the rest of Mansoul. You may encourage one another to remember and follow them for the benefit of Mansoul. Remembering and doing them will prosper your life, and make the time you live longer.

'I have one more thing to tell Mr. Conscience and the rest of you: You must not dwell on or stay focused on any routine or civil instructions that Mr. Conscience teaches you as if the next world depends on them -- yes, after this world is worn out, I plan to make another world for Mansoul. For rules about the next world, you must rely on the teachings of Mr. Secretary. Even Mr. Conscience himself must not expect to find eternal life in what he teaches, because eternal truth only comes from the teachings of the Secretary. And Mr. Conscience must not accept any doctrine or teaching that doesn't come directly from the Secretary unless it comes within the limits of his physical knowledge about routine and civil matters within Mansoul.'

After the Prince had settled all of this in Mansoul, he gave the leaders a cautionary warning about how to treat King Shaddai's Captains who had come with him to Mansoul.

He said, 'These Captains love Mansoul. They are specially selected men, hand-picked from among King Shaddai's army, because they were specially suited to serve in the wars against the Diabolians and preserve the town of Mansoul. Citizens of Mansoul, you must treat these Captains with dignity. Though they are brave and fierce when they need to fight the King's enemies and those who would harm Mansoul, just a little disfavor will dishearten them and weaken their courage. Do not be unkind to my valiant Captains and courageous soldiers. Love them, nourish them, help them, and be considerate of them. Then they will not only fight for you, but they will repel all the Diabolians who want to destroy you and make them run away.

'If ever any of my Captains are too sick or weak to perform the duties they love, don't neglect them, but strengthen and encourage them. Even if they're exhausted and near death, help them and take care of them. They are your protection, like a fence or wall to guard you. Even when they are weak and need your help, don't forget what formidable achievements they're capable of on your behalf when they're in top shape.

[Note -- The Captains (evangelists and gospel ministers) are to be appreciated and taken care of.]

'When they're weak, the town of Mansoul can't be strong. When they're strong, the town of Mansoul can't be weak. Your safety depends on their health and good spirits. If they ever do get sick, it's because they've caught some disease from Mansoul.

'I'm telling you these things because I care about your welfare and your honour. Therefore, be diligent about everything I'm giving you instructions about -- not just your governors and guards and the town as a group, but each of you individually. Your very well-being depends on you faithfully observing the King's orders and commands.

'Next, Mansoul, although I have wrought a reformation among you, there are still Diabolians lurking in your town. They are strong and unrelenting, and are thinking, plotting, contriving, and working together to destroy you even now while I'm here among you -- how much more will they seek your destruction when I'm away? They're capable of bringing you to an even worse state than Egyptian bondage. They are loyal friends of Diabolus, so watch your backs. When Incredulity was the Mayor, they lived in the castle with their prince, but now that I'm here, they're holed up in the walls and corners, and have hidden themselves in caves and dens outside the town walls. Your job regarding these Diabolians is more difficult and hard than your other work: you must subdue them and put them to death, according to the will of my Father. Unfortunately, you won't be able to be completely rid of them unless you pull down all the walls of your town, and I don't want you to do that. So, what should you do? Be diligent, and don't give up. Watch their holes, find their hiding places, attack them, and don't make peace with them. No matter what terms of peace they offer you, reject them, and all will be well between you and me. To help you identify them and distinguish them from the natives of Mansoul, here is a list of some of their leaders: Lord Fornication, Lord Adultery, Lord Murder, Lord Anger, Lord Lewdness, Lord Deceit, Lord Hostility, Mr. Drunkenness, Mr. Wild-Party, Mr. Idolatry, Mr. Witch-craft, Mr. Contention, Mr. Emulation, Mr. Wrath, Mr. Strife, Mr. Treason, and Mr. Heresy. Those are some of the main ones who will try to destroy you forever. They've been skulking around Mansoul, but if you study the laws of King Shaddai, you'll learn enough of their characteristics to identify them when you see them.

[Note -- The enemies still lurking within Mansoul are listed in Galatians 5:19-21.]

'I want you to be aware, Mansoul, that if these villains are allowed to run around and wander through the town at will, they will quickly eat out your insides, like vipers. Yes, they will poison your Captains, cut off the legs of your soldiers, break open the locks of your gates, and turn your flourishing town in a barren wasteland surrounded by a pile of rubble. To help you courageously apprehend these foes wherever you find them, I give you, your Mayor, Mr. Recorder, Will-be-will, and all citizens full authority and commission to seek out, capture, and crucify all varieties of Diabolians whenever and wherever you find them in or around the walls of Mansoul.

In addition to the teaching ministry that I'm going to establish, you have the four Captains who I sent out at first to fight the Diabolians. If they're ever needed, they can privately inform you and publicly preach good, sound doctrine that will provide reliable guidance. They could set up weekly -- or even daily -- lectures in Mansoul to instruct you in worthy lessons that will benefit you in the long term. Also, be careful that you don't spare the evil villains I've told you to crucify.

I've listed those tramps and traitors by name. Be aware that some of them will creep in to mislead some of you -- even some of you who seem zealous for religion. If you're not watchful, they will do you more damage than you can imagine.

[Note -- Be watchful for such things as self-righteousness, spiritual pride, and excessive pride over one's achievements.]

They will appear to you as something different than you've seen them described. Therefore, Mansoul, watch and be attentive. Do not let yourselves be betrayed.'

Chapter 10

After the Prince had made these improvements in the town of Mansoul, and taught them things to help them, he scheduled another day for them to gather together so he could meet them and bestow another badge of honour to distinguish them from all the other people living in the kingdom of Universe. On the appointed day, the Prince gave them a short speech.

'Mansoul,' he said, 'I'm about to do something to show the world that you are mine, and to help you identify yourselves from any false traitors who might creep in among you.'

He commanded his servants to go to his treasury and get glistening, white robes. He said, 'I have gathered and stored these for my town of Mansoul.' The white garments were fetched out of his treasury and shown to the people. He told the people to find their size and put them on. So the people were dressed in fine, white linen, spotless and clean.

Then the Prince said, 'This is my uniform, these clothes identify my servants from everyone else. I give these clothes to all who are mine, and no one is allowed to see my face if he isn't wearing these. So wear them for the sake of me, who gave them to you, and so the world will know you belong to me.'

Mansoul put them on, and they shone like anything! They shone as bright as the sun, as clear as the moon, and as imposingly as a strong army with banners flying.

The Prince added, 'No prince or leader or great one of the Universe gives this clothing except me. That's why it will show the world that you are mine.'

'Now that you have my uniform, let me give you some instructions about them. Make sure you hear and do what I say.

'First: wear them every day, so that you never appear as if you weren't mine.

'Second: Keep them clean. If they look dirty or soiled, it dishonours me.

'Third: Don't let them drag on the ground, picking up dust and dirt.

'Fourth: Don't lose them! You wouldn't want to have to go around undressed and ashamed.

'Fifth: I do not want you to stain them or smear them, but Diabolus would love to see that happen. If that does happen, then quickly do what my law says so that you can stand before me and before my throne. This is the way to be sure I won't leave you or forsake you, and ensure that you'll be able to live here in Mansoul forever.'

And now Mansoul was like the jeweled ring on Emmanuel's right hand. Was there a town anywhere that could compare with Mansoul? Where else was there a people who had been redeemed from the power of Diabolus? What other town was so beloved by King Shaddai that he sent his son to the infernal cave to get them back? What other town had the honour of

Emmanuel making it his home? What other place had he fortified for himself and made strong with the force of his army? Mansoul had a most excellent Prince, golden Captains, strong soldiers, well-tested weapons, and shining, white garments. Those are no minor benefits! Can the town of Mansoul value those blessings enough and prove themselves worthy of them by using them properly?

When the Prince had finished with his improvements, he showed his delight in the result by flying flags on top of every tower. And he showed his pleasure with these other blessings.

First. He visited them frequently. Every day, it seemed, either the leaders of Mansoul were calling on him, or he was sending for them to come to his castle. Sometimes they walked together, discussing the wonderful things he had already done, and other things he promised to do for the town of Mansoul. He often did this with the Mayor, or Will-be-will, and the honest junior preacher Mr. Conscience, and the Recorder. The Prince was so gracious and loving and courteous with the town of Mansoul! Wherever he went, in the streets, or gardens, or orchards, he gave blessings to the poor, and greeted those passing by, and laid hands on those who were sick and healed them. He also encouraged his Captains with his presence and encouraging words every day -- sometimes every hour! A kind smile from him would strengthen and cheer them more than anything else under heaven.

The Prince also gave feasts to bless his people. Hardly a week would pass without a banquet given for his people. You might remember the feast I mentioned earlier, but now these feasts were rather common. Every day in Mansoul seemed to be a feast day! And when they left these feasts, the Prince didn't send them home empty-handed; he'd give them a ring, a gold chain, a bracelet, a white stone, or something. That's how much he treasured Mansoul. Mansoul was lovely to him.

[Note -- gold chain: token of marriage; bracelet: token of honour; white stone: token of beauty; something: token of pardon]

Second. When the town leaders couldn't come to him, he would send large quantities of food out to them: meat from the royal dining hall, wine and bread that had been prepared for his Father's table, all kinds of delicacies, so that their own tables would be covered. Anyone who saw it would say that such a thing had never been seen in any kingdom.

Third. If Mansoul didn't visit as often as he wanted, he would leave his castle and knock at their door to come in to keep the friendship close. If they were home and opened the door to him, he would express his former affection and confirm it with new tokens or signs of his favor.

It was amazing to see him, the Prince of princes, eating and drinking with his people, while all of his mighty Captains, soldiers, trumpeters, singers stood around waiting on them -- in the very place where Diabolus had lived and entertained his Diabolians to the utter destruction of Mansoul. These days, Mansoul's 'cup runneth over.' There were barrels of sweet wine, the finest of wheat, and milk and honey from the rock. Mansoul could only say, 'How great his goodness is! Since I have found favour in his eyes, I have been so honoured!'

The Prince ordained a new officer in the town. It was the good man whose name was Mr. God's-Peace. He was given a position to rule over Will-be-will, the Mayor, Mr. Recorder, the junior preacher, and all the people of Mansoul. Mr. God's-Peace was a not a native of Mansoul himself; he had come from King Shaddai's court with the Prince. He was a fond friend of Captain Belief and Captain Good-Hope. I've even heard that they were related, and I tend to believe it. This man was made a ruler over the town, especially of the castle, and Captain Belief was assigned to be his assistant. I observed that as long as things in Mansoul worked according to this agreeable man's wishes, the town was in a very happy condition. There were no bickerings, no naggings, no interferings, no unfaithful actions in the town. Every man focused on his own tasks. The merchants, officers, soldiers, and workers all kept to their business. The women and children went about their day cheerfully; they would work and sing all day long. Throughout Mansoul, there was nothing but harmony, peace, joy, and good health. It lasted all summer.

[Note -- God's-Peace: a sense of pardon produces peace, hope, love, respect, etc.]

But there was a man in the town named Mr. Carnal-Security. Even after all the mercy that had been shown to Mansoul, this man tried to drag Mansoul into tremendous and appalling slavery and bondage. Here is a brief account of what happened:

[Note -- Carnal-Security brings men into bondage because they rest in comforts, instead of living in Christ by faith.]

When Diabolus had first taken Mansoul, he brought many Diabolians, men like himself, with him. One of these was Mr. Self-Conceit. He was a famous and lively man. When Diabolus noticed how active and confident he was, he sent him on many dangerous missions, and Mr. Self-Conceit managed them better than many of the others. So Diabolus favoured him and promoted him to as high a position as Lord Will-be-will. In those days,

Will-be-will liked him and his success, and even gave him his daughter, Lady Fear-Nothing, as a wife. They were the parents of Mr. Carnal-Security. There were quite a few of these children who had one parent from Mansoul, and one from the Diabolians, so it wasn't always easy to tell who was a native of Mansoul.

Mr. Carnal-Security took after both of his parents -- he was self-conceited like his father, and feared nothing like his mother. He was also very busy -- if there was any news, doctrine, change, or even talk about change, Mr. Carnal-Security would be involved somehow. But he avoided those he considered weak and tended to affiliate with those he thought were on the strongest side.

When King Shaddai and his son made war upon Mansoul, Mr. Carnal-Security was in the town. He kept busy encouraging the people in their rebellion, and hardening them to resist King Shaddai's forces. When he saw that the town of Mansoul had been taken and converted to be useful to the glorious Prince Emmanuel, and how Diabolus was captured and forced to leave the castle in disgrace, and how Mansoul was full of soldiers and weapons, he slyly changed his tune and, just as he had served Diabolus against the Prince, he decided to pretend to serve the Prince against King Shaddai's enemies.

He got a smattering of information about Emmanuel's teachings, and, being a bold person, he ventured into a group of townspeople to try to chat with them. He knew that the town of Mansoul was strong and important, and he knew they would be pleased to hear him bragging about their power and greatness. So he started talking about the stability and might of the town, and how nobody could ever break through the walls, and then he raved about their Captains and weapons, and applauded the fortresses and towers, and finally praised the promises they had from their Prince. He said that with such blessings, Mansoul should be happy forever. He saw that the people liked what he said, so he went all around town, down the streets, from house to house, talking to each and every person, until all of Mansoul was listening to him and becoming almost as carnal as he was himself. From talking, they began having dinners together, and then spending leisure time together, until they were practically inseparable. Emmanuel was still in the town; he saw all of this and he was very aware of what was going on. The Mayor, Will-be-will, and Mr. Recorder were just as fascinated by this Diabolian gentleman as the rest of the city, even though the Prince warned them not to be misled by the Diabolians and their tricks. The Prince had also told them that their security didn't lie in the strength of their walls and fortifications, but in making use of what they had in a way that pleased Emmanuel, and in a way that made Emmanuel feel welcome to keep his presence in the castle. His overall teaching was that they should be careful to remember his Father's love, and they should do whatever they needed to in order to remain in that love. Of course, becoming enchanted with a Diabolian like Mr. Carnal-Security and heeding all of his suggestions was not the way to do that. They should have listened to their Prince, respected and loved him, and stoned that hateful brute to death. If they had been careful to walk in the ways their Prince recommended, then their peace would have been like a river, and their righteousness would have been like the waves of the sea.

When Prince Emmanuel saw that, because of the influence of Mr. Carnal-Security, the hearts of Mansoul had cooled towards him,

First. He mourned over them, and lamented to the Secretary, 'How I wish that my people had listened to me, and that Mansoul had walked in my ways! I would have fed them the finest wheat, and sustained them with honey from the rock.' Then he thought to himself, 'I'll go back to my Father's court until Mansoul reconsiders and acknowledges that they have done wrongly.' So he did. He left them because Mansoul rejected him in these ways:

1. They stopped paying him visits and calling on him at his castle.

2. They neglected him when he went out to visit them, and failed to notice when he didn't visit.

3. He continued to spread banquets for them and call feast days, but they didn't enjoy them even when they bothered to show up.

4. They no longer looked for his advice, but became stubborn and confident in themselves. Now that they felt invincible and strong, and Mansoul seemed secure from any enemy, they assumed she would be stable and immune from danger forever.

Emmanuel had watched as, through Mr. Carnal-Security's influence, Mansoul no longer depended on him or his Father, and no longer valued the blessings he had given them. He grieved for their condition, and tried to make them see how dangerous their current attitude was. He sent his Secretary to them to warn them not to follow such ways, but twice when the Secretary went to look for them, he found them having dinner at Mr. Carnal-Security's house! They were not disposed to reason about issues concerning their best interests. So the Secretary went away sadly. When he told Prince Emmanuel, the Prince was offended and also sad, so he made plans to drift away from their company and return to his Father's court.

These are the things he did to put some distance between himself and Mansoul:

1. Even though he still lived at Mansoul, he stayed at home in his castle more often.

2. When he did speak to them, he wasn't as pleasant and friendly.

3. He no longer sent them food from his table like he used to.

4. When they came to see him, which wasn't very often any more, he wasn't as quick to open his door to them. Before this, he would hear their footsteps approaching and be out the door meeting them before they even had to knock.

Now he acted a little more reserved and cool with them. hoping they might notice and return to him. But, alas! They didn't even notice, so they didn't care. Even the remembrance of the way things used to be didn't come to their minds to show that things had changed. So he left his castle and stayed at a place near the town gate, hoping they would be alarmed at his moving so near the exit and more sincerely seek his company. Mr. God's-Peace also resigned his post, and would no longer act on behalf of King Shaddai in the town of Mansoul.

[Note -- Christ, the Spirit, and peace withdraw from the carnally secure man.]

So the people did the opposite of what they were supposed to, and thus the Prince left them to themselves. But they were so hardened in their way, and so fascinated by what Mr. Carnal-Truth was teaching them, that they barely noticed when he left, and didn't miss him when he was gone.

One day Mr. Carnal-Security gave a feast for Mansoul. There was a man in the town named Mr. Godly-Fear. At one time he had been highly sought after, but these days, people didn't pay much attention to him. Mr. Carnal-Security thought it would be amusing to mock and abuse him, so he invited him to the feast. He came, and during the feast, all the guests were sitting at the table, eating and drinking and having fun -- all except Mr. Godly-Fear. He felt like a stranger, and did not eat or join in the fun. When Mr. Carnal-Security noticed him just sitting there, he spoke to him:

'Mr. Godly-Fear, don't you feel well? You look sick, or depressed, or perhaps both. I have a restorative elixir made by Mr. Forget-Good; if you drink a shot glass of that, it might cheer you up and make you a more fit member of our party.'

Mr. Godly-Fear responded prudently, 'Sir, I thank you for whatever kindness and civility you may offer. But I have no desire for your elixir. I do have something to say to the leaders of Mansoul, though: it is strange to me that you can be so lighthearted and jolly when the town of Mansoul is in such a wretched condition.'

Mr. Carnal-Security said, 'You sound like some sleep and fresh air would do you good. Why don't you lie down and take a nap while we continue our fun?'

Mr. Godly-Fear said, 'Sir, if you had an honest heart, as I do, you couldn't possibly carry on as you're doing.'

Mr. Carnal-Security said, 'Why not?'

Mr. Godly-Fear: 'I'll tell you if you'll listen. At one time the town of Mansoul was strong, and, under the right conditions, impregnable. But you, the townspeople, have weakened it, and now it lies vulnerable to its enemies. This is no time to flatter or be silent. It is you, Mr. Carnal-Security, who have slyly stripped Mansoul of her safety and driven her glory away from her. You might as well have pulled down her defense towers, smashed her gates, and broken her locks.

'How have you done this? Ever since you became an important person in Mansoul, the Prince who has been our strength has been neglected and offended. In fact, now he has left and is gone. If you doubt me, ask yourselves: Where is the Prince? When was the last time he was seen here? When did anyone last hear from him, or taste any of his food? Here you sit, eating with this Diabolian monster, but when was the last time you ate with your Prince? If you had been on your guard, your enemies from the outside could never have made you their prey. But now that you have sinned against your Prince, your enemies within have overpowered you.'

Mr Carnal-Security responded, 'You're unbelievable! Mr. Godly-Fear, won't you ever shake off your negativity? Are you afraid of being attacked? Who here has harmed you? Look -- I'm on your side! You're the only one looking on the negative side, I'm all for being confident and optimistic. Is this a time to be sad? A feast should be a happy time! Why do you have to spoil the mood with such passionate, melancholy words when you could eat, drink, and be merry?'

Mr. Godly-Fear said, 'I have a right to be sad. Prince Emmanuel has left Mansoul. He's gone, and you are the villain who has driven him away. He's gone, and he didn't even tell his nobles that he was leaving. If that's not a sign of his anger, then I don't know anything about godliness.

'Lords and leaders, my speech is really directed at you. Your gradual sliding away from him is what provoked him to gradually distance himself and go away. You didn't even notice it, although he was pulling away gradually over some time. If you had noticed, you could have been renewed by humbling yourselves. But when he realized that no one was even paying attention, or taking the beginning signs of his anger and judgment to heart, he left. I saw him go with my own eyes. And now, although you're full of boasts, your strength is gone. You're like Samson, waving his head around to show off his glorious head of hair -- not realizing that your hair has been cut off and you're bald! You might shake this off and continue to party with this gentleman like you've done in the past, and assume that everything is the same as ever. But since you can't do anything without the Prince, and he is gone, you ought to turn your partying into sad sighs, and weep instead of laughing.'

Mr. Conscience, the junior preacher, was startled at this, and agreed. He said,

'He's right, my friends. I'm afraid that what Mr. Godly-Fear has been saying is true. For my part, I haven't seen my Prince for a while. I can't even remember how long it's been. I'm afraid he's right, and our days at Mansoul are numbered.'

Mr. Godly-Fear: 'You won't find the Prince in Mansoul. He's gone, and it's the fault of the leaders. They rewarded his kindness and grace with unbelievable thoughtlessness.'

Mr. Conscience the junior preacher looked shocked. In fact, everyone there except the host looked pale and heartsick. But they began to recover themselves, and agree with Mr. Godly-Fear, and consider what the best thing to do might be. What should they do to their host for drawing them away from the Prince, and how could they recover the Prince's love? Mr. Carnal-Security just rolled his eyes and went to the next room.

Now they all remembered what the Prince had said: that false prophets who tried to mislead them should be destroyed. So they went out of the house while Mr. Carnal-Security, the Diabolian, was in the next room, and burned his house down around him.

After he was destroyed, they went to look for Emmanuel their Prince. But they couldn't find him. Now they were more convinced than ever that Mr.

Godly-Fear was correct, and their Prince was gone. They began to reflect on the wicked and improper things they had been doing, for now they were convinced that they were the reason he had left them.

They decided to go to Mr. Secretary -- though they had grieved him by refusing to listen to him before -- to see if he knew where Emmanuel was, and how they might get a letter to him. But Mr. Secretary wouldn't meet with them. He wouldn't let them into his royal home, nor would he come out to speak to them.

And now all seemed to be gloom and darkness in Mansoul. Now they realized how foolish they had been, and to see what the company and chatter of Mr. Carnal-Security had done, and what hateful damage had come to Mansoul because of his bragging words. But they still didn't know how much more it was likely to cost them. Now Mr. Godly-Fear began to be valued again. In fact, they practically looked on him as a prophet.

Chapter 11

When the Sabbath day arrived, they all went to hear their junior preacher. He preached a thunderous sermon of judgment to them that day. His text was from Jonah 2:8; 'Those who pay attention to false things turn their back on their own mercy.' He preached with such zeal and power, and his listeners were so dejected, that it was an unusual service. The people were so convicted that they could hardly go home and return to their regular routines and go back to work the following week. They felt so condemned that they didn't know what to do.

Mr. Conscience not only showed them their own sin, but he trembled himself for his own part in it. As he preached, he cried out, 'Of, unhappy man that I am! I did such a wicked thing! Me, a preacher, too! I was appointed by the Prince to teach his law, but I myself lived like a senseless pig! To think that I led the way to sin! I should been crying out against wickedness, but I joined Mansoul in wallowing in it until it drove the Prince away from us.' He accused the leaders and townspeople for their part, too, so that they all felt distressed and ashamed.

About this time, the town was stricken with a disease. Almost every one in the town came down with it. The Captains had a bad case and hovered between life and death for quite a while. If there had been an invasion against Mansoul, there was nothing they could have done about it. Their entire population was sick. There were so many pale faces and weak limbs as staggering townspeople tried to get around in Mansoul. Everywhere were groans and panting and people about to faint.

The white garments the Prince had given them were in a sorry state. Some were torn, and all were dirty. Some were hanging by a thread and about to be blown off by the next wind.

After some time in this sad, desolate condition, the junior preacher called for a day of fasting and humbling themselves before King Shaddai for their wickedness. And he asked Captain Boanerges to deliver a sermon, which he agreed to do. When the day came, what he preached on was Luke 13:7: 'Cut it down; it's just taking up space in the ground.' He explained how the fig tree was barren, and then he showed the consequence: repentance, or complete destruction. And he showed that the punishment had come from King Shaddai himself. All of this made Mansoul tremble. It went right to their hearts, and confirmed what had been preached by others before. So there was sorrow and mourning throughout the town.

After the sermon, the people discussed what they ought to do. The junior preacher said, 'I don't want to do anything without first getting the advice of Mr. Godly-Fear. He understood more about about the mind of King Shaddai before than we did, so he probably does now, as well, when we're turning back to virtue.'

So they called for Mr. Godly-Fear, and he came to them. They asked him what he thought was the best thing to do, and he answered, 'I think Mansoul should send a humble petition to the offended Prince and ask him to turn to help you in his favour and grace, and not to stay angry forever.'

The people thought this sounded like a good idea, so they wrote up their petition. But who should deliver it? They decided on the Mayor. So he went with their petition and arrived at King Shaddai's court, where the Prince had gone. But he found the gate locked and guarded, so he couldn't get in. He asked the guard to let Prince Emmanuel know he was there and what his business was. So a messenger told King Shaddai and Prince Emmanuel that the Mayor from Mansoul desired an audience, and why he had come. The Prince did not admit the Mayor or come to the gate. He only sent this message: 'They have turned their back to me. Now that they're in trouble they want me to arise and help them? Let them go to Mr. Carnal-Security and get help from him. He can be their leader and protector. Since they left me when they were doing well, why bother to come to me now that they're in trouble?'

This response disheartened the Mayor. It troubled him to the point of despair. Now he realized how damaging it was to associate with Diabolians like Mr. Carnal-Security. When he saw that he wouldn't be able to get any help for himself or his friends at Mansoul from King Shaddai's court, he went away weeping. All the way back to Mansoul, he lamented the sad state of Mansoul and their predicament.

As he approached the town, the leaders of the town came out to meet him and find out how it had gone at the court. He told them sadly, and they began to cry out, and mourn, and weep. They went into mourning and went sorrowing through the streets. When the rest of the town found out why they were so upset, they joined them in mourning. Thus, it was a day of rebuke and trouble, and the town of Mansoul was in anguish and distress.

After some time, they calmed down a bit and came together to discuss their options. Again, they asked for advice from Mr. Godly-Fear. He said that there was nothing better than what they had already done. In fact, they shouldn't be discouraged, but they should try again. He said, 'It's the way of King Shaddai to make his people wait and show patience. It should be the way of people in trouble to be willing to wait for him.'

So they took courage and sent another petition. And another, and another, and another. In fact, there wasn't a day or even an hour when you could go out the gate and not meet someone coming or going to petition King Shaddai and ask the Prince to come back. The road was full of messengers going both ways with petitions. This was the primary work project of Mansoul all that long, tedious winter.

If you remember, after Prince Emmanuel had re-taken and re-modeled the town of Mansoul, there were still some Diabolians lurking around in Mansoul. Some had come with Diabolus when he initially invaded the town, and some had been born there of mixed parentage. They had holes and openings in and under the town walls. Some of their names were Lord Fornication, Lord Adultery, Lord Murder, Lord Anger, Lord Lewdness, Lord Deceit, Lord Hostility, Lord Blasphemy, and that notoriously dangerous old villain, Mr. Covetousness. These and many others still continued to live in Mansoul even after Emmanuel had driven their prince Diabolus out of the castle.

Prince Emmanuel had signed a commission ordering Will-be-will and the entire town to capture and kill any of these scoundrels they could find, because they would always be Diabolians by nature, always be enemies to the Prince, and they would forever seek to destroy the town of Mansoul. But the people of Mansoul had not undertaken this commission. They had neglected to weed out these evildoers, so the villains had gradually gained courage and began to show themselves in Mansoul, and before long, the people of Mansoul were associating with them and becoming too familiar with them, to their detriment.

When the Diabolians who were still skulking around Mansoul saw that Mansoul had offended their Prince by sinning, and that he had left, they lost no time in plotting the ruin of Mansoul. They met in the hiding place of Mr. Mischief, another Diabolian, and discussed how they might deliver Mansoul into the hands of Diabolus again. Various schemes were proposed, and at last Mr. Lewdness proposed that the Diabolians who were still in the town should offer themselves as servants to the Mansoulians. 'If Mansoul hires some of us, that will make it that much easier for us to take over the town.' But then Mr. Murder said, 'We can't do that now. Mansoul is more vigilant right now because she was already ensnared by our friend, Mr. Carnal-Security. That's what caused them to offend their Prince, and now Mansoul is trying to be reconciled to the Prince again and thinks she can only do that by killing our people. Mansoul has a commission to capture and destroy us, so let's be wise as foxes, otherwise, we'll be dead, and then we won't be any use at all. But while we live, there might be something we can do.' They discussed the matter back and forth, and finally decided to send a letter to Diabolus showing him the state the town was in, and how displeased the Prince was with them. 'We can also let him know what we plan to do and see if he has any suggestions for us.'

So they wrote up a letter which said:

'To our great lord, the prince Diabolus who dwells in the subterranean cave:

'Great leader and mighty prince, we, the faithful Diabolians who are left in the rebellious town of Mansoul, acknowledge that we receive our very existence from you, and the nourishment we need at your hands. We cannot bear another day to see how your name is disrespected, disgraced, and discredited among the inhabitants of this town. We also dislike your long absence from the town. We do much better when you're with us.

'The reason we're writing to you is that we see a glimmer of hope that this town might be yours again. It has declined greatly from the way Emmanuel had it, and he has left them. Even though Mansoul keeps sending more and more petitions to him, he isn't responding.

'There has also been a plague here. Not only the poor are sick, but even the leaders and captains. We Diabolians seem to be the only ones who are immune. So, between their great transgression on the one hand, and the dangerous sickness on the other, they're an easy target for you. If you have a devious scheme, and you can come with your treacherous companions to take the town, send us word, and we'll be ready to assist you from our end. Or if you have a better plan, outline it to us. We're ready to follow your counsel, even at the risk of our lives and everything else we have.

'This letter was dictated on this date after much consultation at the home of Mr. Mischief, who wishes you well from his place in Mansoul.'

Mr. Profane was chosen to deliver the letter. When he arrived at Hell-Gate Hill, he knocked at the brass gates and Cerberus, the porter, opened the gate and took his letter. Cerberus carried the letter to Diabolus his lord and said, 'This is a greeting from our trusty friends in Mansoul.'

[Note -- Cerberus, 'the hound of Hades,' is a three-headed dog with a snake for a tail.]

All the demons came from all their haunts to hear the news from Mansoul: Beelzebub, Lucifer, Apollyon, and the rest. Cerberus stood by while the letter was read aloud. It was such welcome tidings that a command was given to ring the dead-men's bell unceasingly for joy. The bell was rung and there was great rejoicing that Mansoul was likely to come to ruin. The clapper of the bell clanged out, 'Mansoul is coming to dwell with us! Make room, make room for Mansoul!'

After this ghastly celebration, they got together to discuss a response to send back to their friends in return. There were various ideas, but since urgency was necessary, they decided to leave it to Diabolus, as the proper lord and ruler of the place. So this is the letter Mr. Profane brought back to Mansoul:

'To our offspring, the mighty Diabolians still living in Mansoul. Diabolus, the great prince of Mansoul, wishes you a prosperous and successful result to whatever brave projects and conspiracies you're working against Mansoul. Lord Fornication, Mr. Adultery, and the rest of my beloved descendants, we received your letter here in our desolate den. It was most welcome. In fact, your news was so heartily received that we rang our bell and rejoiced to know we still have friends in Mansoul. We are thrilled to hear of the degenerate state of Mansoul, and to know that they have offended their Prince and driven him away. Their sickness is also welcome news -- as well as your own health and strength. We would be enraptured to get the town back into our clutches again. We will put all of our wits and cunning to work to bring a satisfactory conclusion to your brave beginning.

'Be comforted, my offspring, to know that if we're able to surprise and take Mansoul, we will put all your persecutors to death and make you rulers and governors of the place. If we get Mansoul back again, be sure that we will never be cast out again. We will come with a stronger force this time and tighten our hold more securely than we did the first time. Besides, even Mansoul admits that the Prince has a law that says if we ever get them a second time, they shall be ours forever.

'Therefore, Diabolians, pry even more and spy out the weaknesses of the town. Do what you can yourselves to weaken them more and more. Let us know what, in your opinion, is the most effective means to regain them, whether by persuading them to live a superficial, loose life, or turning them to doubt and despair, or using the gun of pride and self-conceit to blow them up. Be ready to make a hideous assault from within as soon as we're ready to attack from without. We wish you all speed and success in your project. We will use all the hellish powers we possess to get what we desire. Diabolus the enemy of Mansoul sends you advantageous wishes from the pit.

'This letter is sent by joint consent of all the rulers and princes of darkness, to our corrupt friends remaining in Mansoul, by the hand of Mr. Profane, and is signed by me, Diabolus.'

Mr. Profane took this response back to Mansoul. He went to Mr. Mischief's home, where the contrivers were meeting. They were relieved to see their messenger returned safe and sound. Diabolus's response added to their gladness. They all asked after various friends they had in the pit -- Lucifer, and Beelzebub, and the rest -- and Mr. Profane said, 'They're doing well, my lords, as well as they can be in that place. And they rang their bells for joy when they read your letter.'

Since Diabolus's letter encouraged them in their work, they put their heads together to figure out how to complete their treacherous scheme against Mansoul. The first thing they determined was that their intentions needed to be kept a secret from Mansoul. 'Don't let them know about any part of our plan.' But what should they do to ruin and overthrow Mansoul? One said one thing, another said something else. Mr. Deceit said, 'Fellow Diabolians, our co-conspirators in the dungeon suggested three possibilities:

'1. Seek to ruin Mansoul through a superficial, loose life.

'2. Drive them to doubt and despair.

'3. Use the gun of pride and self-conceit to blow them up.

'Now, I think that tempting them to be prideful may be effective, and tempting them to abandon all restraint may also help. But I think that driving them to despair will cut them to the quick. That will make them question whether their Prince really loves them, and that doubt will disgust Emmanuel. If it works, they'll stop sending him petitions, and that will be the end of any requests for help. They'll think, 'Why bother? We might as well do nothing.' And all the Diabolians agreed with Mr. Deceit.

But how could they do that? Mr. Deceit had an answer for that, too. 'Some Diabolians should disguise themselves as gentlemen from a faraway country, and offer themselves as servants to the people of Mansoul, and pretend we want to help them. If the people of Mansoul hire them, their influence may defile and corrupt the town so that their Prince will not only be more offended, but he'll spew them out of his mouth. And once that happens, our prince Diabolus will be able to take them easily. They'll fall like a ripe fig right into his mouth.'

This sounded like a great plan, but it might be too obvious if they all did it. So they picked just a few for this delicate scheme: Lord Covetousness (who disguised himself as Prudent-Thrifty), Lord Lewdness (who disguised himself as Harmless-Mirth), and Lord Anger (who called himself Good-Zeal).

[Note -- Harmless-Mirth: Light talk or behaviour is as destructive to peace as sin itself.]

On market day, these three disguised themselves, took on their assumed names, and went to the market place. They looked fine and healthy, dressed in sheep's wool that was about the same dingy color as the white garments of the people of Mansoul. These men were fluent in the language of the Mansoulians and didn't ask much for wages, so it didn't take them long to find positions as servants.

Mr. Mind hired Prudent-Thrifty, and Mr. Godly-Fear hired Good-Zeal. It took Harmless-Mirth a little longer to get hired because it was the Lent season, but Lent was almost over. Will-be-will hired him to be his manservant. So they all got jobs.

Once these Diabolians were inside the homes of the Mansoulians, they started right in to do as much mischief as they could. They were depraved, vile, and sneaky, and quickly corrupted the families where they were staying. They had the most success with their masters, especially Prudent-Thrifty and Harmless-Mirth. Good-Zeal didn't get on very well with his master, because Mr. Godly-Fear soon picked up on the fact that he was a counterfeit scoundrel. As soon as Good-Zeal realized this, he escaped from the house. If he hadn't, I imagine Mr. Godly-Fear would have hanged him.

When these reprobates had corrupted the town as much as they could, they set themselves to wondering when Diabolus might be arriving so that they could be ready from within. They all agreed that a market day would probably be the best time for an attack. The people would be too busy to fear any surprise attacks, and the Diabolians would be able to gather together without rousing suspicion. And if their plans didn't go off well, they could disperse and hide in the crowd.

With this all neatly planned out, they wrote another letter to Diabolus:

'We, the lords of loose living from our dens, holes, and caves within Mansoul, send greetings to the great and high Diabolus.

'Great lord and nourisher of our lives, we were glad when we read that you were willing to work with us and cooperate in our design to ruin Mansoul.

'We were pleased that you wanted to encourage us in devising the utter destruction and desolation of Mansoul. It is pleasing and profitable for us to see our enemies lying dead at our feet or fleeing before us. Therefore, we are still contriving to pave the way so that it will be easy for your lordship to take Mansoul.

'We studied the three hellishly clever options you outlined in your last letter, and we decided to blow them up with the gunpowder of pride, tempt them to live reckless, wild lives, while driving them to the gulf of despair, which we consider the most effective part of the plan. We have thought of two ways to do this. First, we will tempt Mansoul to be as vile and degraded as possible. Then after you arrive, we can fall on them together. Since you have your pick of nations to serve in your army, we suggest the doubters as most likely to strike an effective attack on Mansoul. Thus, we shall overcome these enemies together -- and if we don't, the pit will open, and desperation will push them in. We've already started the first part of our design: three of our trusty Diabolians are disguised and working in their homes. Lord Covetousness is disguised as Prudent-Thrifty and is working for Mr. Mind; he is almost as covetous now as our friend! Lord Lewdness is disguised as Harmless-Mirth, and is employed by Will-be-will, who is now very shameless. Lord Anger is disguised as Good-Zeal, but he was hired by Mr. Godly-Fear, and that peevish old man took a dislike to him. We have since found out that he ran away before his master could hang him.

> *[Note -- Doubting and distrust are the offspring of unbelief.]*

'These three have advanced our work upon Mansoul. Despite that quarrelsome, disagreeable Godly-Fear, the other two are doing their jobs well, and they're likely to have Mansoul ready even sooner than expected.

'Our next step is for you to arrive at the town on a market day. While they're preoccupied with their business, they'll be too distracted to be worried about an assault, and less able to defend themselves and make things difficult for you. While you're making a furious attack outside the town, we, your loyal and beloved children, will be making whatever commotion and chaos we can from inside. So we'll be able to completely bewilder Mansoul and swallow them up before they know what happened. If you and your serpent heads, dragons, and other lords have a better idea, let us know quickly.

'We send this message to you monsters of the infernal cave, from the home of Mr. Mischief, by the hand of Mr. Profane.'

Chapter 12

While Diabolus and the Diabolians were sending letters back and forth about the best plan to ruin Mansoul, the town itself was in a sad and wretched predicament. They had grievously offended King Shaddai and his son, their enemies had gotten the upper hand within Mansoul, and the Prince was not responding to their petitions. Because of the tricks and subtle influence of the disguised Diabolians posing as servants, their cloud of doom seemed to grow darker, and their Prince seemed farther and farther away.

The plague was still raging among the people of Mansoul and their Captains, but their enemies only seemed to grow more lively and healthy. They seemed to be the ones in control.

By this time, Mr. Profane had left to deliver the letter to Diabolus's black den. When he got to Hell-Gate Hill, Cerberus was there to meet him as before.

By now, they were old friends, and they fell to chatting about Mansoul and the design to ruin her.

'Greetings, old friend!' said Cerberus. 'You've come back to Hell-Gate Hill again? I'm glad to see you!'

Mr. Profane: 'Yes, my lord, I'm back. I have a letter about the concerns of Mansoul.'

Cerberus: 'What's their condition right now?'

Mr. Profane: 'They're right where we want them. Their godliness is heavily decayed, which is just what our hearts could wish for. Their Prince is disgusted with them, which is also gratifying. Our own people have infiltrated their homes as servants. We're just a step from owning the town! Our trusty friends in Mansoul are daily making plans to betray Mansoul to our prince, and the bitter sickness continues to spread and weaken the people. All in all, things are looking likely to succeed, and I think we will finally prevail.'

Then Cerberus, the dog of Hell-Gate said, 'This is the perfect time to attack. I hope the enterprise comes off without a hitch, and success comes very soon. I hope it's over soon for the sake of the poor, suffering Diabolians who live in fear for their lives in that traitorous town of Mansoul.'

Mr. Profane: 'The project is almost complete; the Diabolians within Mansoul are working day and night, and the people of Mansoul are as gullible as silly doves. They're distracted with their own problems and don't have the slightest idea that their town is about to be attacked and destroyed. There's every reason for Diabolus to hurry and get to Mansoul as soon as he can.'

Cerberus: 'That sounds promising. I'm glad things have progressed so well! Go on in to the lords, Mr. Profane. They'll give you a hearty welcome. I've already given them your letter.'

So Mr. Profane went into the den, and Diabolus greeted him with, 'Welcome, trusty servant! Your letter has gladdened my heart!' The other lords of the pit also greeted him. Mr. Profane bowed to all of them and then said, 'Let Mansoul fall to my lord Diabolus, and may he be her king forever!' At that, the demons within that hollow gorge of hell gave a loud, hideous groan of delight (that's how they make music) that was loud enough to make the mountains shake as if they might fall apart.

After they had read and considered the letter, they discussed how they ought to reply. The first to speak was Lucifer.

He said, 'The first step of the plan seems to be succeeding -- the Diabolians are using every way they can to make Mansoul more vile and filthy. That is the best way to destroy a soul. Our old friend Balaam turned that way and prospered many years ago. We should make this a general rule; nothing can make that scheme fail except grace, and I sincerely hope there's none of that in the town. But I'm not convinced that the distraction of market day makes the best time to attack. I think we should debate that idea. The whole project depends on that step. If we don't pick the most opportune time, the whole thing may fail. The Diabolians back in Mansoul think that market day is the best time because the people will be busy and unprepared for any surprise attack. But how do we know they don't double their guards on market days? It seems like an obvious precaution in general, and their present situation may make them more wary. In fact, what if their men are always armed these days? If that's the case, you may be disappointed in your attempts, my lords, and you may endanger the Diabolians who are in the town.'

Then Beelzebub said, 'You may have a point, but we don't know if they're more wary or not. It's worth discussing. We need to know how aware Mansoul is of her decayed state, and whether she's at all suspicious about the plot we're planning against her and whether that suspicion has motivated her to set guards at her gates, and double those guards on market days. But if they're completely clueless and asleep, any day would work -- although a market day would be best. That's my opinion.'

Then Diabolus said, 'How can we know how suspicious they are?' Someone suggested asking Mr. Profane, so they did, and this was his response:

'As far as I can tell, Mansoul's faith and love has deteriorated, and their Prince has rejected them. They keep sending him petition after petition, but he hasn't been in any hurry to answer them. And I haven't seen much sign of them reforming their ways.'

Diabolus: 'I'm glad they're not making much progress in reforming, but I'm still nervous about their petitioning. And yet, their loose, careless lifestyle is a sign that there's not much heart in what they're doing, and things don't mean much if there's no heart in them. But let's continue discussing, men.'

Beelzebub: 'If it's as Mr. Profane says, it doesn't really matter which day we choose to make our assault. Neither their prayers nor their strength will help them much.'

When Beelzebub had finished, Apollyon continued. 'My opinion concerning this matter,' he said, 'is to proceed carefully and softly, not in a hurry. Let our companions continue carrying on in Mansoul, polluting and defiling it by drawing it further and further into sin -- nothing will destroy and devour Mansoul as much as sin. If this is done, and if it takes effect, Mansoul will get lazy about keeping watch, or petitioning, or anything else that might make her more safe and secure. She'll forget all about Emmanuel. She won't care for his company, and if she starts living like that, the Prince won't be in any hurry to rush to her aid. Our trusted companion, Mr. Carnal-Security, drove the Prince out of town with one of his tricks. Why shouldn't Lord Covetousness, and Lord Lasciviousness keep him out? And I'll tell you something else you don't know: if just two or three Diabolians are tolerated and allowed to stay in Mansoul, they'll do more to keep Emmanuel away and make it easier for you to make Mansoul your own than a whole army sent to help us. So let that first plan be carried out steadily and diligently, with all the devious scheming imaginable. Let them continually send more and more of their companions in to toy with the people of Mansoul. In that way, it might not even be necessary to make war against them. Or if war is still necessary, the more sinful they are, the more weakened they'll be and unable to resist us, and we'll be able to overcome them more easily. Suppose the worst happens and Emmanuel shows up to help them? Perhaps the same means, or something similar, can be used to drive him away from them again. In fact, if they lapse into sin again, maybe he'll be driven away from them forever for the same reason he was driven away the first time. And if he goes away, he'll take his battering rams, slings, Captains, and soldiers with him -- leaving Mansoul completely unprotected and vulnerable. And when Mansoul realizes that her Prince has completely forsaken and abandoned her, she's sure to open her gates to you like she used to. But this can't be done quickly; it's a plan that has to be carried out slowly.'

Diabolus was getting impatient and angry. He said, 'My men, and powers of the cave, my trusted companions, I have listened to your long, tedious suggestions with much impatience. But my vacuous mouth and empty stomach craves to repossess Mansoul so desperately that, whatever happens, I'm not willing to wait on lingering projects to see if they work out or not. I must, however I can, and as soon as possible, fill my insatiable emptiness with the soul and body of Mansoul. So who's with me? I'm going to recover my town of Mansoul right now!'

When the evil lords and princes of the pit saw the furious desire Diabolus had to devour the poor town of Mansoul, they stopped raising any further objections and agreed to help him however they could, though it must be admitted that Apollyon's plan would have damaged Mansoul far more. But they were willing to loan him whatever strength they had, knowing that some day they might need his help in return. They began discussing battle plans: how many soldiers they had, and which were the strongest to help

Diabolus go against the town of Mansoul. They decided that, according to the letter the Diabolians had sent, no one was more fit for this expedition than the terrible army of doubters. Twenty to thirty thousand seemed to be a good number. They wanted Diabolus to immediately start beating his drum to summon men from the land of Doubting, which lies in the vicinity of Hell-Gate Hill. These lords and princes would also participate by leading the army of Doubters. They wrote a letter and sent it to the Diabolians lurking in Mansoul and then waited for Mr. Profane to come back and relay what plan the Diabolians were working on. This is their letter:

'From Diabolus and the company of princes of darkness who reside in the horrible, dark dungeon of hell, to our trusted companions in and around the walls of Mansoul who are impatiently waiting to hear our villainous answer to their venomous and poisonous plan against Mansoul.

'Dear friends whom we boast about and in whose actions we delight in all year: Your letter delivered by our beloved friend Mr. Profane was most welcome to us. When we read its contents, we made such a hideous yell of gratification from our gaping hollow-bellied place that the mountains around Hell-Gate Hill almost shattered into pieces.

'We could only admire your loyalty to us, and the great subtlety of your minds that serve us against the town of Mansoul. You have devised such an excellent plan for overcoming those rebellious people that even all of our wits here in hell couldn't think of anything better. Ever since we read your suggestions, we have done nothing but approve and admire them.

'In order to encourage you in your shrewd craft, we must inform you that we discussed and debated your plan from one side of the cave to the other, but none of us could come up with anything more suitable and effective to take and possess the town of Mansoul.

'Everything we discussed other than your plan was rejected and discarded. Diabolus the prince only accepted your scheme. In fact, his vast gorge and cavernous belly were ambitious to put your strategy into action.

'We are letting you know that our burly, furious, and unmerciful Diabolus is raising twenty thousand doubters to come against Mansoul and relieve you. They are all powerful men who are accustomed to war, and can therefore endure the battle. Diabolus is working this out as quickly as possible, because his heart and spirit are committed to this plan. Continue to stick to us and give us advice and support, and when this is all over, we will promote you to rulers of Mansoul.

[Note -- Doubters: Disbelief of God's word, power, truth, faithfulness, and love, is like a whole host of enemies.]

'We have one more thing to ask of you. Continue to use whatever power, guile, and and skill you can as well as delusive persuasions to draw Mansoul into more sin and wickedness so that their sin may bring forth their death.

'We conclude that the more vile, sinful, and corrupt Mansoul is, the more hesitant Emmanuel will be to aid them either by coming himself or sending anyone else. As well, the more sinful they are, the weaker they will be and the more unable to put up any resistance when we assault them to swallow them up. Perhaps their Shaddai will even remove his protection from them altogether and call his Captains and soldiers home with their battering rams and slings, and leave them vulnerable and exposed. Then they'll be open to us and fall like a ripe fig into our mouth. It will be easy to come upon her and overtake her.

'As far as when we should arrive at Mansoul, that's not decided yet. Some of us think market day, or the night after a market day, would be best. Just be ready so that as soon as you hear our drums beating outside the town, you can create a chaotic confusion inside. Then Mansoul will be completely distressed; she won't know which way to turn for help. Lord Lucifer, Lord Beelzebub, Lord Apollyon, Lord Legion, and all the rest of us send you greetings. So does Lord Diabolus. We wish both of you the same success and rewards we're now enjoying.

'We and all the legions here with us greet you from our ghastly imprisonment in this most grim pit. We wish you to be as hellishly prosperous as we'd like to be ourselves. From the messenger, Mr. Profane.'

Then Mr. Profane readied himself to deliver the letter to the Diabolians within the town of Mansoul. He came up the stairs from the deep mouth of the pit to exit and travel to Mansoul, and there was Cerberus, guarding the entrance. Cerberus greeted him and asked him how things were going beneath, and what plans were being worked against the town of Mansoul.

Mr. Profane: 'Things are going as well as can be expected. The lords approved of the letter I brought from the Diabolians, and I'm returning to Mansoul to tell them so. I have the response here in my pocket to deliver to them; I think they'll be glad to read it. The letter is encouraging them to go ahead with their plan, and to also be ready to cause mayhem within the town as soon as they know Diabolus is within striking range of the town.'

Cerberus: 'You mean Diabolus intends to go there himself?'

Mr. Profane: 'He certainly does! And he's taking twenty thousand tough doubters with him, all hefty warriors hand-picked from the land of Doubting, who will serve him on this mission.'

That made Cerberus glad, and he said, 'Such brave preparations in store to attack the town of Mansoul! I wish I could be leading a thousand of them; then I could show my own valour against the famous town of Mansoul.'

Mr. Profane: 'Maybe your wish will come true. You certainly look fearless enough, and my lord is looking for brave, tough soldiers to go with him. But I need to go -- my business is a matter of urgency.'

Cerberus: 'Yes, you'd better go. Farewell, I wish you all the speed possible and I send all the trouble this place can afford to go with you. When you get to the house of Mr. Mischief, the place where the Diabolians are planning to meet, tell them that Cerberus hopes to serve with them, and if he can, he'll be with the army that invades Mansoul.'

Mr. Profane: 'I'll tell them. I know the Diabolians will be glad to hear that, and they'll be anxious to see you, too.'

After a few more of these compliments, Mr. Profane said good-bye, and Cerberus exchanged more pit wishes and bid him speed on his journey. Mr. Profane then took off directly for the town of Mansoul.

When he got there, he went immediately to the house of Mr. Mischief and found the Diabolians already assembled and waiting for his return. He greeted them and delivered his letter, and added this compliment: 'My lords, the high and mighty principalities of the pit, greet you as true Diabolians. They wish you the most proper of their greetings for your great service, grand attempts, and brave achievements that you've accomplished to restore Mansoul to our prince Diabolus.'

Mansoul was in a dire situation. She had offended her Prince and he was gone. By her foolishness, she had invited the powers of hell to seek her complete destruction.

It's true that Mansoul was somewhat aware of her own sin, but the Diabolians had gotten under her skin. Mansoul cried, but Emmanuel was gone and her cries had not yet brought him back. She didn't know if he would ever come back to his Mansoul again. She also didn't realize how strong or ambitious the enemy was, or how busy they had been in actualizing the plot of hell that they had planned against her.

They continued to send petition after petition to the Prince, but there was no response. They neglected to reform their ways, which is just what Diabolus wanted. He knew that if they regarded sin in their hearts, their King would not hear their prayer. So Mansoul grew weaker and weaker, and were tossed about like a tumbleweed rolling in the wind. Although they cried out to their King, they embraced Diabolians in their bosoms -- so what was their King supposed to do for them? There seemed to be an odd mixture in Mansoul -- Diabolians and Mansoulians would walk the streets together. They began to seek civil relationships with the Diabolians, thinking that since the sickness had killed so many in Mansoul, it was no use being contentious with them. The weaker Mansoul became, the better for their enemies. Their sins worked for the advantage of their foes. The Diabolians began to look forward to possessing Mansoul for themselves. They mingled with the people of Mansoul while planning for the day they would be in charge. The number and strength of the Diabolians seemed to be increasing while the number and strength of Mansoul seemed to be dwindling. More than eleven thousand people -- men, women, and children -- had already died from the sickness in Mansoul.

But now King Shaddai sent Mr. Prywell, a lover of Mansoul, to go up and down through Mansoul listening to see if there were any threats against it. He was a jealous sort of man, and was afraid of some tragedy happening to Mansoul, either from the Diabolians within, or from enemies outside the town. As Mr. Prywell was listening here and there, he ended up at Vile Hill in Mansoul one night. This was a place where Diabolians liked to meet. He heard some mutterings in the darkness, so he came closer to the house that was there to hear more. He hadn't been listening for long when he heard someone inside confidently affirm that very soon, Diabolus would possess Mansoul again, and that when that happened, the Diabolians intended to kill all the Mansoulians and their Captains, and drive the soldiers out of town. The voice also said there were twenty thousand fighters coming with Diabolus to accomplish all of this, and they'd see it before the month was up.

When Mr. Prywell heard this, he was certain it was true. So he immediately went to the Mayor's house and told him. The Mayor sent for the junior preacher and broke the news to him. The junior preacher alerted the whole town of Mansoul since he was now the only preacher in Mansoul because the Lord Secretary was grieved and laying low. Here's the way Mr. Prywell alerted Mansoul: that very hour, he had the lecture bells rung to call the town together. He gave them a brief warning to be watchful because of Mr.

Prywell's news. 'A horrible plot has been contrived against Mansoul,' he said, 'a plan to massacre all of us in a single day. This isn't just gossip, because Mr. Prywell said it. He has always been faithful to Mansoul, you know him to be a serious and cautious man. He's no tale-teller, or spreader of false reports. No, he's the kind of person who loves to get to the bottom of matters, and doesn't chat about hearsay, but only talks about solid facts.

'I'll call him and you can ask him for yourselves.' So he called for him, and he came and told the news so directly, and affirmed the truth of it with so much confirming evidence that Mansoul was convinced that it was true. The junior preacher also supported him, saying, 'Sirs, it isn't irrational for us to believe it, because we have provoked King Shaddai to anger and our sin has run Prince Emmanuel out of town. We have had far too much contact with Diabolians and abandoned the Prince's former mercies. It's no wonder, then, that the enemy within and the enemy without should plot and plan our ruin, and what better time to do it than now? The sickness is in our town right now, and has weakened us. Many well-intentioned men are dead, and the Diabolians have grow stronger and stronger lately.

'Besides,' said the junior preacher, 'I have heard from the truthful Mr. Prywell one additional piece of information: what he overheard leads him to believe that several letters have been exchanged between the furies and the Diabolians about destroying us.' When Mansoul heard this, they couldn't deny it. They lifted up their voices and wept. Mr. Prywell confirmed everything the junior preacher had said. So they started crying again, and doubling up their prayers and petitions to King Shaddai and his son. They broke the news to the Captains, commanders, and soldiers in the town, asking them to prepare, and to be strong and brave. They said they would make sure they had whatever armour and weapons they needed and to prepare themselves to battle Diabolus by night or day, whenever he should attack.

The Captains, who truly loved Mansoul, shook themselves like mighty Samson, and met together to plan how to defeat those arrogant and hellish schemes that were on the way through Diabolus and his companions against the sick and weakened people of Mansoul. This is what they decided:

1. The gates of Mansoul should be shut and locked, and anyone coming in or out should be strictly examined by the Captains of the guards. They hoped that the managers of the plot might be caught and perhaps tell them who the ringleaders were.

2. A strict search should be made for Diabolians throughout Mansoul. Every house should be systematically searched from top to bottom. This might turn up some who were involved in the plot.

3. They also decided that whenever any Diabolians were found, including those in Mansoul who might have been harbouring the confederates, they should be punished in the public market-place to shame them and to act as a warning to others.

4. Mansoul determined to have a time of fasting and penitance throughout the entire town to plead and humble themselves for their sins before the Prince and his Father. Anyone who did not fast, but was found wandering the streets as if it was business as usual, would be assumed to be Diabolians, and treated as such.

5. Mansoul decided to send urgent penitance and petitions for help to King Shaddai, and to let him know what Mr. Prywell had told them.

6. They decided to give formal appreciation to Mr. Prywell on behalf of the town for diligently seeking the welfare of their town, and, since he was so naturally inclined to keep an eye out for their best interests and undermine their foes, they would grant him a commission as Scoutmaster General, for the good of town.

All these things were done. They shut and locked the gates, they conducted a search for any Diabolians, they publicly punished any they found, they fasted, they sent petitions to their Prince, and they promoted Mr. Prywell. Mr. Prywell did his job with great diligence and faithfulness. He threw his whole heart into his work, not just within the town, but he also went outside the town walls to scout around.

Chapter 13

A few days later, Mr. Prywell made a journey to Hell-Gate Hill, where the doubters were, and heard about what had been talked about in Mansoul. He realized that Diabolus was almost ready to begin his march against the town. He rushed back to Mansoul, called the Captains and leaders of Mansoul, and told them where he had been and what he had heard and seen. He told them that Diabolus was almost ready to march, and that he had made Mr. Incredulity, who had broken out of prison, the general of his army. His army consisted of doubters, and there were over 20,000 of them! Diabolus was planning to bring the evil princes from the infernal pit with him, and make them captains over his doubters. He confirmed that several from the dark den would come along with Diabolus as a volunteer militia to conquer Mansoul and make them submit to Diabolus, their prince.

He also told them that the doubters had shared with him that Mr. Incredulity had been made general because no one was more loyal to the tyrant, and because he had an insatiable hatred against the welfare of Mansoul. He still remembered how Mansoul had imprisoned him, and he meant to be revenged.

But the evil princes would only be commanders; Incredulity would be over all of them because he was more able to harass Mansoul than any of the other princes.

When the Captains and leaders of Mansoul heard Mr. Prywell's news, they thought it would be best to enact the laws that the Prince had made against the Diabolians. So they made a thorough search of all the houses in Mansoul, looking for Diabolians. They found two -- Mr. Covetousness was found in Mr. Mind's house (but he had changed his name to Prudent-Thrifty), and Mr. Lustfulness was found in Will-be-will's house (but he had changed his name to Harmless-Mirth). The Captains and leaders put them in the custody of Mr. True-Man the jailer. He was so harsh with them, and put so many heavy chains on them, that they both wasted away and died in prison. Their masters, according to the agreement of the Captains and leaders, were punished in the public market-place to shame them and make them a warning to the rest of Mansoul.

For penance, they had to publicly confess their faults and promise to change their lives.

Then the Captains and leaders continued their search through Mansoul for more Diabolians, whether they were lurking in caves, holes, or anywhere else they might hide around Mansoul. But, although they could spot their footprints and follow those to their holes and even smell them at the mouths of their caves, yet they weren't able to catch them. Their ways were too crooked, their holds were too strong, and they were too quick at slipping away.

By now Mansoul ruled over the Diabolians who were left with such a stiff hand that they were glad to shrink into corners and hide away. One time they had been able to walk openly, but now they were forced to sneak out only at night. One time Mansoul had been their friend, but now they were their deadly enemies. That was a positive change that Mr. Prywell's news made in Mansoul.

By this time, Diabolus had finished arranging his army with the captains and field officers he liked best. He was the highest lord, and Incredulity was the general of his army. These are some of their officers:

1. Captain Rage led the election doubters. His banner was red, his standard bearer was Mr. Destructive, and his coat of arms was a red dragon.

2. Captain Fury led the vocation doubters. His standard bearer was Mr. Darkness, his banner had pale colours, and his coat of arms was a flying fiery serpent.

3. Captain Perdition led the grace doubters. His standard bearer was Mr. No-Life, his banner was red, and his coat of arms was a black den.

4. Captain Insatiable led the faith doubters. Mr. Devourer was his standard bearer, his banner was red, and his coat of arms had open jaws.

5. Captain Brimstone led the perseverance doubters. His standard bearer was Mr. Burning, his banner was red, and his coat of arms was a stinking blue flame.

6. Captain Torment led the resurrection doubters. His standard bearer was Mr. Gnaw, his banner had pale colours, and his coat of arms was a black worm.

7. Captain No-Ease led the salvation doubters. His standard bearer was Mr. Restless, his banner was red, and his coat of arms was a ghastly image of death.

8. Captain Sepulchre led the glory doubters. His standard bearer was Mr. Corruption, his banner had pale colours, and his coat of arms had a skull and crossbones.

9. Captain Past-Hope led the felicity doubters. His standard bearer was Mr. Despair, his banner was red, and his coat of arms had a hot iron and hard heart.

Over these there were seven superior captains. They were Lord Beelzebub, Lord Lucifer, Lord Legion, Lord Apollyon, Lord Python, Lord Cerberus, and Lord Belial. He set these over the captains, Incredulity was general over them, and Diabolus was king of them all. They had volunteers who were of the same caliber, and they led armies of 100 or more.

They left Hell-Gate Hill where they had assembled and marched straight towards Mansoul. Thanks to Mr. Prywell, Mansoul had been warned of their coming. So they had extra guards at the gates, and slings mounted in advantageous places where they could hurl stones at the enemy.

The Diabolians within the town weren't able to do as much damage as they had hoped because Mansoul was alert and on to them. But the poor people were badly frightened at the first appearance of their foes, especially when the enemy sat right at the gates and beat on their drums. This was amazingly hideous to hear. It scared men as far as seven miles away who were awake to hear it. Their colourful flying banners were also terrifying and demoralizing to see.

Diabolus made his approach at Ear Gate and attacked it furiously. He supposed his companions inside were ready to do their part, but the Captains had taken care of that. So Diabolus did not have the help he expected, and his army was met with flying stones from the slings. Although the Captains were weakened from the sickness that had plagued Mansoul for so long, they fought gallantly. So Diabolus was forced to retreat and go out of the reach of the slings.

He fortified himself outside the town and built up four siege mounds against the town. He called the first one Mount Diabolus after himself to frighten the townspeople, and the other three were called Mount Alecto, Mount Megara, and Mount Tisiphone, named after the dreadful furies of hell. In this way he began to harass Mansoul and torment them like a lion terrorizing his prey. But the Captains and their armies resisted so daringly, and did so much damage with their slings, that they forced him to retreat against his will, and Mansoul began to take courage.

The tyrant set up his banner on the top of Mount Diabolus, which was raised against the north side of the town. His banner had a hideous flaming shield with a picture of Mansoul in flames.

Then Diabolus commanded his drummer to approach the walls of Mansoul every night and beat a threatening summons. He had him do this at night because in the daytime the Captains were attacking him with slings. Diabolus said he wanted to summon the trembling Mansoulians to a parley, and maybe after a few nights, they would get weary of the drum beats and finally give in and surrender.

So the drummer rose up every night and beat his drums. While the drums were beating, those looking towards Mansoul would see only darkness and sorrow. The only sound more fearful than that drum beat was the voice of

King Shaddai. Mansoul could do nothing but tremble and look forward to being swallowed up.

After the drummer had beat his drums, he made this speech to Mansoul: 'My master bids me to tell you that if you willingly surrender, he'll make things easy for you. But if you resist, he is determined to take you by force.' But the people of Mansoul had gone to their Captains in the castle, so there was no one to hear the drummer or give him a response. So the drummer went back to his master at the camp.

When Diabolus realized that his drums weren't going to bend Mansoul to his will, he sent the drummer back the next night, but without his drum, to tell the people that he wanted to talk. But the talk only amounted to a summons to surrender. The townspeople didn't bother to listen; they remembered what they suffered when they heard the first few words.

The following night, Diabolus sent Captain Sepulchre. He came to the walls of Mansoul and said,

'Inhabitants of the rebellious town of Mansoul! I summon you in the name of Diabolus to open your gates and let the prince come in. If you resist, we will take your town by force and swallow you up like the grave. If you intend to surrender, let me know. If not, then let me know.

'The reason for this summons is because my prince is your true prince and master. You admitted it yourself. The assault of Emmanuel, when he treated Diabolus so dishonourably, has not convinced him to give up his right to refrain from recovering his property. Think it over, Mansoul. Will you surrender peacefully or not? If you give up quietly, we'll be friends, just like old times. But if you refuse and resist, then don't expect anything but fire and sword.'

This made the weary town of Mansoul even more discouraged, but they didn't give him any answer. So he went back to his camp.

The people of Mansoul consulted with their Captains and with each other, and decided to ask their Secretary for advice, but he was grieved and unsettled about them. The people begged these three favours from him:

1. That he would look favourably upon them and not keep himself hidden so much. Also, that he would listen while they let him know about their miserable situation. But he said he was 'still uncomfortable, and therefore was unable to be at ease with them like he had been.'

2. They wanted his advice about their urgent situation, now that Diabolus had come with twenty thousand doubters. They said Diabolus and his men were cruel and they were afraid of them. But the Secretary only said, 'You must look to the law of the Prince and see what you've been told to do there.'

3. They wanted the Secretary to help them write up a petition to King Shaddai and his son, and sign his name as if he was one of them because, as they said, 'we have sent many petitions, but we can't get an answer. Surely one with your signature would fare better.'

But all he would say was, 'they had offended Emmanuel, and grieved himself, the Secretary, as well. Therefore, they would have to get themselves out of their own mess.'

This response felt like a millstone upon them. It felt so crushing that they didn't know what to do. At the same time, they didn't dare comply with Diabolus's demands. So Mansoul was in quite a fix: her enemies were ready to swallow her up, and her friends weren't ready to help her.

Then Mr. Understanding, the Mayor, stood up. He had reflected on what Mr. Secretary had said from every angle until he found a bit of comfort in it. 'This must be what was meant when Mr. Secretary told us that we would have to suffer for our sins,' he said. 'But it sounds to me like we'll probably be saved from our enemies in the end; after a few more trials and sorrows, Emmanuel will come and help us.' The Mayor took a more critical perspective of the Secretary's words because he had a prophetic gift, and because the Secretary's words always had a general timeless meaning, yet the townspeople could sometimes look closer and find a specific meaning for their exact situation.

Then they went to the Captains and told them what the Secretary had said. The Captains had the same opinion as the Mayor. They began to take courage and make preparations to make a daring attack on the enemy's camp to destroy the Diabolians and doubters that the tyrant had brought to destroy Mansoul.

They all went their separate ways: the Captains went to their preparations, the Mayor, the junior preacher, and Will-be-will went to their homes. The Captains were itching to be doing some adventurous work for their Prince; they enjoyed noble battles. So they got together and decided to respond to Diabolus with slings and weapons. The very next morning, they set out and slung rocks at him. Just as the sound of Diabolus's war drum is hideous to Mansoul, there is nothing as hideous to Diabolus as the whizzing of

Emmanuel's golden slings. Diabolus had been slowly moving closer to the town, but now he was forced to retreat a little farther away from Mansoul. This was encouraging! The Mayor set the town bells to ringing and asked Mr. Conscience to send word to the Secretary to thank him, because his words had strengthened and encouraged the Captains and leaders of Mansoul against Diabolus.

> *[Note -- the golden slings hurling rocks are God's promises. There is nothing as hideous to God's enemies!]*

When Diabolus saw his aggressive captains and soldiers frightened and cowering under the stones coming from the golden slings, he thought to himself, 'I'll try to ensnare them in my net with flattery.'

So, after a little while, he came down to the wall of Mansoul without his drummer and without his captains, but with sweet, coaxing words of peace. He said in a sugary-sweet voice, that he didn't want revenge; he only cared about the welfare and best interests of the town. That was his only concern. He just wanted an opportunity to address the people of the town. So they came, and he addressed them:

'Oh, people of Mansoul, you are the light of my heart! I have watched so many nights, and traveled so far, just hoping that I could do something to help you! Why should I want to harm you by declaring war on you? Just quietly and willingly surrender yourselves to my care. As you remember, you used to belong to me. For a long time, you enjoyed having me as your ruler, and I enjoyed having you for my subjects. You had all the earthly delights you could wish for. Anything that might make you happy and content, I tried my best to provide for you. You didn't have difficult, dark, troublesome, heartbreaking times when you were with me -- but trouble and heartbreak are all you've had since you revolted from me. And you will never have peace until you and I are together again. I beg of you to embrace me again. If you will just join me as before, I'll increase the privileges you had before. I'll give you plenty of license and liberty, and you'll have pleasures galore. I won't rebuke you for any of the incivilities with which you offended me, not ever! And those friends of mine that are lurking in dens and holes and caves because they're afraid of you -- they won't hurt you any more. I'll force them to be your servants. They'll give you whatever they have, and share anything that comes their way. I don't need to tell you what a comfort they'll be to you -- you know them, and sometimes you have enjoyed their company. Why should we be at odds with each other? Let's renew our relationship and be friends again.

'Be patient with me. As your friend, I'm going to take the liberty of speaking more freely to you. I feel compelled to share freely because of the love I have for you, and my friends feel the same way. Don't let this trouble keep us apart. Why should you be afraid of war when we can be friends? I am determined to have you back, either the easy way as friends, or the hard way with war. Don't fool yourselves that your Captains are a match for me, or that Emmanuel will come back to help you. Be realistic.

'I am here with a strong and formidable army, headed by the most terrifying princes of the pit. My captains are faster than eagles, stronger than lions, and greedier for blood than a pack of wolves. Next to them, Og of Bashan is nothing; Goliath is nothing. A hundred such heroes couldn't stand against my captains. So how can you, Mansoul, expect to escape from them?'

After this flattering and deceitful speech, the Mayor gave him this response: 'Diabolus, you master of deceit, we've dealt with your flattering lies before and we know how destructive they are. Why should we listen to you again? Why should we disobey our King Shaddai again and join up with you? If we did that, our Prince would reject us forever. And if this place that he made for us is rejected by him, how could it ever be a pleasant place for us to live? Besides, you are empty and barren of truth and we'd rather die at your hand than accept your flatteries and lying tricks.'

When the tyrant saw that he wasn't making any headway by talking with the Mayor, he fell into a hellish rage and determined to come back later with his army of doubters and attack Mansoul.

He called his drummer and had him beat his drum to call his army to battle. This made the people of Mansoul quake in fear! Diabolus stationed his men for battle. He placed Captain Cruel and Captain Torment at Touch Gate, and told Captain No-Ease to relieve them if needed. He positioned Captain Brimstone and Captain Sepulchre at Nose Gate, and grim-faced Captain Past-Hope at Eye Gate. He also set up his banner there.

Captain Insatiable was to take care of Diabolus's carriages, and take custody of anyone who was taken prisoner.

Mansoul kept Mouth Gate as a fortified gate for townspeople to go in and out with petitions to their Prince. That's also where the captains had set up their slings, since it was higher and enabled them to get a better aim at the enemy. So Diabolus wanted to stop up that gate with dirt.

Chapter 14

While Diabolus was outside the town of Mansoul preparing to make his assault, the citizens of Mansoul and their Captains were just as busy within the walls. They mounted slings, set up their banners, sounded their trumpets, and positioned themselves in the most efficient way to do battle. Will-be-will watched for the enemy hiding inside the town, hoping to kill them as they lurked in their dens or caves, or in holes inside the walls of Mansoul. Ever since he repented for his part in their sin, he showed as much responsibility and bravery as anyone else in Mansoul. He caught the Diabolian Jolly and his brother Griggish, who were the sons of his servant Harmless-Mirth (he had changed his name from Mr. Lustfulness). Although Harmless-Mirth had been imprisoned and died in confinement, the sons were still working for Will-be-will and living under his roof. Will-be-will took them with his own hands and crucified them. He was especially eager to destroy them because after their father had been thrown in jail, those two brothers started playing pranks and annoying Will-be-will's daughters. Will-be-will was not the kind of person to enjoy killing people rashly, so he kept an eye on those two to see if what he had heard was true. Two other servants, Mr. Find-Out and Mr. Tell-All, caught them acting improperly more than once and told their master. Once Will-be-will had the evidence he needed, he took those two young Diabolians to Eye Gate and killed them where Diabolus would see them, and in defiance of Captain Past-Hope and the hideous banner flying there.

This obedient action of the brave Will-be-will disconcerted Captain Past-Hope, discouraged Diabolus's army, struck fear into the hearts of the Diabolians lurking within Mansoul -- but put strength and courage into the hearts of the Prince's Captains. When they saw that Mansoul was determined to fight, they gathered together to do battle outside the walls. And this was not the only proof of Will-be-will's sincere concern for the town or loyalty to his Prince, as will be shown later.

While Prudent-Thrifty was working at Mr. Mind's house, he had two children with Mr. Mind's daughter Hold-fast-Bad -- their names were Gripe and Pilfer-All. After Prudent-Thrifty had been thrown in jail, the two children stayed behind with Mr. Mind. When those children saw how Will-be-will had treated the children in his own household, they feared the same fate, so they made preparations to run away that night. But Mr. Mind knew what they were planning, so he guarded them all night. Knowing that the law commanded their deaths because they were at least half-Diabolian, in the morning, he took them to Eye Gate and hanged them.

The townspeople were greatly encouraged by this act of obedience and, in that spirit, tried to capture more Diabolian troublemakers, but the villains went further into hiding and couldn't be found. So Mansoul set up a diligent watch and went on with their own business.

I mentioned that Diabolus and his army were disconcerted when Will-be-will killed the two young Diabolians, but Diabolus's discouragement turned into mad rage against the town, and he fought all the more furiously. But the townspeople had taken heart. Now their hopes and expectations had heightened, and they feared the Diabolians less, so they also fought harder. Their junior preacher gave a sermon on Genesis 49:19, 'Gad will be attacked by marauding bands, but he will attack them while they retreat.' This showed that, although Mansoul might have a hard time at first, victory would at last be on their side.

Diabolus commanded his drummer to beat out an ominous charge against the town. So the Captains played a counter-charge on their silver trumpets. Diabolus's army rushed towards the town to attack, and the Prince's Captains and the townspeople fought back from within the town. Now nothing was heard from Diabolus's camp but horrible rage and blasphemy. But within the town, all that could be heard was good words, prayer, and singing of psalms. The enemy responded with horrible objections and their terrible drum, but the town countered with their slings and blasts of silver trumpets. All in all, the battle lasted for several days with only brief intermissions, during which the townspeople refreshed themselves and the Captains prepared for the next assault.

Emmanuel's Captains were wearing silver armour, and their soldiers were wearing steel armour. Diabolus's soldiers were wearing iron armour to protect against the stones coming from the slings. Within the town, there were some who were wounded, and there was no doctor because Emmanuel wasn't there. But one of the trees had leaves with healing properties, and that kept some of the people alive. Infection was a serious problem, and the leaves didn't help with that. Of the townspeople, Mr. Reason was wounded in the head. The Mayor had been shot in the eye. Mr. Mind had a stomach wound. The junior preacher had been shot in the chest, but it had missed his heart. None of these wounds was life-threatening.

Some of the general townspeople had been killed.

A considerable number were wounded and killed in the Diabolian camp. Captain Rage and Captain Cruel were wounded. Captain Accursed was forced to retreat and make camp further away from Mansoul. Diabolus's banner was beaten down, and his standard bearer, Captain Much-hurt, was killed when a stone struck him in the head. That grieved and shamed his prince Diabolus.

Many of the doubters were killed, though there were still enough left to be a real threat to Mansoul. Now that victory seemed to be on the side of Mansoul, the Captains and Mansoulians took courage and fought more bravely, but a dark cloud of gloom covered Diabolus's camp and made them angry and more vicious. Mansoul took the next day to rest. They commanded the bells to be rung. The Captains joined in the celebratory mood by shouting joyously around the town and blowing their trumpets.

Will-be-will continued seeking out Diabolians within the town. He found one whose name was Mr. Anything, who was mentioned before -- he's the one who brought the three fresh recruits to Diabolus from Captain Boanerges's army and persuaded them to enlist under the tyrant and fight against King Shaddai. He also captured the notorious Loose-foot, who operated as a spy and messenger for the Diabolian army. Will-be-will sent both of these prisoners to Mr. True-Man to be kept under guard until the most advantageous time to crucify them -- a time when it would be sure to discourage their enemies.

Although the Mayor couldn't get around so well with his wound, he made himself useful by giving orders to the Mansoulians to be diligent at their watches, stay on their guard, and if the occasion offered itself, to prove themselves brave men.

Mr. Conscience, the preacher, did his best to keep everything he had taught them fresh in the people's hearts and minds.

After a while, the Captains and tougher soldiers in the town decided to make an excursion out to the camp of Diabolus during the night. This was a foolish plan because night is the best time for the enemy, but worse time for Mansoul. But they were determined to do it because their courage was high from their last victory.

When the appointed night arrived, the Prince's Captains cast lots to see which of the soldiers would be leading this desperate and hopeless mission, and the lot fell to Captain Belief, Captain Experience, and Captain Good-Hope. Mr. Experience had been promoted to Captain when the Prince was living in Mansoul. So they ventured out to go among the army who were sieged against them and ended up in the middle of the enemy's main forces. Diabolus and his men were at their best at night. They had gotten wind that the Captains were coming and were prepared for them. So the Prince's soldiers had a hard time of it. They were struck from every side while the hellish drums beat furiously. But the Captains still blew their silver trumpets, and the battle went fiercely on both sides. Captain Insatiable waited by the carriages for some fresh prey.

The Prince's Captains fought bravely, beyond what one would have expected. They wounded many of Diabolus's men and made his whole army retreat. But somehow, while Captain Belief, Captain Good-Hope, and Captain Experience were pursuing the enemy from behind, Captain Belief stumbled and fell so hard that he wasn't able to get up. Captain Experience finally managed to help him up, but this incident put their soldiers in disorder. Captain Belief was also wounded and in so much pain that he couldn't hold back his cries, and the fearful sound made the other two Captains think he was dying, and they lost heart. Diabolus saw all of this, so he decided to grab the opportunity and take a stand. He faced about and started chasing the Prince's army with all the fury of hell. He came up to Captain Belief, Captain Good-Hope, and Captain Experience and slashed at them, wounding them all. Between their discouragement, their disorder, and now the wounds they received and loss of blood, they barely made it back to the hold safely.

When the rest of Mansoul's soldiers saw their three Captains wounded, they thought a retreat was the wisest thing to do. So they went back to Mansoul and that was the end of that mission. But Diabolus was so encouraged with the night's work that he assured himself that Mansoul would be his in a very few days, and it would be an easy conquest. The next day he boldly approached the town and demanded entrance, and wanted them to surrender the town to him. The Diabolians traitors who had been hiding within the town also took heart and began to act boldly.

But the valiant Mayor retorted that if Diabolus wanted anything from Mansoul, he'd have to take it by force. Even if Emmanuel wasn't there with them, as long as he was alive, they would never consent to yield up Mansoul to anyone else.

Then Will-be-will stood up and said, 'Diabolus, you lord of the pit and enemy of everything good, we poor citizens of Mansoul know you too well. We're familiar with the way you govern, and we know the end results of submitting to you. We know better than to yield our town up to you. When we were ignorant of your tricks we allowed you to conquer us, like a bird who steps into a snare because he doesn't see it. But now we've been turned from darkness to light, and from the power of Satan to the light of God. We have suffered much trouble and loss because of your subtlety and the deceit of your Diabolians lurking within our town, but we will never give up, lay down our weapons, and surrender to so horrendous a tyrant as you. We'll die first! Besides, we still have hope that, at the right time, deliverance will come to us from King Shaddai's court. Therefore, we will continue to fight!'

These brave speeches from Will-be-will and the Mayor quenched the boldness of Diabolus a little, though it kindled his furious rage. It also helped the townspeople and Captains. It was like balm to Captain Belief's wound. This moment, when the Captains had come home in defeat and the enemy were emboldened and surrounding the town, was just the right time to speak boldly.

Will-be-will had also acted bravely inside the town. While the brave Captains and a few men had been out in the field on their daring mission, Will-be-will had been armed inside the walls seeking out and striking any Diabolians he could find. He wounded Mr. Cavil, Mr. Brisk, Mr. Pragmatic, and Mr. Murmur. He also wounded other lesser Diabolians. The reason he was able to this is because, while the Captains had been out fighting, the Diabolians thought it was safe to come out and cause an uproar in the town. So they had come out of hiding and gathered in a group to go rollicking through Mansoul causing as much mischief as possible. Thus, Will-be-will was able to spot them and cut them down hastily before they could all disperse and go back into hiding.

Will-be-will's brave act helped to revenge the wrong that Diabolus had done to the Captains, and let the Diabolians know that Mansoul wasn't going to give up after the loss of a battle or two. Thus, the tyrant's arrogant confidence was taken down a notch, compared with how he would have bragged if his Diabolians had wounded the whole town of Mansoul the way he wounded the three Captains.

Diabolus resolved to have another try with Mansoul. 'I beat them once,' he thought. 'I might be able to beat them twice.' He commanded his troops to be ready at a specific hour of the night to make another attack on the town, and told them to focus their efforts on Touch Gate and try to break in there. The code word for this mission was Hell-Fire. He said, 'If we successfully break in upon them, either with some or all of our force, don't forget our code word. I don't want anything to be heard in Mansoul except, Hell-Fire! Hell-Fire!' The drummer was also commanded to pound his harrowing drum beat without ceasing, the standard bearers were commanded to display their hideous banners, and the soldiers were to do their part to terrorize the town.

When night had come, and everything was prepared according to the tyrant's wishes, he made his assault on Touch Gate. After a short struggle, he broke through because the gate was weakened and yielded without much effort. He placed Captain Torment and Captain No-Ease on guard there and attempted to press forward, but the Prince's Captains attacked him so that his entrance was hindered. The Prince's men resisted to the best of their ability, but, to tell the truth, their three best and bravest Captains were wounded, so those who were left were overpowered by the tyrant's soldiers and captains and weren't able to keep them out of the town. So Prince Emmanuel's men and Captains retreated to the castle, which was the town's stronghold. They went there partly for their own security, but mostly to keep Diabolus out of the castle, since that was the Prince's home and the central place in Mansoul.

After the Captains had fled into the castle, the enemy had little resistance and were able to take the rest of the town. They spread into every corner, crying out, 'Hell-Fire! Hell-Fire! Hell-Fire!' Nothing could be heard above their dire shouts of 'Hell-Fire!' and the pounding drum. And now Mansoul felt the dark cloud of their doom. There didn't seem to be any reason for hope. Diabolus forced the inhabitants to feed and house his soldiers. The junior preacher's house had as many doubters as it could possibly hold. So did the Mayor's and Will-be-will's. Any place where there was a corner, a cottage, a barn, or even a pigsty, was now full of Diabolus's vermin. They turned the people of Mansoul out into the streets and slept in their beds, and ate at their tables. Poor Mansoul! Now she felt the full fruits of her sin, and knew what poison was in Mr. Carnal-Security's alluring words. Diabolus's soldiers ruined whatever they got their hands on. They set fire to some places in town, and they killed some of the children! Why wouldn't they? What kind of pity or conscience could freakish doubters have? Many of the women in Mansoul were so abused and molested that they died, and their bodies lay in the streets all over town.

Now Mansoul seemed to be nothing but a den of monsters, an asylum of hell, and a place of total darkness. Mansoul lay like a barren wasteland. Nothing grew there but thorns, briars, weeds, and stinking plants. When the Diabolians turned the people of Mansoul out into the streets, they had mauled and beaten most of them. Mr. Conscience was severely wounded, and his wounds got infected so that he was in constant pain. If it hadn't been for King Shaddai's mercy, he would have been killed. The Mayor almost had his eyes put out. If Will-be-will hadn't escaped into the castle, he would have been slashed to pieces, because he was targeted as one of the most zealous enemies of Diabolus and his crew. And his zeal had indeed been impressive and showed how brave he could be.

At that point, a person might have walked all through Mansoul without seeing any sign of a religious man. Mansoul was in a fearful state! Every corner swarmed with grotesque doubters. They could be seen walking up and down the town by the clusters in their appalling red coats and black coats. They filled the town with hideous noises, vulgar songs, fraudulent stories, and blasphemous language against Shaddai and his son. And the Diabolians that had been lurking in hidden holes and dens in and under the town walls came out and showed themselves. They walked right out in the open with the doubters that had infiltrated Mansoul. They were more freely able to swagger boldly around town and haunt the homes than even the honest natives of Mansoul.

But Diabolus and his beasts weren't satisfied. They weren't treated kindly like the people had treated the Captains and soldiers of Emmanuel. In fact, the townspeople harassed them when they could. The Diabolians didn't have access to any supplies unless they took them from the people by force. The people hid things from them, and what they couldn't hide, they were resentful about having taken from them. The poor Mansoulians would have liked to be rid of the doubters and Diabolians and had their homes back, but now they were captives in their own town, and they were forced to tolerate it. But they showed their dislike and indignation.

The Captains inside the castle continually slung stones at the villains. Diabolus never gave up trying to break open the gates of the castle, but Mr. Godly-Fear had been promoted to gate guard, and he had so much courage and integrity that Diabolus's attempts were fruitless. It's too bad Mr. Godly-Fear wasn't in charge of the whole town!

This sad state of things lasted for two and a half years. The Diabolians used the whole town for their evil purposes. The townspeople were driven into holes, and Mansoul's glory was trampled and flattened. There was no rest or peace or cheer for the people. If the Diabolians had kept the town in a siege from outside the walls, it would have been enough to famish them. Imagine how much worse to have the Diabolians actually inside the town, living in the homes, fighting the town from within! That was the pitiable situation of Mansoul.

> *[Note -- The life of a Christian will always be a seat of war as we struggle against the world, our own flesh, and the devil; but an evil attitude of unbelief is like a spiritual Goliath, which we should constantly pray Christ to subdue.]*

Chapter 15

After two and half years living in this deplorable condition, and not being able to get their petitions through to the Prince, the leaders of Mansoul gathered together to discuss their misery and the dreadful judgment looming in their future. They considered putting together another petition to Prince Emmanuel, but Mr. Godly-Fear reminded them that the Prince didn't acknowledge petitions in matters like theirs unless the Secretary's signature was on it. 'In fact,' he said, 'this is why your petitions haven't prevailed in all this while.' So they said they'd write a petition and get the Secretary to sign it. But Mr. Godly-Fear said that the Secretary wouldn't sign anything that he hadn't written up himself. 'And don't bother trying to forge his signature,' he said, 'because the Prince knows his Secretary's signature too well to fool him. My advice is to go to the Secretary and beg him to help you.' The Secretary was still living in the castle, where the Captains and all the soldiers were.

They thanked him and did as he suggested. They went to the Secretary and let him know that Mansoul was in a deplorable condition, and hoped he would write a petition for them to send to Prince Emmanuel and his Father, King Shaddai.

The Secretary asked, 'What do you want me to say?' And they said, 'You know yourself the state Mansoul is in. You know how we're backslidden and degenerated from the Prince. You also know that Diabolus has attacked us and made Mansoul his seat of war. You know how our people have been abused, and how much they've suffered. Even the Diabolians who were in hiding have become bold enough to walk up and down our streets right out in the open. We'd like you to use your wisdom and write what you think is best for us.' The Secretary said, 'I will. I'll write it and sign it.' They asked, 'when should we come back to get it?' But he answered, 'You need to stay here while I write it. You need to put your own desires into it. The handwriting and signature may be mine, but the ink and paper must be yours. Otherwise, how can you say what's in your petition? Besides, I can't write it myself because I'm not the one who has offended the Prince.' He also added, 'No petition goes from me to the Prince, and then to the Father, unless the people who are petitioning join their own hearts and souls in the matter, because that has to go into the letter.'

The people heartily agreed with this advice, and a petition was written up for them. But who should deliver it? The Secretary suggested Captain Belief, since he was a well-spoken man. They asked him, and he said, 'I gladly accept the commission. Even though I'm wounded and lame, I'll do this as quickly and as well as I can.'

The petition said this:

'Dear Sovereign Lord, patient and long-suffering Prince; your lips are full of grace, and mercy and forgiveness belong to you, even though we have rebelled against you. We aren't worthy any more to be called your Mansoul, nor are we fit to receive even the most common benefits from you. But we beg you, and your Father, to take away our transgressions. We are aware that you could destroy us forever for our sins, but please don't do it because it wouldn't honour your name and reputation. Instead, please take this opportunity to have compassion on our miserable condition. We're surrounded and oppressed everywhere we turn. Our own backslidings shame us and show us our guilt. The Diabolians within our walls frighten us, and his army from the pit distresses us. Your grace can be our salvation, and we don't know where else to go for help.

'Furthermore, gracious Prince, our Captains are weakened, discouraged, and sick. Recently, some of them were beaten and wounded by the tyrant's soldiers. The brave Captains in whom we trusted are disabled. But our enemies are strong and thriving. They boast arrogantly, and threaten to divide us up as their booty. They have conquered us with their army of doubters. We don't know how to handle them. They're all grim-faced and unmerciful, and defy us and you.

'Our wisdom is gone, and our power is gone because you have left us. We have nothing left to us except sin, shame, and confusion. Please take pity on us, Lord. Take pity on your poor, pitiful town of Mansoul, and save us out of the hands of our enemies. Amen.'

This petition, having been signed by the Secretary, was carried to King Shaddai's court by the brave and powerful Captain Belief. He left by Mouth Gate, which was the town's sally port, and went to the court of Emmanuel. Somehow Diabolus must have heard about it. He said to the townspeople, 'You stubborn-hearted rebels! Do you still think your petitions will have any effect? I'll put an end to your sending petitions.' He knew who was delivering the petition, and that made him both infuriated and afraid.

So he commanded that his drummer start pounding out the dreadful beat again -- the beat that terrified Mansoul. But if Diabolus commands his drummer to beat, Mansoul has no choice but to put up with it. So the drum was beat and at the summons, all the Diabolians gathered together.

Then Diabolus began speaking to them. 'Hearty Diabolians, I must inform you that those rebels in Mansoul have hatched a treacherous plot against us. Although you know the town is ours, those miserable Mansoulians have dared to attempt to send a message to Emmanuel for help. Now that you know of their disloyalty, you'll know how to treat them. Trusty Diabolians, I command you to distress the town even more. Afflict them with your mischief, abuse their women, abduct their maidens, kill their children, beat up their old men, burn their town, and make whatever trouble you can. Let that be our reward to those conspirators for their desperate defiance against us.'

That was the accusation he made, but so far all he had done was to complain and rage about it.

After he had said this, Diabolus went up to the castle gates and demanded that they be opened to him on pain of death to allow him and his men to enter. Mr. Godly-Fear, who had charge of the gate, refused. He said the gate would never be opened to him or his men, and, furthermore, after Mansoul had suffered for a little while, she would be made perfect, and strengthened, and settled again.

Diabolus said, 'Then deliver up to me the men who sent that petition against me, especially Captain Belief, who carried it to your Prince. Deliver that villain up to me and I'll leave our town.'

One of the Diabolians, Mr. Fooling, said, 'My lord is offering you a fair deal. Isn't it better for one man to die than for your whole town to be destroyed?'

But Mr. Godly-Fear only said, 'How long would Mansoul be safe once she had trusted Diabolus? We'd rather lose this town than lose Captain Belief. Once he's gone, we'd lose the town anyway.' Mr. Fooling had nothing to say to that.

> *[Note -- lose Captain Belief: when the shield of belief (credence) is wanting, the soul is exposed to all the fiery darts of the wicked one. "This is the victory--even your faith."]*

Then the Mayor said, 'You devouring tyrant, you might as well know that we will never listen to anything you say! We are determined to resist you as long as we have a Captain, a man, a sling, or a stone to hurl at you.' Diabolus answered, 'Are you trusting and waiting for help and deliverance to come? You may have sent for Emmanuel, but you have too many counts of wickedness for innocent prayers to come from your lips. Do you think your plan has even the slightest chance of succeeding? No, your wish will fail, and your attempt will fail because it's not just me who's against you --

no, you have offended Emmanuel as well. So what's left to hope for? How will you escape?'

Then the Mayor said, 'Yes, we have sinned, but that won't help you because our Emmanuel said in faithfulness that whoever comes to him for help would never be ignored. He also told us, you invader, that all kinds of sin and blasphemies would be forgiven to the sons of men. Therefore, we don't dare give in to despair. Instead, we wait for and hope for deliverance.'

By this time, Captain Belief had returned from King Shaddai's court with an envelope. When the Mayor heard this news, he left the wall where the tyrant was yelling to the people of Mansoul, and went to the castle. He greeted Captain Belief, asked how he was doing, and whether there was any good news from the King. He had tears of discouragement in his eyes as he asked. The Captain said, 'Cheer up! All will be well in due time.' Then he picked up the envelope, waved it in front of him with a smile, and set it on the table. The Mayor and Captains who were there took this to be a good sign. The Mayor went out to seek all the other Captains and leaders to let them know that Captain Belief had returned and had news for them. So they all came to the castle, greeted him, asked about his journey, and wanted to know the news from King Shaddai. He gave them the same answer: that all would be well in due time. When everyone had arrived, he opened the envelope and drew out five notes, addressed to specific individuals who were there.

The first note was for the Mayor. It said that Prince Emmanuel was pleased that the Lord Mayor had been so faithful and trustworthy in his role, and so responsible in his care for the people of Mansoul. The Prince was glad he had been so bold in his resistance against Diabolus, and he would shortly be rewarded.

The second note was for Will-be-will saying that Prince Emmanuel was aware of how valiant and courageous he had been for the honour of his absent Lord when Diabolus had used his name with contempt. The Prince was pleased that he had been so faithful to the town of Mansoul and so diligent to capture the Diabolians who were lurking within the walls of Mansoul. He knew how Will-be-will had executed some of the major troublemakers with his own hands, and had set a good example to the Mansoulians and discouraged the enemy. The note said he would shortly be rewarded.

The third note was for Mr. Conscience, the junior preacher, and it said the Prince was heartened that he had performed his duties so honestly and faithfully. Prince Emmanuel was pleased that he had so dutifully discharged the trust committed to him by counseling, opposing, and warning the people of Mansoul about the Prince's laws. He was glad to hear that Mr. Conscience had called for fasting, prayer, and mourning when Mansoul was in rebellion, and that he had called on Captain Boanerges to help him with such an important task. He would also be rewarded shortly.

The fourth note was for Mr. Godly-Fear. The Prince had seen that he had been the first to detect that Mr. Carnal-Security's deceit and clever tricks had started the initial breach toward Mansoul's defection and deterioration. The Prince hadn't forgotten his tears and mourning for the state of Mansoul. He was pleased that Mr. Godly-Fear hadn't failed to detect the villain's his plot to undermine the town of Mansoul, even while he had been in Mr. Carnal-Security's own house, seated at his own table in the midst of merrymaking and festivities. The Prince had noticed how he resisted the tyrant's evil threats, and motivated the people to petition the Prince and ask for help and peace, and he would be rewarded shortly.

There was a fifth note addressed to the whole town saying that the Prince had known of their repeated appeals to him. Their petitions would bear more good fruit in time. The Prince was encouraged that their hearts and minds were finally fixed upon him and his ways, even though Diabolus had worked so hard to undermine them. Neither flatteries nor trials and hardships had made them yield to Diabolus's cruel schemes. There was a footnote at the bottom instructing that the Prince had left the town in the hands of Mr. Secretary, and under direct supervision of Captain Belief. He wrote, 'Be sure to submit to their guidance, and in due time you shall receive your reward.'

After the brave Captain Belief had delivered the notes, he retired to Mr. Secretary's lodgings and conversed with him. They were intimate friends and had a better idea how things would go in Mansoul than the people did themselves. Mr. Secretary loved Captain Belief dearly and frequently shared delicacies with him from his own table. Even when he was discouraged with the townspeople, he always had a smile for the Captain. After a long talk, the Captain went to his own quarters to rest. Then they met again and the Captain asked what King Shaddai had said to Mr. Secretary. After a couple words of personal assurance of favour, the Secretary said, 'I have promoted you to Lieutenant General over all the forces in Mansoul. From now on, everyone in Mansoul will obey whatever you say. You will be the one to lead Mansoul in, and lead them out. You will be in charge of the war for your Prince and for the town against the power of Diabolus. The rest of the Captains will be under your command.'

Chapter 16

Now the people of Mansoul began to realize how closely connected Captain Belief was with King Shaddai's court and Mr. Secretary. Nobody else seemed to be able to communicate as directly to the Prince or bring such promising news. They regretted that they hadn't respected him and made better use of him before when they were in such distress. They sent their junior preacher to Mr. Secretary to let him know that, from now on, everything they were and all they had were to be submitted to the management, protection, supervision, and guidance of Captain Belief.

So the junior preacher passed on this message, and Mr. Secretary responded that Captain Belief would be the leader of King Shaddai's army, and in charge of the welfare of Mansoul. The junior preacher bowed in thanks, and returned to relay this to the townspeople. But all of this was done under cover and in secret because the enemy still had great power over the town.

Meanwhile, when Diabolus was boldly confronted by the Mayor, and saw the fortitude of Mr. Godly-Fear, he fell into a mad rage. He called his forces to a council of war to get his revenge on the town. So all the evil princes of the pit met together, with Mr. Incredulity at the head of them, and all the captains of his army in attendance. The conclusion of their council was that they needed a plan to conquer the castle, because they couldn't rightly claim to possess the town as long as the castle was still in possession of their enemies.

One beast suggested one plan, another suggested something else, and there was no agreement. So Apollyon, the president of their council, stood up and spoke. 'My brothers, I have two suggestions. Let's withdraw from the town and go back to our camp to finalize our plans. Our presence here in town will do us no good while the castle is still in the hands of the enemy, and there's no way we'll be able to take it as long as so many brave Captains are within it and Mr. Godly-Fear has charge of the gates. Once we have withdrawn into our camp in the plains, they'll be relieved of some of their immediate fear and loosen their vigilance. They may even let down their guard so much that they fall back into their sinful ways and hasten their own downfall. But even if that doesn't work, our leaving might draw the Captains after us, and you remember what happened the last time the Captains went out seeking us. Once they're out of the town, we can lay an ambush behind the town, and when they're a safe distance away, we can rush in and take the castle.'

But Beelzebub stood up and said, 'It'll be impossible to draw all the Captains away from the castle; some will undoubtedly determine to stay there to protect it. It would be useless to make such an attempt unless we could get all of them out.' He thought they should think of something else. After all their thinking, the best idea seemed to be the one Apollyon had suggested: to get the townspeople more entrapped into sin. As Beelzebub said, 'It makes little difference whether we're in the town or out in their field, or whether we fight skillfully or kill a large number of their men. As long as there's even one Mansoulian who can lift a finger against us, Emmanuel will take their side, and if he comes to their defense, it's all over with us. So this is what I think. The best way to bring them into bondage to us is to create ways for them to fall into sin. We might as well have left the doubters at home if we can't get them into the castle. Doubters are no good from a distance; they're like challenges that can be answered with logical arguments. But if we can only get them into the town and make them dwell there and spread their influence, we'll be sure to conquer. So let's withdraw into the plains -- but without the expectation of the Captains following us. Let's go out to the camp, but advise our trusted Diabolians within the town to stay busy working to betray the town to us. That really is the only hope we have.' The whole group had to agree that the most effective way to get the castle was to get the town to sin. How might this be done?

Lucifer said, 'Beelzebub's advice is sound. I think the best way to make it happen is to withdraw our forces from Mansoul, stop terrifying the people with threats, or drum beats, or anything else. We'll go back to the fields and pretend we aren't even paying attention to them, since I've seen that terrifying them only makes them more vigilant and prepared. And here's another angle: Mansoul is a market-town; they delight in trade and commerce. What if some of our Diabolians pretended to be from some far-off country bringing their wares to the town to sell? It wouldn't make any difference how much they charged, even if they only made half of what the items were worth. Those chosen to play these parts would need to be men who are clever and loyal to us. I can already think of two likely candidates for this job -- Mr. Penny-wise-pound-foolish, and Mr. Get-i'the-hundred-and-lose-i'the-shire. The one with the long name is just as good as the other one. Mr. Sweet-world and Mr. Present-good are also accommodating and shrewd, and, at the same time, they're our true friends and helpers. Let them and a few others take on this business for us. Let them draw Mansoul into business and commerce, and get them prosperous and rich. That's the way to get the better of them! Remember how we controlled Laodicea that way, and how many we hold in this snare even now? When they've begun to grow prosperous, they'll forget their misery, and, as long as we're not terrifying them, they'll breathe easy, lighten up, and neglect to be diligent about their night watches and castle guards.

'In this way, we can burden Mansoul with bounty and abundance. They'll be forced to turn their castle into a warehouse rather than a fortress fortified against us and housed with soldiers. If we can just transport our goods and commodities there, the castle will eventually be ours. And if the castle is stuffed with provisions and wares, even during a sudden assault, there'd be no room for the Captains to take shelter there. Do you remember the old saying, 'The deceitfulness of riches chokes out the word,' and 'When the heart is stuffed with plenty, and excess, and the concerns of this life,' then all kinds of trouble will come upon them while they're least expecting it?

'Also, my lords,' he continued, 'you know that once Mansoul has an abundance of our things, they'll need to hire our Diabolians as stewards and servants to maintain those things. What Mansoulian is full of material things of this world, who doesn't also have Mr. Profuse, or Mr. Prodigality as his servant, or some other Diabolian like Mr. Voluptuous, Mr. Pragmatical, or Mr. Ostentation? Any one of them can take the castle and destroy it, or make it unfit as a place for Emmanuel to live in. In fact, one of these men could take the castle sooner than a whole army of twenty thousand men. So, my advice is that we quietly withdraw ourselves and not make any more attacks or threats -- at least not for now. Instead, let's work on this new scheme, and see if that doesn't make them destroy themselves.'

This idea was met with enthusiasm by all of them, and was applauded as a very masterpiece of hell. What a handy idea, to choke Mansoul with the material treasures of this world, and to crowd her heart with the good things they involve. But look how things work out: just as this Diabolian council was breaking up, Captain Belief received a letter from Emmanuel! The letter said that in three days, the Prince wanted to meet him in the field near Mansoul. 'He wants to meet me in the field near Mansoul?' exclaimed the Captain. 'What does he intend to do? Why does he want to meet me in the field?' He took the letter to Mr. Secretary and asked what he thought, since he was a seer in all matters that involved King Shaddai as well as the welfare and comfort of Mansoul. So the Captain showed him the letter and wanted his opinion about it. 'I don't know what it means,' said the Captain. The Secretary looked it over and said, 'The Diabolians have had a great discussion against Mansoul today. They've been contriving the utter ruin of the town. Their scheme is to set Mansoul in a direction that will surely make her destroy herself. They're planning to depart out of the town and camp out in the fields again. They'll lie there until they see whether their scheme works or not. You are to be ready on the third day to go to the field with your armies, and then attack the Diabolians. The Prince will also be in the field by then, and he'll have a mighty force of his own to fight against them. So he'll attack from the front, and you'll attack from behind, and between both of your armies, the Diabolian army will be destroyed.'

Captain Belief went to find the rest of the Captains and tell them about the letter he had received from Prince Emmanuel. And he added, 'That letter was like a bewildering dark mystery until Mr. Secretary explained it to me.' He told them what the letter instructed them to do, and the Captains were glad to hear it. Captain Belief commanded that all the King's trumpeters should go up to the tops of the battlements and, there, where both the Diabolians and Mansoulians could hear them, they should play the best music they could create. So the trumpeters did as they were commanded. They got themselves up to the top of the castle and began to blow their trumpets. Diabolus flinched and said, 'What can be the meaning of this? They're not playing a call to arms, or a charge -- what do those nutcases mean by being merry and glad?' One of his men said, 'They're making joyful noises because their Prince Emmanuel is coming to help the town of Mansoul. They seem to be singing that he is coming at the head of an army, and his help is very near.'

The people of Mansoul were concerned to hear the melodious charm of the trumpets. They said to each other, 'This can't harm us; surely this can't mean harm to us.' But the Diabolians said, 'What should we do?' and the answer was, 'We'd better get out of the town!' 'Yes,' said another, 'we planned to leave the town anyway to put our scheme into effect. When we're out of the town, we'll be in a better position to fight if an army does arrive to attack us.' So they left the very next day and stayed out on the plains outside the town near Eye Gate. Besides the trumpets, the reason they left the town was because they didn't control the castle yet and because 'it will be more convenient to fight from there, or flee, if we need to, if we're out in the open fields.' The town would have been more of a trap than a safe place of defense if the Prince came and surrounded them. So they went out into the plains, far enough away to be out of reach of the slings which had harassed them so much before.

The appointed time when the Captains were to fall upon the Diabolians had just about arrived. The Prince's soldiers eagerly prepared themselves for action because Captain Belief had told them during the night that they would meet their Prince the very next day. This made them even more eager to engage the enemy, because the idea of meeting the Prince in the field tomorrow was like oil to a flaming fire. They hadn't seen their Prince for such a long time, and this made them even more excited. Now that the time had come, Captain Belief and the rest of his men positioned themselves in the field before the sun was up. When everything was ready, Captain Belief went to the head of the army and gave the Captains the code word to pass along to their soldiers. The word was, 'The sword of the Prince Emmanuel, and the shield of Captain Belief,' or, to the Mansoulians, 'The word of God and faith.' Then the Captains began to surround the rear of Diabolus's army.

Captain Experience had stayed behind in the town because of the wounds he had received in the recent skirmish with the Diabolians. But when he realized that the other Captains were preparing for action, he quickly called for his crutches, and went out to the battlefield! He said, 'Why should I lie around here while my brothers are fighting, and when Prince Emmanuel is going to show up himself in the field with his servants?' But when the enemy saw the wounded man coming on crutches, they were even more daunted. They thought, 'what kind of wild spirit has taken hold of these desperate Mansoulians, that they come out to fight us on crutches?' The Captains handled their weapons bravely, crying out and shouting as they struck blow after blow, 'The sword of Prince Emmanuel, and the shield of Captain Belief!'

When Diabolus saw that the Captains had come out of the town and were valiantly surrounding his army, he concluded that he could expect nothing from them except blows from their 'two-edged sword.'

So Diabolus attacked the Prince's army with deadly force, and the battle began in earnest. And who should Diabolus meet first in the battle except Captain Belief on one side, and Will-be-will on the other. Will-be-will's blows had the strength of a giant. He had a strong arm, and he focused on fighting the election doubters because they were Diabolus's bodyguards. Will-be-will kept them busy fighting him off. When Captain Belief saw Will-be-will engaged, he joined in the attack from the other side. Captain Good-Hope had attacked the vocation doubters. They were tough men, but the Captain was valiant and just as tough. Captain Experience helped him, and they forced them to retreat. The rest of the armies were just as hotly engaged, and the Diabolians fought fiercely. Then Mr. Secretary commanded that slings should be used from the castle -- and his men were good enough shots to throw stones at a hair's breadth. But, after a while, the enemy that had been forced to flee from the Captains began to rally and attack the rear of the Captains' army so that the army began to waver. But they remembered that they would see their Prince soon, so they gathered their courage and fought back more fiercely than ever. Then the Captains shouted, 'The sword of Prince Emmanuel, and the shield of Captain Belief!' At that, Diabolus fell back, thinking more aid had come. But he didn't see any sign of Emmanuel. Now the battle hung in doubt, and there was some retreat on both sides. During this brief rest, Captain Belief bravely encouraged his men to keep up the fight, and Diabolus told his men the same thing. Then Captain Belief made the following speech to his soldiers:

'Gentlemen soldiers, and my brothers in this battle, I am rejoiced to see such a strong and valiant army fighting for our Prince because of their love for Mansoul. You have fought as well as I expected and shown yourselves to be men of truth and courage against the enemy. For all of their boasting, they can't boast of many spoils from this battle. Gather your courage, and prove yourselves men just once more, because in a few minutes, you will see Prince Emmanuel in the field. We must make one more assault against the tyrant Diabolus, and then Emmanuel will come.'

As soon as the Captain had made this speech, the messenger Mr. Speedy came to announce that Emmanuel was at hand! When the Captain heard this news, he told the other field officers, and they passed the news on to their soldiers. At this, the soldiers perked up like men who had come back to life. The Captains and soldiers rose up, ran towards the enemy, and cried out as before, 'The sword of Prince Emmanuel, and the shield of Captain Belief!'

The Diabolians also tried to gather up their endurance for one last stand, but this last attempt to resist fell short. They lost their courage and many of the doubters simply fell down dead. After an hour of hard fighting, Captain Belief glanced up, and -- look! Prince Emmanuel was coming! His banners were flying, trumpets blowing, and his men were rushing so rapidly to the area of fighting where they were needed most that their feet hardly seemed to touch the ground. Captain Belief led his men back in the direction of the town, leaving Diabolus in the field. Emmanuel came upon Diabolus so that his army was between Emmanuel and Captain Belief. Both attacked Diabolus and fought their way towards each other, and it wasn't long before they met in the middle, still trampling down Diabolus's army as they came.

When the other Captains saw that Emmanuel had arrived, and that he and Captain Belief had surrounded Diabolus, they shouted, 'The sword of Emmanuel, and the shield of Captain Belief!' so loudly that the ground shook and almost split open. Diabolus saw that he and his monstrous army were outnumbered, so he and his beasts made their escape, forsaking their army of doubters and leaving them to be slain by the Prince and Captain Belief. Soon not one of them remained alive. Their bodies were spread all over the ground, looking like manure spread out to fertilize a field.

When the battle was over, things settled down into order. The Captains and leaders of Mansoul came together to greet Prince Emmanuel right there in the field with a thousand joyous welcomes to see him back in the borders of Mansoul again. He smiled down at all of them and said, 'Peace be with you.' Then they all accompanied the Prince and his forces as they started towards the town of Mansoul. The gates were thrown open to receive him, and the people were thrilled at his blessed return. Here is how they welcomed him.

First, with all the gates of the town and the castle open wide, the town leaders came forward to greet the Prince. As he drew closer, they all recited Psalm 24 -- 'Lift up your heads, O ye gates; and be lifted up, ye everlasting doors; and the King of glory shall come in.' And, 'Who is the King of glory?' and they answered themselves, 'The Lord, strong and mighty; the Lord mighty in battle. Lift up your heads, O ye gates; lift them up, ye everlasting doors,' and so on.

Second, the most skilled musicians in the town were commanded to entertain the Prince with song. The leaders kept up the Psalm, asking 'Who is the King of glory?' and answering each other, and the other people of Mansoul quoted Psalm 68, 'They have seen thy goings, O God; even the goings of my God, my King, in the sanctuary.' So the Prince was escorted into the town amid much rejoicing and music.

Third, the Captains attended the Prince as he entered. Captain Belief and Captain Good-Hope went in front of him, Captain Charity and his companions came behind, with Captain Patience last of all, and the other Captains on either side of him. All this time, banners were flying, trumpets were playing, and the soldiers were shouting joyfully. The Prince was wearing his gold armour, and his chariot had silver pillars, gold flooring, and a purple covering. His smiles showed his love for the people of Mansoul.

Fourth, when the Prince arrived at the entrance to Mansoul, he found all the streets scattered with lilies and other flowers, and wreaths and boughs hanging from the trees along the streets. There were people standing in every doorway, and each door was decorated with something unique and lovely to make his way beautiful and festive. They also cheered welcomes as he passed by, shouting, "Blessed be the Prince who comes in the name of his Father, King Shaddai!'

Fifth, the leaders of the town were at the gates to welcome the Prince as he entered the town -- the Mayor, Will-be-will, Mr. Conscience the junior preacher, Mr. Mind, and other important men of town. They bowed, kissed his feet, thanked him and blessed him, and praised his mercy for having pity on their misery rather than abandoning them for their sin. Then he was escorted to the castle, which was his royal palace and his home. Mr. Secretary and Captain Belief had already prepared it for his presence. So he entered in.

Sixth, the entire town, including the common people, came to the gates of the castle to weep and lament over their own wickedness that had forced him to leave their town. They bowed seven times, cried aloud, and asked his forgiveness, begging him to confirm his love for Mansoul.

The Prince replied, 'Do not weep, go your way. Have a feast! Eat delicious food, drink sweet wine, and send some of your feast to those who have nothing to celebrate with, because the joy of the Lord is your strength. I have returned to Mansoul with mercies, and my name will be raised up, exalted, and glorified because of it.' He kissed and embraced all the people.

He also gave each of the town leaders and officers a gold chain and jeweled ring. He sent their wives earrings, jewels, bracelets, and other things. He gave all the native citizens many precious treasures.

When the Prince had done all of these things for the famous town of Mansoul, he said, 'Wash your garments, put on your jewels, and then meet me at my castle.' So they went to the fountain set up in the town and washed their clothing until it was white again, and then went back to the castle and stood before him.

And now there was music and dancing throughout the whole town of Mansoul because their Prince had returned to bless them with his presence and his smiles. Bells rang, and the sun shone warmly on them all day and the next.

The town was more diligent now about seeking out any Diabolians who still lurked in the walls and holes around Mansoul, and thoroughly destroying them. There were a few who had escaped during the battle.

Lord Will-be-will was even stricter than he had been before. His heart was completely set on seeking them out and killing them. He pursued them night and day and gave them no peace.

Things were settled and put back into order in the town, and the Prince commanded that the dead be gathered up and buried -- those who had been killed by the Prince and Captain Belief and their men. The bodies needed to be disposed of so that their fumes and stink wouldn't infest the air and annoy the people. The people were also instructed to do the best they could to wipe out every memory, and even any record of the names, of their enemies.

Chapter 17

The Mayor, the wise and trusted friend of Mansoul, commanded that Mr. Godly-Fear and Mr. Upright should oversee the project of disposing of the bodies, and specific individuals should be assigned to go out into the fields to bury the bodies lying around the plains. Some were appointed to dig graves, some to lift the bodies and carry them to the graves, and some were to go around to make sure that no bones or parts of Diabolians or doubters were overlooked. If any parts were found, the searchers were put up a marker so that others could bury them out of sight. This way, the names and remembrances of those villains would be blotted out from under the heavens, and the children born in Mansoul wouldn't even know what a limb or body of a doubter or Diabolian looked like. This was done, and the field was cleansed. And now Mr. God's-Peace resumed his old duties, as he had done before.

And so, the election doubters, the vocation doubters, the grace doubters, the perseverance doubters, the resurrection doubters, the salvation doubters, and the glory doubters were buried in the plains all around Mansoul. Their cruel weapons -- arrows, darts, mauls, firebrands, and other instruments of death -- were buried with them, as well as their armour, their banners, Diabolus's standard, and anything else they could find that carried the taint or smell of a doubter. Unfortunately, their captains -- Captain Rage, Captain Cruel, Captain Cursed, Captain Insatiable, Captain Brimstone, Captain Torment, Captain No-Ease, Captain Sepulchre, and Captain Past-Hope -- had escaped, along with the seven leaders of their armies -- Lord Beelzebub, Lord Lucifer, Lord Legion, Lord Apollyon, Lord Python, Lord Cerberus, and Lord Belial -- and old Mr. Incredulity, their general.

Meanwhile, the escaped tyrant arrived at Hell-Gate Hill with his old friend, Incredulity. They descended into their den and condoled with their companions about their misfortune and the great loss they had suffered by the town of the Mansoulians. They talked and whined, and shortly fell into a passionate rage and determined to be revenged for their losses. They called a council to decide what might be done against the town of Mansoul. Their gaping paunches couldn't wait to hear what Lucifer and Apollyon would contrive to further destroy Mansoul. Their raging hellish thought every day was to fill themselves with the body, soul, bones, flesh, and last remaining tidbit of Mansoul. They decided to make another attempt with a mixed army of doubters and blood-men. Here is an account of them.

> *[Note -- Blood-men represent the earthly, carnal, sensual, devilish nature, which is hostile to God -- and which we are so often enslaved to.]*

The doubters are so called because their natural temperament and nature is to challenge and question every one of the truths of Prince Emmanuel. They live in the land of Doubting, far to the north between the land of Darkness, and the 'valley of the shadow of death.' Sometimes those two are considered the same place, but they're actually two separate places, lying slightly apart from one another. The land of Doubting lies in between them. The army that came with Diabolus came from there.

Who are the blood-men? They're an evil race who are so named because of their destructive nature, and their hunger to unleash their fury against the town of Mansoul. They live in the country of Loath-good under the constellation of Sirius, the dog star, and they guide their actions by astrology. Most of their country is far away from the land of Doubting, but the two countries meet in one spot at Hell-Gate Hill. The blood-men and the doubters are allies. Both of them challenge and question the faith and loyalty of Mansoul, which makes them very qualified to serve Diabolus.

Diabolus beat his war drums to raise another army from these two countries, and gathered twenty-five thousand to attack Mansoul. Ten thousand were doubters, and fifteen thousand were blood-men. Several leaders were chosen to be their captains, and Mr. Incredulity was made the general of the entire army.

The captains of the doubters were five of the demons who had led the last army -- Captain Beelzebub, Captain Lucifer, Captain Apollyon, Captain Legion, and Captain Cerberus. The captains they replaced were made lieutenants and ensigns.

Diabolus wasn't relying on the doubters to be his principal fighters; in the last battle, the Mansoulians had beaten them. He only used them to increase the number of his army and to help in a pinch if needed. His real hope was in his blood-men. They were all rugged soldiers who had done daring feats in past wars.

The captains of the blood-men were Captain Cain, Captain Nimrod, Captain Ishmael, Captain Esau, Captain Saul, Captain Absalom, Captain Judas, and Captain Inquisition.

1. Captain Cain headed two groups -- the zealous blood-men, and the angry blood-men. His banner had shades of red, and his coat of arms was a murderous club.

2. Captain Nimrod headed two groups -- the tyrannical blood-men and the encroaching blood-men. His banner also had shades of red, and his coat of arms was a massive bloodhound.

3. Captain Ishmael headed two groups -- the mocking blood-men and the scorning blood-men. His banner was red, and his coat of arms was an image of someone mocking Abraham as he sacrificed Isaac.

4. Captain Esau headed two groups -- the resentful blood-men (who grudged anyone who got something they didn't) and the vindictive blood-men (who take out private revenge on others). His banner was red, and his coat of arms had an image of someone lurking in secret to murder Jacob.

5. Captain Saul headed two groups -- the jealous-without-cause blood-men, and the devilishly furious blood-men. His banner was red, and his coat of arms was three bloody darts aimed at harmless King David.

6. Captain Absalom headed two groups -- the murderous blood-men (who would kill even a parent or friend for notoriety), and the two-faced blood-men (who will flatter someone before stabbing them). His banner was red, and his coat of arms was a son pursuing his father to kill him.

7. Captain Judas headed two groups -- the cut-throat blood-men (who will kill anyone for money) and the back-stabbing blood-men (who would betray even a friend with a kiss). His banner was red, and his coat of arms was thirty pieces of silver and a noose.

8. Captain Inquisition headed only one group, but all the different kinds of blood-men made up his army. His banner was also (surprise!) red, and his coat of arms was a good man burning at the stake.

The reason Diabolus rallied so quickly and gathered another army so soon after his defeat was because of the confidence he had in his blood-men. He had a lot more faith in them than he had had before in the doubters, although the doubters had been useful to him in strengthening the population of his kingdom. But he knew the reputation of the blood-men -- they rarely went out to kill without returning with bloody weapons. They were like pit bulls that fasten onto anyone without letting go -- father, mother, brother, sister, prince, governor, yes, even on the Prince of princes. He was even more encouraged because one time, they had forced Prince

Emmanuel out of the kingdom of Universe. 'So why shouldn't they be able to force him out of the town of Mansoul, too?'

[Note -- the confidence he had in his blood-men: the iniquity in our own hearts is like fuel for the enemy to kindle.]

So General Incredulity led this army of twenty-five thousand against Mansoul. Mr. Prywell had gone out to spy, and he spotted them and brought Mansoul news that they were coming. So Mansoul shut and locked their gates and prepared to defend themselves against this new army of Diabolians.

Diabolus brought his army and set upon the town of Mansoul. The doubters were positioned around Touch Gate, and the blood-men stationed themselves at Eye Gate and Ear Gate.

When the army were in position, General Incredulity sent an insistent summons urging Mansoul to yield to their demands. If they resisted, he threatened to burn down Mansoul with fire. The blood-men weren't interested in Mansoul's surrender; they just wanted to destroy them and kill every last one of them. Even if Mansoul agreed to surrender, that wouldn't quench the thirst of these men. They must have blood! They felt they would die without the blood of Mansoul. That's why they're called blood-men. General Incredulity was planning to use this blood-thirsty army as his final card to play if his weapons didn't work.

When the townspeople received this urgent demand, they weren't sure how to react. But after a half hour of frantic consultation with one another, they all agreed to deliver this summons to the Prince, with a footnote at the bottom: 'Lord, please save Mansoul from these blood-thirsty men!'

The Prince took the note, read it, considered it, and noticed the brief footnote at the bottom. He called Captain Belief, and told him to take Captain Patience with him to the part of Mansoul that was threatened by these blood-men. The Captains did as they were commanded, and the two of them stationed themselves near the gates that were under attack.

Then Prince Emmanuel commanded Captain Good-hope, Captain Charity, and Will-be-will to station themselves on the other side of the town. 'And I,' he said, 'will set my flag up on the top of the battlements of the castle while you keep an eye out for doubters.' When this was done, he commanded brave Captain Experience to bring his men to the middle of the market place and have them run through their routine military drills every day where the townspeople could see them. This turned out to be a long siege, and the enemy made many fierce attempts to break into the town, especially the blood-men. The people in Mansoul had some close calls with them, especially Captain Self-Denial, whose job was to guard Ear Gate and Eye Gate against the blood-men. Captain Self-Denial was young, but strong, and a native of Mansoul. When the Prince had returned to Mansoul the second time, he had chosen him over a thousand other Mansoulians and promoted him to Captain for the welfare of the town. This Captain was strong, extremely brave, and willing to take risks for his town. Sometimes he would venture out and meet them face to face, attacking them, fighting hand-to-hand combat, and even killing a few of them. This was no easy task, and took some sacrifice. He already had several of their wounds on his face and other parts of his body.

[Note -- While we fight the Lord's battles, sin dwelling within us continues to wound us; pride and self-righteousness won't leave us alone: we need the blood of Christ to cleanse our best efforts.]

After waiting a time to test the faith, hope, and love of the people of Mansoul, the Prince called his Captains and soldiers together. He divided them onto two companies. Early the next morning at the appointed time, he sent them out to meet the enemy, saying, 'Half of you attack the doubters, and the other half of you attack the blood-men. Those of you who go against the doubters, kill as many as you can your hands on. But those of you going out against the blood-men, don't kill them, but take them alive.'

So in the morning, the Captains went out as they were commanded against their enemies. Captain Good-Hope, Captain Charity, Captain Innocent and Captain Experience with all of their men went after the doubters. Captain Belief, Captain Patience, Captain Self-Denial, and all their men went after the blood-men.

Those that went against the doubters gathered into a group and marched out onto the plains to attack them. But the doubters remembered how the Prince's men had won the last battle, and they turned and fled as soon as they saw the army. The Prince's men followed in pursuit and slew many on the run, but they couldn't catch all of them. Some of the doubters who escaped returned home, and the others straggled in small groups up and down the country until they wandered upon various barbarous peoples and practiced their devilish actions. The barbarians didn't even try to resist them, they merely submitted and allowed themselves to be enslaved. Sometimes in later times a group of them would travel in companies and show up at the gates of Mansoul, but they were never able to get in because if Captain Belief, Captain Good-Hope, or Captain Experience even showed themselves, the doubters would run away.

[Note -- allowed themselves to be enslaved: The wicked, and those who don't know God, are led captive by Satan at his will, blinded to their misery, and clueless to their remedy. They might as well be asleep in whose delusive arms of the god of this world. Many of them stay sleep until death and judgment awaken them, to behold their awful and remedial state.
Lord, pity them!]

The Prince's men who fought against the blood-men did as they were commanded. They didn't kill any of them, but tried to capture them. But when the blood-men didn't see Emmanuel himself in the field, they assumed that Emmanuel wasn't anywhere near Mansoul. So they considered that the Captains were acting on the folly of their own reckless whims, and they were more scornful of them than afraid of them. But the Captains took no notice of that. They surrounded them and captured them. They even took care of the few escaping doubters who came to their aid. By the time the blood-men realized this was no joke, it was too late to flee. They put up a bit of a struggle, but, though they can be malicious and cruel when they have the upper hand, they're cowards at heart when they find themselves outmatched. So the Captains caught them and brought them to the Prince.

When the Prince saw them, he noticed that they were from three different counties in the same country.

1. Some were from Blind-man-shire and tended to act in ignorance.

2. Another sort came from Blind-zeal-shire, and they were very superstitious.

3. The third kind were from the town of Hate, which is in the county of Envy. Everything they did was done out of spite and bullheadedness.

When those who had come from Blind-man-shire realized where they were and who they'd been fighting against, they trembled and sniveled as they stood before Prince Emmanuel. If any of them asked for mercy, the Prince touched their lips lightly with his golden scepter as a sign of favour..

The ones from Blind-zeal-shire acted quite differently -- they insisted that they had every right to do what they had done because Mansoul's laws and customs were so different from everyone else's. Very few of them could be made to understand that they had done anything wrong, but any of them who did and who asked for mercy also obtained the Prince's favour.

Those who had come from the town of Hate stood before the Prince neither weeping, nor arguing their case, nor repenting. Instead, they stood there chewing their tongues in their anguish and rage because they hadn't been able to do what they wanted to Mansoul. These blood-men and those from the other two groups who hadn't asked for pardon for their faults were held captive to give some kind of account for what they had done at a future court date when the Prince would judge everyone in the kingdom of Universe. At that time, each of the blood-men would have to stand before the Prince by himself to answer for what he had done.

So much for this second army that Diabolus sent to overthrow Mansoul.

Chapter 18

There were three or four doubters who had fled, and after running from place to place for awhile, they finally realized they had successfully escaped. So they decided to disguise themselves as Mansoulians and live among them in Mansoul. They ended up at the house of an aged Diabolian in Mansoul named Evil-Questioning. He hated Mansoul and worked undercover for Diabolus. These Diabolian doubters came to his house -- you can be sure they had gotten directions to get there. Evil-Questioning made them welcome, sympathized with their misfortune, and fed them the best he had in his house. After they had chatted a bit and gotten to know each other a little, Evil-Questioning asked if they were from a specific town in the land of Doubting that he knew of, and they said, 'No, we're not actually all from the same shire. I'm an election doubter.' The next one said, 'I'm a vocation doubter, and my friend here is a salvation doubter.' And the last one said, 'And I'm a grace doubter.' Evil-Questioning said, 'it doesn't matter which shire you're from, boys, I can see that you're all down on your luck. I am with you wholeheartedly, everything I have is at your disposal, and you're welcome to stay here with me as long as you want.' So they thanked him and were glad to have found a safe shelter within Mansoul.

Then Evil-Questioning asked, 'How many were in your army when you came to attack Mansoul?' and they answered, 'There were twenty five thousand -- but only ten thousand were doubters. The other fifteen thousand were blood-men. Their country borders ours near Hell-Gate Hill, but, poor guys, we hear they were all captured, every last one, by Emmanuel's forces.' 'Ten thousand!' exclaimed Evil-Questioning. 'That's quite a large company! How did such a large army dwindle so much and fail to conquer your foes?' They answered, 'Our general was the first one to run for the hills.' 'What!' exclaimed Evil-Questioning, 'who was that cowardly general?' 'He was the Lord Mayor of Mansoul at one time,' they said; 'don't call him cowardly. I don't know that anyone anywhere has done more service for our prince than General Incredulity. If he had been captured, they would have hanged him for sure, and that's a wretched ordeal.' Then old Evil-Questioning said, 'I wish all ten thousand doubters were well armed and I was leading them into battle against Mansoul. I'd give them a fight to remember!' 'I'm sure that would be something to see,' said the doubters, 'but what good are wishes?' 'Shhh, not too loud,' said Evil-Questioning; 'you must be secretive and quiet while you're here, or you'll be discovered and captured!' 'Why?' asked the doubters. 'Why!' exclaimed Evil-Questioning, 'Why! Because the Prince and his Secretary, and their Captains and all their soldiers are in the town even now. The town is crawling with them! And besides them, there's a guy named Will-be-will, a cruel enemy of ours, and the Prince has made him keeper of the gates and commanded him to seek out and destroy any and all Diabolians he can find. If he gets any idea that you're here, there's no hope for you. You wouldn't be able to buy your way free.'

As it happened, one of Will-be-will's soldiers, a man named Mr. Diligence, had been standing under the eaves of the house that night and heard everything that had been said between Evil-Questioning and the four doubters.

Mr. Diligence was a soldier that Will-be-will had a lot of confidence in and loved dearly because he was courageous and persistent about searching for Diabolians.

When Mr. Diligence had heard all the talk between Evil-Questioning and the four Diabolians, he reported it to Will-be-will immediately. 'Are you sure, my trusted friend?' asked Will-be-will. 'Yes, I know what I heard, and if you'll come with me, you'll hear it for yourself.' 'They're still there? I know Evil-Questioning very well; we were good friends back in the days of our apostacy, but I don't know where he's living these days.' 'But I do,' said Mr. Diligence. 'Come with me, and I'll lead you to his den.' 'Then let's go!' said Will-be-will, 'lead me there and let's catch them!'

So they both went together to Evil-Questioning's house, Mr. Diligence leading the way in the darkness. When they got under the eaves, Mr. Diligence said, 'Listen! Do you recognize the old man's voice?' 'I sure do!' said Will-be-will. 'It's been a long time since I've heard it. One thing I know about him: he's clever and tricky! Don't let him give us the slip!' 'Don't worry, I won't let him get away,' said Mr. Diligence. 'How are we going to find the door?' asked Will-be-will. 'I have a plan for that,' said Mr. Diligence, and he showed him where the door was at. Then both of them broke open the door, rushed in, and caught all five of them together. Will-be-will put them under arrest, and they bound them and brought them to Mr. True-Man, the jailer, to confine overnight. In the morning, the Mayor was informed of their capture. He rejoiced at the news, not only because of the doubters who had been captured, but because old Evil-Questioning had been a troublemaker to Mansoul and caused much grief to the Mayor. He had been sought frequently, but had never been apprehended until now.

The next step was to bring these five Diabolians to trial. So the day was set and the prisoners were brought forward before the judge. Will-be-will could have executed them as soon as he found them, but he thought it might bring the Prince honour to bring them to judgment publicly, and it would also discourage the enemy.

Mr. True-Man brought them in chains to the front of the town hall, the place of judgment. The jury was selected, the witnesses sworn in, and the trial began. It was the same jury that had tried Mr. No-Truth, Mr. Pitiless, Mr. Haughty, and the rest of their companions.

The first one to be questioned was old Evil-Questioning, since he was the one who had hosted and comforted the four doubters. They read him his accusation, and told him he had the right to object if he had anything to say in his defense.

'Mr. Evil-Questioning, you, an intruder in the town of Mansoul and a Diabolian who hates Prince Emmanuel and works to destroy Mansoul, are charged with harbouring the King's enemies even after laws were passed forbidding such.

'1. You have questioned the truth of Mansoul's doctrines and laws.

'2. You wished Mansoul had ten thousand doubters attacking her.

'3. You received, entertained, and encouraged Mansoul's enemies who came to you from their army. How do you plead? Guilty or not guilty?'

'Sir,' said Evil-Questioning, 'I don't understand the accusation. It has nothing to do with me. You said the accused is Evil-Questioning, but my name is Honest-Inquiry. The two names may sound similar, but I can assure you that there's a world of difference between the two. Even in the worst of times, there's no harm in a little bit of honest inquiry; surely that's not worthy of death.'

> *[Note -- Sinners may give false names to their sin and make it sound less ugly, and thus deceive themselves, but God is not mocked.]*

Will-be-will, as one of the witnesses, spoke up. 'Honourable Judge, jurors, and magistrates of the town of Mansoul, you have heard the prisoner deny his name because he thinks that will shift the blame from him. But I know he's the man concerned, and I know his name is Evil-Questioning. I have known him for more than thirty years. I am ashamed to say it, but he and I were great friends when Diabolus, that tyrant, was ruler of Mansoul. I testify that he is a Diabolian, an enemy to our Prince, and a hater of Mansoul. Back during the rebellion, he used to spend three weeks together at my house. We would talk frequently back then, and the content of our talk was much the same as what he and the four doubters were discussing. I admit, I haven't seen him in awhile. I suppose that when Emmanuel came to Mansoul, he changed his address in the same way he is now trying to change his name. But this is the man, sir.'

The court asked him, 'Do you have anything to say in your defense?'

'Yes, I do,' said Evil-Questioning, 'everything I'm accused of is just the word of a single witness. It is not legal in Mansoul to put a man to death on the word of just one witness.'

Then Mr. Diligence stood up and said, 'Sir, as I was making my rounds on my watch during the night, I was on Bad Street, and I happened to hear some murmuring coming from this gentleman's house. I thought, 'what's going on here?' I went up closer to listen, thinking I might discover some Diabolian plot, which I did. So, as I said, I drew closer, and when I got right up near the wall, I realized that there were some foreigners in the house. I had no problem understanding what they were saying, since I've done some traveling myself. When I heard such strange language in a tumble-down, tottering old hovel as this old man lived in, I put my ear up to the window and heard them talking. Mr. Evil-Questioning was asking these doubters who they were, where they had come from, and what business brought them to Mansoul, and they told him. He fed and welcomed them, and asked how many of them there were. They said their army had been ten thousand strong. Then he asked them why they weren't attacking Mansoul, and they told him. He called their general a coward for fleeing when he should have stayed to help fight with his prince. Then I heard this Evil-Questioning wish that all ten thousand of that army were in Mansoul, with him at their head, leading them into battle. Then he hushed them and told them to keep quiet and stay hidden, because if they were captured, they would be killed, and no amount of money would be able to save them.' And the court said, 'Mr. Evil-Questioning, now we have two witnesses against you, and both witnesses agree.

'1. He swears that you welcomed those men into your house and fed them, even though you knew they were Diabolians and enemies of the Prince.

'2. He swears that you said you wished ten thousand of them were in Mansoul.

'3. He swears that you advised them to be secretive and quiet so they wouldn't be captured by the Prince's servants. All of these suggest that you are a Diabolian yourself. If you had been on the Prince's side, you would have apprehended these villains.'

Then Evil-Questioning said, 'To the first charge I answer that these men were strangers and I took them in. When did it become a crime to welcome strangers in Mansoul? I also fed them -- what's wrong with being kind? Yes, it's true that I wished there were ten thousand of them were in Mansoul. But I never said why I wished they were here, Perhaps I wanted them to be here so they could all be captured for the good of Mansoul. It's not your place to make assumptions about what I might have meant. And, yes, I did tell them to be secretive and quiet so they wouldn't be captured by the Captains. But perhaps that's because I'm a soft-hearted person who doesn't wish to see anyone killed, and not because I desire the Prince's enemies to escape capture.'

Then the Mayor said, 'Welcoming strangers is a good thing -- but welcoming the Prince's enemies is treason. And as far as the rest of what you've said, you're just twisting words to avoid and forestall the judgment you deserve. But even if the only thing we could prove about you is that you were a Diabolian, that in itself would be enough to convict and execute you. But to welcome, feed, support, and shelter foreign Diabolians who came here to destroy our Mansoul -- that can't be tolerated.'

Then Evil-Questioning said, 'Oh, now I see how this works -- I'm to be punished and killed just because of my name, and because I'm kind to strangers.' But that was all he said.

Then they called the foreign doubters forward. The first was the election doubter. His charges were read through an interpreter, since he spoke a different language. He was accused of being an enemy of Prince Emmanuel, a hater of Mansoul, and opposed to Mansoul's laws.

> *[Note -- Election by free grace, i.e., those whom God has predestined to salvation by His foreknowledge.]*

The judged asked how he would plead. He confessed to being an election doubter, and said that he had been brought up in that religion for his entire life. He added, 'if I must die for my religion, then I suppose I shall die a martyr, and that makes my death worth the sacrifice.'

The Judge said, 'To question and challenge the doctrine of election subverts one of the most wonderful doctrines of King Shaddai -- the doctrine of God's will, power, and comprehensive knowledge. It removes the liberty for God to deal with his creatures as he wants. It weakens the faith of the town of Mansoul, and makes salvation dependent on works rather than grace. It denies God's word, and unsettles the minds of the people of Mansoul. Therefore, the law justifies your death.'

Then the vocation doubter came forward. His charge was similar to the other, except that he was specifically charged with denying Mansoul's calling.

The Judge asked what he had to say for himself.

He replied, 'I have never believed that there such a thing as a special and powerful calling of God to Mansoul personally. There's a general set of guidelines set down in the word to avoid evil and to do good in order to gain success and happiness.'

The Judge said, 'You are a Diabolian and you have denied part of one of the most primary truths of the Prince. His calling was distinct and compelling, and that call has been instrumental in motivating, awakening, and filling Mansoul with the grace to desire to be in communion with her Prince. It is this calling that stimulates Mansoul to serve him, to do his will, and to find her happiness in pleasing her Prince. Because you have hated this doctrine, you must die.'

Then the grace doubter was called forward and his charges were read. He responded, 'Although I am from the land of Doubting, my father was descended from a Pharisee and lived decently there among his neighbours. He taught them not to depend on grace but to rely on decent living and keeping the law, and he taught me, that, too. And I firmly believe that Mansoul will never be saved freely by grace.'

The Judge said, 'The Prince's law is quite clear:

'1. It is plain in the negative sense that salvation is not of works.

'2. It is plain in the positive sense that it is by grace that Mansoul is saved. Your kind of religion has to rely on the works of the flesh, because attempting to keep the law is a work of the physical flesh. Your way of earning salvation robs King Shaddai of his glory, and hands that glory over to a sinful man. Your way robs the Prince of needing to sacrifice his own life to meet all the requirements for salvation, and transfers that over to sinful man, too. Your way rejects the work of the Holy Spirit and magnifies the work of the physical flesh, and the legal rationale. Furthermore, you are a Diabolian, the son of a Diabolian, and because of your Diabolian precepts, you must die.'

The jury went into the next room to deliberate, and brought back a charge of guilty for all of them. The Recorder stood up and said to the prisoners, 'You prisoners have been charged and found guilty of high crimes against Prince Emmanuel and against the welfare of Mansoul. For these crimes of treason you must die.'

[Note -- We are to lay aside every weight, and every entangling sin.]

The time and manner of their execution was set. The place assigned for the doubters was the spot where Diabolus had gathered his armies against Mansoul, but Evil-Questioning was to be hanged at the end of Bad Street near his own front door.

Chapter 19

After Mansoul had thus gotten rid of her enemies and troublemakers, a strict command was given that Will-be-will and Mr. Diligence should seek out and capture any of the town Diabolians still lurking in Mansoul. These were men such as Mr. Fooling, Mr. Let-Good-Slip, Mr. Slavish-Fear, Mr. No-Love, Mr. Mistrust, Mr. Flesh, and Mr. Sloth. Mr. Evil-Questioning's house was to be demolished and his offspring were to be detained. His sons were Doubt, Legal-Life, Unbelief, Wrong-Thoughts-of-Christ, Forge-Promise, Carnal-Sense, Live-by-Feeling, and Self-Love. Their mother was No-Hope. She had been raised by her uncle Mr. Incredulity after her father, old Mr. Dark, had died.

So Will-be-will and Mr. Diligence went out on their errand. They found Mr. Fooling loitering in the streets and hanged him in Want-wit-Alley, near his own house. Mr. Fooling is the same man who wanted Captain Belief handed over to Diabolus in exchange for Diabolus calling off his attack. They found Mr. Let-Good-Slip shopping in the market, and executed him on the spot. His wealth was given to an honest poor Mansoulian named Mr. Meditation to improve living conditions for him, his wife Piety (who was the daughter of the Recorder), and their son, Think-Well. They hadn't participated in the apostasy and had a good reputation in the town, so nobody begrudged them the money.

Mr. Forge-Promise was a notorious villain who counterfeited King Shaddai's money, so after he was caught, they made a public example of him. He was set in the pillory, and then whipped by all the children and servants in Mansoul, and then hanged. This may seem overly harsh, but honest traders in Mansoul knew too well how much damage can be done in a very little time by a counterfeiter. And my personal opinion is that all such counterfeiters deserve the same treatment.

Will-be-will captured Carnal-Sense, but somehow he broke free and escaped. That reckless villain is still somewhere in the town, lurking in the Diabolian dens by day, and haunting honest men's homes by night. A notice was pinned up in the market-place announcing that anyone who caught and killed Carnal-Sense would be personally invited to dine at the Prince's table and be promoted to guard the treasury of Mansoul. Many attempted to find him and win the reward, but although he was sometimes spotted, nobody was ever able to catch him.

Will-be-will caught Mr. Wrong-Thoughts-of-Christ and put him in prison. He lingered there for a long time before finally dying of consumption.

Self-Love was captured and imprisoned, but he had so many friends and allies in Mansoul that his sentence was deferred until finally Mr. Self-Denial stood up and declared, 'If villains like him are going to be leniently spared, then I'm resigning.' He grabbed Self-Love from the midst of his supporters and knocked him on the head and killed him. A few Mansoulians grumbled amongst themselves about it, but no one dared complain openly while Prince Emmanuel was in town. When the Prince heard about Self-Denial's brave act, he promoted him and made him a ruler in Mansoul. The Prince was also pleased when he heard how many Diabolians Will-be-will had terminated.

This emboldened Self-Denial, and he eagerly set out to help Will-be-will pursue Diabolians. Together, they captured and imprisoned Live-by-Feeling and Legal-Life. They tried to capture Mr. Unbelief, but he kept slipping out of their grasp. So he and a few other more subtle Diabolians remained lurking in Mansoul until the time when Mansoul left the kingdom of Universe. But they had to stay hidden in their dens and holes. If they ever showed themselves in any of the streets, the whole town would be up in arms after them. Even the children would cry out as if they were after a thief, and wish out loud for someone to stone him to death. And now Mansoul finally arrived at some degree of peace and quiet. Her Prince continued to live within her borders. Her Captains and soldiers faithfully did their duties, and Mansoul was busy with the trade she kept up with the far off countries. She also stayed productive in her manufacturing projects.

[Note -- They tried to capture Mr. Unbelief, but he kept slipping out of their grasp: we, as feeble believers, will struggle with unbelief until we have our incorruptible bodies.]

When Mansoul had finally rid herself of so many of her enemies and troublemakers, the Prince arranged a day to meet with the people in the market-place. He wanted to give them instructions on some other matters that would enhance their safety and comfort, and help to condemn and destroy the Diabolians who had been born within Mansoul. On the appointed day, the townspeople met together. The Prince rode down in his chariot, and his Captains attended him on his right and on his left. Then he called their attention to listen, and after a few mutual expressions of affection, the Prince began:

'I have given many great privileges to you, beloved Mansoul. I have singled you out and chosen you, not because you're so worthy, but just because I wanted to. I have saved you, not only from the dread of my father's law, but from the power of the tyrant Diabolus. I have done all of this because I loved you and determined in my heart to do good to you. I have offered complete satisfaction for your souls so that nothing will draw you away from the path that leads to the pleasures of paradise, and I have brought you to myself. The price I paid to redeem you is not an earthly price, like money made of silver and gold. No, I freely spilled my own blood on the ground to make you my own. In this way, I have made peace between you, my Mansoul, and my father, and assigned mansions to you that are with my father in the royal city. In that place, my Mansoul, there are things so wonderful that no one has ever seen them, and no person could even imagine the wonder of them.

'Mansoul, you have seen first-hand what I did for you -- how I delivered you out of the hands of your enemies, even when you had rebelled against my father and were happy to be taken over and even destroyed. I approached you first via my law, and then by the good news of my gospel of peace, in order to awaken you and show you my glory. You know what you were then, you remember the wicked things you said, what you did, and how many times you defied me and my father. And yet, your own eyes can confirm that I didn't leave you that way. I came to you, put up with your abuse, waited for you patiently, and finally accepted you merely because of my grace and favour. I refused to allow you to be lost, even though you yourselves would have been willing to let that happen. To prevent that, I surrounded you and plagued you from all sides so that you would get tired of the way you were living. I harassed you to bring down your heart until you were willing to ally yourselves with my goodness and happiness. And once I had completely conquered you, I turned around and used my new power over you for your own advantage.

'You also see how many of my father's army I have moved into your borders -- Captains, rulers, soldiers, as well as defense machines and excellent tools to overcome and bring down your enemies. You understand what I mean, Mansoul. They are your servants as well as mine. They are here because their natural inclination is to defend you, purify you, strengthen you, and make you sweeter for me. Their purpose is to make you suitable to be in my father's presence, blessing, and glory. That, Mansoul, is what you were created for.

'You have also seen first-hand, Mansoul, how I have overlooked your backslidings and healed you. Yes, I was angry with you, but I have turned my anger away from you because even in your backslidings, I still loved you, and my anger and indignation ceased when I destroyed your enemies. It wasn't your goodness that drew me back to you after I had withdrawn from you and hidden my face from you. The backsliding was all your own doing, but bringing you back and recovering you was all my doing. I created the means for you to come back to me. I was the one who made a wall between us when you started to turn to things that did not please me. I was the one who made your sweetness turn bitter, turned your bright sunshine into darkness, made your smooth, easy way thorny and challenging -- but I'm also the one who frustrated all of the enemies who tried to destroy you. I'm the one who set Mr. Godly-Fear to work in your town. I'm the one who pricked your conscience and stirred up your understanding, your will, and your affections after your immensely grievous decay. I'm the one who put that spark within you to seek me so that you might find me, and when you found me, you found your own health, happiness, and salvation. I'm the one who fetched the Diabolians out of Mansoul a second time, and I'm the one who conquered them and destroyed them right in front of you.

'And now, Mansoul, I'm returning to you in peace. Your sins and violations are forgotten, as if they had never happened. And it won't be just like it was the last time I was with you -- no, this time will be even better!

'In a little while, Mansoul -- it will be after a number of times have passed over you, so don't let it worry you -- I will dismantle this famous town of Mansoul, every stick and stone. And I will carry all the stones, the timber, the walls, even the dust and the people, to my own country, into the kingdom of my father. I'll rebuild it there in more strength and glory than it ever had here. When it's set up there, it will be fit for my father to live in. That's why it was built in Universe to begin with. In my father's kingdom, I will make it a wonderful marvel, a monument to mercy, and it will admire its own mercy. The natives of Mansoul will see things then that they never saw here. Then they will be the equals of those who were superior to them here. And when you're there, Mansoul, you'll have the kind of communion with me, and with my father, and with his Secretary that wasn't possible here. It couldn't happen here even if you lived in Universe for a thousand years.

'When you're there, Mansoul, you won't ever be afraid of murderers, or Diabolians and their threats, ever again. There won't be any more threats or plots or schemes against you. You won't hear alarms of invading armies, or the war drums of the Diabolians beating. You won't see Diabolian commanders flying their war flags. There won't be any siege mounts set up against your walls, or Diabolian messengers terrifying you with demands for your surrender. You won't need Captains, or weapons, or soldiers. You won't ever have to deal with sorrow or grief. No Diabolian will ever be able to sneak into your midst, burrow under your walls, or be seen within the borders of your town ever, ever again. Life there will last longer than you'd want it to last here. But even though it goes on and on, you won't get tired of it because it will always seem sweet and fresh, and not fraught with difficulties.

'In that place, Mansoul, you will meet others similar to you who have shared your sorrow; others that I chose, and redeemed, and set apart for my father's royal city, like I did for you. They will be happy to know you, and when you meet them, you'll be glad, too.

'There are other things, too, that my father and I have provided that haven't been seen since the beginning of the world. They're being stored in the royal city, sealed up with his other treasures for you, until you're there to enjoy them. Where I'm setting up your rebuilt town of Mansoul, are those who love you and rejoice in you now, but will be even more thrilled when they see you exalted to honour! My father will send them to fetch you, and their own arms will be the chariots that take you there -- you'll be riding on the wings of the wind! The place they bring you will be the haven you've always wanted.

'And now, Mansoul, I've told you what will happen to you in the future, if you're able to hear and understand it. Now I'll tell you what I expect of you for the present time, what your duties and practices should be until I come and get you according to what is written in the Scriptures.

'First, keep the white clothing I gave you bright and shining. Do this if you are wise. They have been made of the best quality linen, but they can't keep themselves clean and white -- you have to do that. Keeping them spotless and pure will be your wisdom and honour, and it will glorify me. When your clothing is white, the world will recognize that you are mine. Also, when your garments are bright and pure, then I am delighted in your ways because then your comings and goings to and fro will be like a bright flash of lightning that will catch the eye of everyone and make them take notice, and dazzle their eyes. So, clothe yourselves as I instruct you, and make straight steps for yourselves according to my law. If you do that, your beauty will be pleasing to my father. He is your Lord, and he is the one you should worship.

'In order to keep your clothing clean, I have provided a fountain for you to wash them in. Make sure you wash them in that fountain frequently. Don't go around in soiled, defiled garments. That dishonours and disgraces me. It's also uncomfortable for you to walk around in filthy clothes. I repeat, Don't let the garments I gave you be contaminated or muddied by sin. Always keep them clean. And keep ointment on your head.

'Mansoul, I have delivered you many times from the schemes, plots, and conspiracies of Diabolus. I don't ask you for anything in return except that you don't pay me back evil for the good I've done for you. Keep my love in mind, and think about my continued kindness to my beloved Mansoul. That will motivate you to live and walk in a way that's worthy of the benefits I've loaded you with. It used to be that cords tied the sacrifice to the altar -- let the thoughts of my love be the cords that tie you to the sacrifice of self-denial and right living. Reflect on what I'm telling you.

'Mansoul, I lived a human life, I died for you, and now I'm alive again. I won't die for you again. I'm alive now, and because I live, you will not die. Since I live, so will you. My blood when I died on the cross bought you back for my father. Now that there's peace between you and my father, you will live through me. I will pray for you, fight for you, and continue to do good to you.

'Nothing can hurt you except sin. Nothing can grieve me except sin. Nothing can degrade you in the perception of your enemies except sin. So be careful of sin, Mansoul!

'Do you know why I still allow Diabolians to lurk in your town walls? It's to keep you on your toes, to test your love for me, to keep you on your guard, and to make you value my noble Captains, their soldiers, and my mercy.

'It is also to remind you of what a deplorable condition you were in once, back when a huge number of Diabolians lived not only in and around your town walls, but inside the stronghold of your castle.

'Even if I were to kill all the Diabolians who lived within your walls, there would still be some outside the town, and they would bring you into bondage. If all the Diabolians inside the town were gone, you'd let down your guard and the ones outside the town would find you asleep and not watching, and they'd swallow you up in a moment. That's why I left a few Diabolians within your walls -- not to harm you (though they will if you listen to them and serve them), but to help you. And they will be a help if you stay vigilant and resist them. Whatever they might tempt you to do, my plan isn't for them to drive you farther away from me. It's to draw you closer, to help you learn about warfare, to drive you to prayer, and to make you aware of how powerless you are compared to me. Be careful about this, Mansoul!

'So show how much you love me; don't let the Diabolians who are within your walls draw your affection away from the Prince who redeemed your very souls. Instead, let the mere sight of a Diabolian heighten your love for me. I came, not once, not twice, but three times to save you from the toxic arrows that would have killed you. So stay loyal to me, Mansoul, against the Diabolians, and I will stay loyal to you in front of my father and his entire court. Let your love for me inspire you to resist temptation, and I will love you in spite of all of your infirmities.

'Mansoul, remember what my Captains, my soldiers, and my weapons have done for you. They have fought for you, they have suffered because of you, they have put up with a lot of abuse from you just so they could help you. If you hadn't had them to help you, Diabolus would certainly have made mincemeat out of you. So take care of them. When you're doing well, they will be well. When you're sick, they will be indisposed, and when you're afflicted, they will be weak. Do not cause my Captains to be unwell, Mansoul, because if they're not in top shape, you can't be well, and if they're weak, you can't be strong. If they're fatigued, you can't be invincible and valiant for King Shaddai. And don't assume that you can always live by your own rational sense. You must rely on my word. Even when I'm not right here, you must believe that I still love you, and that you're on my mind and in my heart forever.

'Don't forget, Mansoul, that you are greatly loved by me. I've already taught you to watch, to fight, to pray, and to make war against my foes. Now I'm telling you -- believe that my love for you is constant. Mansoul, I have set my heart and my love on you! Stay alert and watchful. I won't lay any further burdens on you than that. Stand firm until I come back for you.'

End.   Paraphrased by Leslie Noelani Laurio, September 2018

Printed in Great Britain
by Amazon